THE EIGHTH
SEXTON BLAKE
OMNIBUS

TWO COMPLETE SEXTON BLAKE NOVELS

THE FUGITIVE
W. Howard Baker

and

FIRE OVER INDIA
W. Howard Baker

THE EIGHTH SEXTON BLAKE OMNIBUS

BOOK ONE
THE FUGITIVE
W. Howard Baker

•

BOOK TWO
FIRE OVER INDIA
W. Howard Baker

HOWARD BAKER, LONDON

THE EIGHTH SEXTON BLAKE OMNIBUS

THE FUGITIVE
W. Howard Baker

and

FIRE OVER INDIA
W. Howard Baker

SBN 09 300080 4

First published in this Howard Baker edition, 1970

Published by arrangement with Fleetway
Publications Limited, London, England,
who claim exclusive rights in the designation
'Sexton Blake'.

Howard Baker books are published by
Howard Baker Publishers Limited,
47 Museum Street, London W.C.1

Printed in Great Britain by
The Anchor Press Ltd., and bound by
Wm. Brendon & Son Ltd.,
both of Tiptree, Essex

THE FUGITIVE

W. Howard Baker

ONE

The Malibu Club was a long, low-ceilinged room down fifteen cracked marble steps from a dirty pavement.

It had imitation dark-oak panelling on the walls, and something which had once been a cherry-coloured carpet on the floor. Its ceiling was painted a flaking white and, in between the ceiling and the carpet, there was a pocket of air which had known better days.

Some of the clientele had known better days, too, and, for the price of a drink, they would describe them.

Men would touch razor-scars won at pre-war dog-tracks, and wax romantic. Women would open their crumbling parlour-maids' faces above ochre modesty vests, and pluck at long strings of beads with fingernails black-edged like old-time mourning cards—do this, and talk fancifully of days that were gone.

But one or two members of the Malibu Club could also be coaxed to talk privately and in a well-informed, factual manner of other, more recent events—if the right amount of friendly persuasion was offered.

More recent events, that is to say, of a thoroughly criminal nature. And the right amount of friendly persuasion was never less than twenty-five pounds.

In short, there were one or two snouts on the Membership Roll of the Malibu Club; professional informers; sly, sidling men whose conversation *might* more than amply repay any detective for time and money spent in their company. Which was why Sexton Blake was in the habit of slipping into the Club every now and again. Just for a confidential chat in one of the many back rooms.

But particularly note that word—'might'.

This was the reason that a young man called Edward Carter —but better known to his friends as 'Tinker'—was also

7

present at the Malibu on this particular evening. Tinker was Blake's junior partner, and while Blake himself was here to ask questions, Tinker was here to make sure he bought accurate answers.

It wasn't that Blake didn't trust his informant: now talking to him with engaging sincerity across a table in a small and otherwise empty back room. It was just that he liked to be sure.

Sniffy Petersen had the reputation of being the greatest twister unhung since Judas Iscariot. Sniffy Petersen was a very slippery snout.

*   *   *

Earlier on in the evening, back in the book-lined study of his flat above Baker Street, a fine fire ablaze in the hearth and Pedro, the redoubtable bloodhound asleep at his feet, Blake had talked very seriously to Tinker.

'Tomorrow could see the end of the Carfax Case,' he had said. 'But everything depends on whether Petersen plays ball with me tonight. So get on his tail as soon as he leaves me, and report back. If he goes straight home, then the information he's promised me will be on the up-and-up. I know my Sniffy. But if he stops off anywhere, or if he phones anyone . . .' Blake had paused very significantly, and his eyes had narrowed. '. . . Then I want to know all about it. Okay?'

And Tinker had nodded.

Now he sat in a shadowed corner of the Malibu Club, close to the foot of the steps from the street, and he sipped a whisky, spinning it out.

Blake and Petersen were nowhere to be seen, and Tinker was a cut above the ordinary *habitué* of the Malibu, but nobody bothered him. In particular, the management didn't question his right to be there.

At the Malibu, the management asked questions of nobody. This was the first of its two golden rules.

The other appeared on a dozen fly-specked cards posted up in the most likely and unlikely places throughout the premises: *The Malibu Club Closes at Midnight*.

On this night, Sniffy Petersen and Sexton Blake casually emerged from their back room just fifteen minutes before that time.

Petersen made straight for the stairs to the street. Nevertheless, he didn't look like a man in a hurry. Every movement he made—everything about him—was calculated to draw the very minimum of attention to himself. If you hadn't actually looked at him and consciously seen him you'd be prepared to swear later that he hadn't been there at all.

He passed within feet of where Tinker had been sitting until a few moments earlier, and if he'd seen Blake's young partner he would have recognised him, and done some thinking about it. But he didn't. From long experience, Tinker knew all that there was to know about tailing a man. He would pick up his quarry out on the street.

Unremarked and unnoticed, in the same instant that Blake and Petersen had emerged from their back room, Tinker had gone.

*   *   *

Sexton Blake had paused by the bar.

He signalled Carlo, the barman. 'A double whisky.'

In the mirror behind the bar, he saw Sniffy Petersen start up the steps to the street.

Well, he told himself, we'll soon know if the Carfax business is really going to be buttoned up before midday tomorrow. As soon as Sniffy sets one foot out of this place, Tinker will be hard on his tail, and——

But there all thoughts of Sniffy Petersen and the Carfax Case came to an abrupt and untimely end—for the present. Tinker could take care of the present.

Blake had just seen someone else—and something else—to do some thinking about.

Reflected in the mirror behind the bar, he saw a young woman coming down the steps from the street, and coming down them so hurriedly that she almost skidded on them and tumbled headlong.

But it wasn't this which riveted Blake's attention.

9

His eyes were fixed on the young woman's face, and on what he could see there.

And what he could see was blind, elemental, unreasoning terror.

She wore a black wool-fleece coat, cuffed and collared in grey velvet. It hung open to reveal a light-grey woollen dinner dress beneath.

She was tall, beautiful, with honey-blonde hair, and skin which was smooth and clear and white.

She wore black suède court shoes which had four-inch stiletto heels, and high up on her coat, just six inches above her heart, she wore a single crimson flower.

It was the same shade of crimson as her lipstick, and it was meant to do something for her appearance, and it did—but not in the way that she had intended when she had pinned it into place.

It brought out the unnatural pallor of her face, and the stark terror in her dark-blue eyes.

She reached the bottom of the steps from the street, and there she came to a hesitant halt. Simultaneously, Carlo slid out from behind his bar and walked towards her.

His movements were easy, fluid; unhurried. He was very conscious of the fact that he was tall, and handsome in a dark and perfect almost effeminate way. Dozens of young women had told him how beautiful he was. He had a way with women, old as well as young, and this was reflected in the way that he carried himself. There was arrogance in his walk, and also a certain coiled-spring virility. He walked like a lithe black panther sure of its prey.

He reached the young woman's side, smiled, and inclined his body from the waist—briefly. It was something special. He didn't do it often.

Then he said something. The first time he said it, she didn't hear. Looking at her, Blake could see that she wasn't even listening. Carlo had to repeat himself, and he didn't trouble to do that often either. Not with the ordinary, everyday kind of person who entered the Malibu Club.

But it was plain from the outset that this young woman was

far from being ordinary. She was too beautiful and too well-dressed for that.

And there was the fear in her eyes.

There was nothing ordinary about her.

And in the time that it took Carlo to repeat himself, her eyes slid jerkily from table to table—searching for someone—and then swiftly ranged over the men and the women grouped in front of the bar.

She saw Blake in passing. Their eyes met for a tiny fragment of time. Then her gaze flicked fearfully on.

Whoever she was looking for, Blake thought, was not someone she wanted to see. He knew all the signs.

This was a woman afraid. A woman running from something or someone.

This was a fugitive.

Her eyes, raking the club, went in fear of seeing some known and recognisable enemy.

Then suddenly, shakily, she allowed herself to relax. She took a deep, steadying breath. She turned her head and said something to Carlo, and he pulled back his lips over perfect white teeth as he smiled. She followed Carlo across the floor, and her legs were long; her movements graceful.

She took a high stool at the bar, and Carlo brought her a drink. It was a whisky, and she downed it quickly. Carlo poured her a second one, and she took this more slowly. She sat there, twisting the glass in her hand, sipping at the drink with her back to the stairs.

Away on Blake's right, a woman laughed in one of the club's innumerable alcoves. It was an immoderate sound: high-pitched, loud and shrill. Blake looked up and saw a frown crease Carlo's forehead.

He saw him lean forward almost imperceptibly and touch something beneath the counter, and realised that he'd switched on the Musak. The sound of a tap-room piano jangled its way into the room. Carlo turned up the volume.

Blake sipped his drink, and then, without quite knowing why, he shot a glance over his left shoulder.

A man stood at the foot of the stairs.

11

He was a short man, and he was immensely broad. He wore a belted black overcoat, and his shoulders filled it out squarely. He looked like a squat black triangle standing upon its apex.

Above the collar of the coat there was a roll of fat which passed for a neck, and, above that, a hard, cruel face, deep-set with sadistic cold and pale eyes.

He had his hands in the pocket of his overcoat, and he was looking directly to where the well-dressed, honey-blonde young woman sat at the bar, unconscious of him, sipping at her second drink. Carlo began to move along the counter towards him, and then suddenly seemed to change his mind. He turned his back on the new arrival, and busied himself with some glasses. He polished them and repolished them. They didn't need it. The new arrival had looked at him—nothing more.

The man came on into the club, and he walked wide-legged across to the bar. He said 'Rum!' and his voice was a growl at the back of his throat.

Then he took his large, capable hairy hands out of the pockets of his overcoat, and laid them flat on the counter. Deliberately, he half-turned and looked at the tall, young blonde again.

This time, she saw him. She couldn't fail to. He was only five feet away from her.

Blake, looking at her in the same moment, saw her deep blue eyes frost over. It was as though something within them had died. The hand which held her glass began to tremble.

And that, for Blake, clinched the matter.

He thought that it was about time he knew something of what was going on, and who the short, squat man was.

He signalled Carlo. He caught his eye in the mirror above the bar, and beckoned him over. 'Another whisky,' he said. And then, as the barman made to move away: 'The man who just came in . . .?'

He let the whispered question hang in the air. He had posed it without moving his lips.

Carlo reached for a clean glass. 'A double whisky, sir? Certainly, sir.' Then, in a rapid mumble, he added: 'Joe Turk. Keep away from him.'

He brought back the drink. He did it quickly. As he fumbled with Blake's change, he said: 'He's a bad one. An enforcer for one of the mobs. Nailed a bloke to the floor once. Six-inch nails, hammered in straight through the knee-caps.'

'And the woman.'

'I don't know, sir. Never seen her before. She says she's a member, but ...' Carlo raised his voice. 'Like some water with that, sir?'

'No thanks.'

A gravel voice grated all the way along the bar. 'I'd like some service!'

Joe Turk again.

'Yes, sir.'

'Fill it up.'

Still half-turned away from the bar, still eyeing the tall, frightened blonde on her stool with a brooding, bitter intensity, Turk pushed his empty glass away from him across the counter. Carlo took it hurriedly, filled it, brought it back.

No money was asked for, or offered.

Without turning round, without looking at the drink, the squat man took it. He downed it in a gulp. He rapped the glass on the top of the bar, and Carlo filled it again. All the while, Turk never shifted his malignant stare from the young woman not six feet away from him.

Blake could feel the tension building up within the narrow confines of the room. Something—or someone—was going to snap. And it was going to be soon.

Carlo snapped off the Musak. The piano jangled to an abrupt halt, and the sudden inrush of silence was frightening. He cleared his throat loudly. 'Last orders, ladies and gentlemen, please!' His voice cracked on the last word. It came out high, almost as a squeak. It sounded funny, but nobody laughed.

Turk turned around. 'Another!' He looked up and caught Blake staring at him in the mirror above the bar. He held Blake's eyes with his own for a long moment, and silently he menaced the detective.

13

Mind your own business! his eyes said. *Keep out of this. It doesn't concern you!*

Then his eyes jerked away as the tall blonde slipped off her stool hurriedly. She tried to appear calm. She tried to take her time across the floor to the foot of the stairs.

But she couldn't.

She stumbled on the stairs in her haste to reach the street.

Turk watched her go. Then he swallowed his drink and started to follow. When he reached the stairs he went up them fast.

Blake thought it was time he went, too. He thought that he didn't like being threatened, however silently. He thought that the young woman who had just left the club was shortly going to be in dire need of a friend, and that he had been elected—unopposed—to that position.

No one else within the Malibu had so much as moved.

He swung away from the bar then, and he crossed the floor to the stairs, moving quickly. Carlo watched him go.

Planning to interfere, was he? Well, that was his business. Carlo certainly wanted no part of it. He had encountered Turk before, and he was poison.

It was quite true that he had literally nailed a man to the floor: a club owner out Stepney way who wouldn't pay for 'protection'. Everyone running a club in or around London knew the story, and knew it was Turk who had done it. So, for that matter, did the police.

But they had never managed to bring the crime home to him. Even when you're crippled for life in that way you don't start singing to the coppers; not if you've got any sense.

All right, so you're crippled. But there are worse things. Like being blinded by a charge of buckshot fired full in your face.

And you're still breathing, aren't you? Sing loud and clear to the coppers and, chances are, that you soon won't be.

Carlo was very pale. He moistened his lips. He tried hard not to think of what a shotgun at close range would do to his almost too perfect features.

He gave himself a quick drink.

14

He was always game for a tumble. He was always in the
market for a nice easy piece of high-class tail. But there was
limits to what he was prepared to do to obtain it.

He wasn't going to tangle with Joe Turk.

Chat up the birds, yes. Lay a hand on them masterfully.
Bow and act suave—on occasion.

But get his face chewed up like a ploughed field . . .?

He drained his glass in a hurry.

He didn't even mentally wish Blake the best of luck. He was
careful not to. He didn't want to get himself involved. Not at
all. Not even that much. Not with Joe Turk.

Though he didn't wish Blake the best of luck, he was sure—
certain sure—that he'd need it.

*　　*　　*

The entrance to the Malibu Club was behind Sexton Blake
now. He stood in the dark street.

About twenty yards away the blonde was walking quickly.
Her high heels stabbed the cement, and beat a rapid, nervous
tattoo. Five yards behind her, overtaking her effortlessly, went
the man Carlo had called Joe Turk.

As Blake started off in pursuit, a long black car rounded the
corner of the block and bore down upon the girl and the man
who was following her.

As it passed Blake, he saw that it contained two men—one
in front, driving, and one behind. It braked hard a few feet
beyond the hurrying woman and, as it did so, she realised her
danger and tried to turn.

Instantly, the man called Turk leapt forward. His arms
enveloped her. One of the rear doors of the car came open with
a rush, and he made to hurl the woman on to the back seat.

She tried to scream, but the sound was choked off as he
thrust one of his large, hairy hands over her mouth.

Blake began to run.

He heard the sharp sound his feet made as they struck at the
pavement. He prayed he would be in time. The woman lashed
out with her long legs, and someone within the car revved the
engine impatiently.

15

The man called Turk did his best. As Blake raced towards him he freed one of his arms and struck the woman viciously. Her whole body slumped. Again he tried to throw her into the rear of the car.

Then Blake arrived, and the squat man let his burden fall as he swung to meet him.

The detective heard the woman's head crack against the pavement, and he saw Turk's hand dive for a pocket and come out holding something which glittered as it caught the light. It was a short wooden truncheon, not more than a foot long, and one end of it—the business end of it—was embedded with razor blades.

It was a fearsome weapon.

Turk made a great sweeping slash with it, and Blake had to jump back hurriedly to keep out of the way. But, in the next second, he struck.

Turk had thrown himself off-balance, and Blake took advantage of the fact. He made his right hand into a stiff, unyielding edge of bone, and he chopped down with it. He caught Turk across the side of his blubbery neck, and all of his one hundred and seventy pounds was behind the blow. The squat man gasped and staggered, and his unholy weapon flew wide, out of his grasp. It tinkled like glass as its half a hundred cutting edges hit the road.

Blake hit the squat man again, and this time it was with a fist which was bunched and as hard as iron. He slammed him over the heart and then, as he sagged, he brought his other fist all the way up from the floor in an uppercut which exploded on his opponent's jaw.

Turk collapsed backwards. He fell against the side of the car. Blake went after him.

Then there was a great, roaring sound in the detective's ears. In his eagerness to finish off his attacker he had forgotten all about the occupants of the car. Something struck him across the head. A great white blinding light burned briefly behind his eyes.

He fell to his knees, and tried to take hold on a chunk of air. It slipped through his fingers, and he collapsed on his face.

Dimly, he was conscious of voices shouting, and of the thunder of the car's engine. Then someone—breathing hard—cradled his head, and forced a mouthful of strong, fiery liquid between his teeth.

He coughed rackingly, tasting brandy. Then he got his eyes open.

He was looking straight up into the face of Tinker.

His eyes jerked sideways.

The car, and Joe Turk, had both gone.

TWO

Blake got to his feet. His head ached abominably. He touched it gingerly, and was sourly pleased to observe that at least he wasn't bleeding.

He said to Tinker, 'Where did you spring from?'

'Sniffy Petersen went straight home,' Tinker said. 'Fast. Like a racing pigeon. He's got a new wife. You didn't tell me.'

'I didn't know,' Blake said. 'And I'm not sure that "wife" is the right word anyway.'

'Well, whatever it is, he's got a new one. Some dish,' Tinker added judiciously. 'She opened the door to him. Must have been waiting for the sound of his footsteps in the street. And the way they carried on before they got the door closed again ... well. Sniffy won't be out and about again tonight.'

'No telephoning or stopping off on the way?'

'None. And with the job finished so quickly I came back here just on the off-chance——'

'To tell me.'

'That's right.'

'Lucky you did,' Blake said. 'Lucky for me. They had me down. They could have put the boot in—and would.' Then his head jerked round painfully. 'Where's the girl? They didn't get the girl?'

Tinker looked at him quickly. 'No, she's over there.' And he pointed. 'In that shop doorway. She was pretty shaken up.' He smiled faintly. 'But I pulled her round. Before I came back to you, as a matter of fact. I hope you don't mind, but I thought——'

'That my head has had a few hard knocks in its time and can stand a few more,' Blake said drily. 'I know. And I take it that the enemy made for the hills as soon as you put in an appearance?'

'Something like that,' Tinker agreed. 'I clouted one of them pretty hard, just in passing, and they weren't inclined to stay any longer.' He paused. 'Like to tell me what this is all about?'

'I don't know myself yet,' Blake said. 'I don't know who the girl is, or why the men in the car were out to get her. I know that one of the men was a character called Joe Turk, an enforcer, apparently, for one of the mobs. But that's all I do know.'

'I got the number of the car,' Tinker said off-handedly.

'You did? Then what are we doing just standing here nattering?' All the time, Blake had his eyes on the girl in the doorway. 'Chase it up, will you? You know what to do.'

'I ought to by now.'

'And find out all you can about Joe Turk, too.'

'Okay.' Tinker regarded Blake thoughtfully. 'And you'll be able to manage? Here, I mean. And'——he jerked his head—— 'and with her?'

'Yes, I'll be able to manage all right,' Sexton Blake said. 'And thanks, Tinker.'

His young partner had already started to move away from him.

Making for the shop doorway which sheltered the girl, Blake crossed the pavement.

* * *

Her perfume came to him just before he reached her. It was a pleasant perfume: faint, sharp and fragrant.

He had kept an eye on her while he'd been talking to

18

Tinker, but had delayed in approaching to give her a chance to recover as much of her poise as she could.

It seemed to be important. He didn't want to come upon her while she was at a grave disadvantage. He sensed that it might be important to her.

This was no ordinary young woman.

He caught himself thinking this not for the first time that evening and, again—not for the first time that evening—he found himself wondering if she was also going to be out of the ordinary so far as he himself was concerned.

It could be that way.

He knew himself very well, and he had sensed this too.

He halted in front of her. 'Are you all right?'

She leant against the shop window, head up, eyes almost closed. But she had her breathing under control. And the same was almost true of her voice.

'Just resting,' she said. 'And—and waiting to thank that young man.'

'He's gone, I'm afraid.'

Her eyes came open, and they were strangely wary. 'I saw you talking,' she said. 'You know him?'

'Very well.'

'And I saw you in the club.'

'Yes.' Blake was frowning. 'Are you sure you're all right? You took a nasty knock.'

'I'll be fine in a minute.'

'I'll get you a cab.'

'No—no. I'm all right. Really I am.' Quickly she pushed herself up from the window. 'No need for a cab. I'd rather walk.'

'If you're sure that you can . . .' Blake said dubiously. 'Here, let me help you.'

But she flinched away from him, and her voice wavered. 'Please don't worry about me. I can manage. Good night.'

She took four steps away from Blake—quick steps—and then swayed. She would have fallen if he hadn't stepped forward and taken hold of her.

Her body was taut and resistant beneath his hands.

'Please'—she got out—'please leave me alone. Please——'

But Blake had just spotted a cab as it cruised round the corner. He flagged it down. As it stopped, a sad face peered out at them, and a voice issued out from beneath a melancholy ragged moustache. 'Evenin' guv. How's business?'

'Why, Alf! Good evening to you!'

The young woman turned her head, and looked from one man to the other. Then the taxi-driver seemed to notice her for the first time. 'Lor, miss,' he said, 'you are in a bit of a state!'

He climbed down from his seat, came round the cab and opened the door. 'Hop in, miss.' He turned to Blake. 'Where to, guv? Baker Street?'

'I'm taking this young lady home,' Blake said, and looked at her. She still hadn't entered the cab. 'I'm afraid I don't know——'

He stopped, and waited for her to say where she lived.

But she hesitated, and the taxi-driver stepped into the breach. He seemed to divine what it was that was troubling her. He said kindly: 'Mister Blake is all right. You could trust him with your life, if you had to. I've known him for the best part of fifteen years. That right, guv?'

Blake didn't answer. He was watching the woman make up her mind.

Then she smiled a little shakily. 'Lowndes Square, Knightsbridge. I have a flat there.'

She climbed into the cab, and Blake followed her. He relaxed against the cushions as the driver climbed back into his seat and took off the handbrake. He said, 'You know my name, but I don't know yours.'

'Paula Dane, and'—she hesitated again, then she said—'and I'm grateful to you, no matter how ungrateful or suspicious I seem. It's just that——'

'I know,' Blake told her. 'And I'd be exactly the same.'

And he shrugged.

'Some men try to kidnap you,' he said. 'Or, at least, that's what it looks like. They use a car, and you struggle as one of them tries to bundle you into it, and you get knocked out. Next thing you know, there's a strange young man bending over you, reviving you, and the hoodlums seem to have gone. But it's all very odd.'

He shrugged again.

'You take this young man for a friend at first—until he leaves you to assist another man sprawled on the pavement. Then you're not so sure. Where did this other man come from? You saw him back in the club. Is he in cahoots with the enemy?

'He could be.

'The young man goes off abruptly, without letting you thank him. Very strange. Especially as you've seen him talking to the other man first. They seem to know each other. Is something being planned?

'Then this other character comes across to you, and suspicions harden. For one thing, you get knocked out when one man tried to bundle you into a car, and now this one seems hell-bent on getting you into a cab . . .'

He let his voice tail away, and the young woman by his side said, 'Am I really so obvious?' Then she answered her own question, ruefully, 'Yes, I suppose I am.'

Abruptly, she said, 'I've seen you somewhere before.'

'We've been into that. It was back at the Malibu.'

'No . . . somewhere else.' She frowned briefly. 'I'll remember.'

Then, suddenly, she shivered. 'Back at the Malibu——' She didn't go on.

'Remembering Turk?' Blake said gently.

'Turk?'

'The man you were so afraid of. I believe he is known to his Soho acquaintances as "Joe Turk".'

'I didn't know his name.' Paula was silent for a moment, and then she said slowly, as if feeling her way, 'How do *you* know it?'

'Don't start that again,' Blake said. 'I just asked. I could see the effect that he had on you, and I don't blame you for being afraid. He was a very nasty piece of work. The barman told me about him, and recommended that I keep out of his way.'

'That barman!' Paula said. 'That club! Ugh!'

'Not very prepossessing, is it? Though I think you're being a little unkind about Carlo, the barman. He's not such a bad type.'

'To a man, perhaps not. But to me——'

'He's not every woman's type, I agree,' Blake said. 'Some would find him a little too sure of himself.'

'You can say that again!' Then Paula said, 'But if you're not all that fond of the place, why do you go there?' She added quickly: 'You don't have to tell me. I'm just poking my nose into things which don't concern me.'

'I go there on business,' Blake said.

'Oh . . .' Paula sounded as though she didn't believe him.

'When you know me a little better,' Blake said, 'and when you know what my business is, then I think that you'll understand. But—for now—let's just say that some people can be persuaded to talk, and that I like to listen.'

'Is that a cue for me?'

'You don't have to tell me,' Blake said. He chose her own phrase, and he used her own intonation. His gentle mockery brought a smile to her lips.

Then she said swiftly, 'There's not really a lot to tell.'

'No?'

'No. And you can take that look out of your eyes. I mean it!'

Blake looked at her sidelong. 'Not a lot to tell, eh? Joe Turk's a professional thug, and back at the Malibu wasn't the first time you'd seen him. It seems to me that he's out to get you. I'm not saying this just to frighten you, but——'

'You don't need to try to frighten me,' Paula said soberly. 'I'm scared to death!'

'Then what's it all about? I might be able to help.'

Paula didn't say anything at all for a long moment. She looked out of the cab window and saw the Victoria and Albert Museum slide past as the taxi moved on down Brompton Road towards Knightsbridge. Then she said, almost absently, 'The barman warned you about this man, Joe Turk? Warned you to keep away from him?'

'Yes.'

22

'He warned you to—to mind your own business, in fact?'

'More or less.'

'But you came out, all the same,' Paula said. 'I heard some-one running. That was you?'

'Yes.'

'Why?' Paula asked. 'Why did you interfere? You needn't have done. No one else bothered.'

Blake didn't answer her. Instead, he looked out of the window on his side of the cab and said: 'We must be getting pretty near to your place by now. We've just passed Harrods.'

Paula looked at him thoughtfully. Then she laid her hand on his. 'I'll tell you all that there is to tell,' she said. 'You'll come up? I can offer you a cup of coffee. The real thing. Not inst.'

Blake smiled. 'But you don't——'

'I know,' Paula said. 'I don't have to. But I'm going to all the same. Because I want to. Does that satisfy you?'

The cab slid in to the kerb in front of a large, modern block of flats, and Blake helped her out.

Later, she lounged back on a curved four-seater settee and pushed out her legs in front of her. Ruefully, she examined her nylons. They were badly laddered. Blake sipped his coffee, and complimented her on it. She smiled, picked up a silver cigarette box, and offered it to him.

He accepted a cigarette, and lit hers for her. Then he re-laxed into the deep comfort of his armchair and looked around him.

It was a nice room.

The floor was covered in rich red carpeting, and here and there round the room there were small fleecy-white rugs.

The walls were plain, a very pale green, set off with white doors and skirting boards, and along the length of one of the walls there ran a series of glass-fronted bookcases.

Beside Blake's chair, there was a small, light-wood table and, beyond it, close to the long windows, there was a baby grand piano and a writing desk.

Elsewhere in the room there was order, and security, and a sort of overriding peace, but on the writing desk all was con-fusion. There was a small portable typewriter, and a squared-off pile of new paper; there were used sheets of all shapes and sizes, some torn and some crumpled. On the very edge of the desk, two pencils balanced, and both had broken points. On the floor beside the desk, there lay an open dictionary, and something which appeared to be a printers' type-specimen book.

'That's where I do my homework,' Paula said suddenly, and Blake realised that she had been watching him.

'You must forgive me,' he said. 'I'm being my usual self. Insatiably curious—and very rude.'

'Do you like it—all apart from my untidy writing desk, I mean?'

Blake began to make a casual answer, and then he suddenly realised that this young woman really wanted to know. It wasn't a casual question. She was really interested to know what he thought of her room.

'I do like it,' he said, and he meant it. 'Even the writing desk.'

Paula laughed. Then she said, 'I suppose you're really waiting for me to begin my story, only you're much too polite to show your impatience.'

Blake didn't say anything, but he smiled.

'Well—all I know is that the man you saw tonight—the man who you told me is called Joe Turk—is trying to kidnap me,' Paula said. She was trying hard to be casual. 'It's rather frightening,' she said, in the tone of voice she might have used to describe a new film.

She said: 'Last night, I was coming home very late, and a man followed me up here from the Tube. I could hear him behind me, but I didn't think anything of it at first. I'm not one of these girls who imagines the worst all the time. In fact, you could say I didn't think anything of it at all—not until he attacked me about two hundred yards back down the road.'

She drew on her cigarette quickly, and shivered.

'What happened?' Blake wanted to know.

'He just grabbed me,' Paula said, 'and started dragging me towards this parked car. I hadn't noticed it until then. You know how you see things, yet, somehow, don't really see them?

Well, this car was parked on the opposite side of the road, well away from all the other cars parked there, and there were two men inside it.'

'The same car as tonight?'

'I don't know. I don't think so.'

'Hmm,' Sexton Blake said. 'But two men inside the car, like tonight. And the man who attacked you——?'

'He was the same. The man you call Joe Turk.'

'I see,' Blake said. 'Well, go on.'

'He had dragged me halfway across the road to the car,' Paula said, 'when another car shot round a corner. It was travelling at speed and swinging all over the road. The driver was drunk, I should think. Anyway, it saved me. Because it came straight at us, you see. How it missed us I'll never know. But Turk—he let go of me. He had to, to get out of the way. And I just ran and ran.'

'Hmm . . .' Blake said again.

'But that isn't all,' Paula said. 'I was pretty shaken up last night. Who wouldn't be? Well—you can imagine. But I didn't think of what had happened as a part of any predetermined plan. I certainly didn't think of kidnapping. You can guess what I thought, can't you?'

'I think so,' Blake told her slowly.

'What I thought was that I'd just had a providential escape from a fate worse than death. Turk and the other two men in the car . . .'

She shivered again.

'Did you report what had happened to the police?'

'No . . .' She hesitated. 'Again, maybe you can guess why.'

'You thought of the attack on you as a prelude to what would have been a very nasty sexual assault,' Blake said slowly. 'If it had happened. But it hadn't. Now you wanted to forget all about it as fast as possible.'

'Do you blame me?'

Blake shrugged. 'I know it happens all the time.'

'I thought of it as a thoroughly unpleasant but isolated incident,' Paula told him. 'It was what happened tonight that made me think again.'

25

'At the Malibu Club?'

'At the Malibu—and before,' Paula said.

'What happened "before"?'

'I'd been working late'—she gestured towards the littered writing desk—'with my homework. I hadn't taken any time out to get myself a meal. About half past ten I decided I'd go out and have supper—somewhere special. Really treat myself. There's a very good place I know at the top of Kensington Church Street. Not the High Street end.'

'And?'

She stubbed her cigarette out. She said: 'I took a cab there. No trouble. And supper was fine. But, afterwards, when I came out on to the pavement, there waiting for me was the man who'd grabbed me last night. Joe Turk.'

'And?' Blake repeated.

'I—well—I don't know'—she sounded very uncertain now —'I suppose that I panicked. He started to move towards me, and I tried to get back into the restaurant. But he was there before me and, well, I just ran. There was a cab cruising by, and I yelled, but the driver either didn't hear me, or didn't want to, and I kept on running. And that man—Joe Turk— was after me.'

Her voice wavered.

'I doubled down side-streets, thinking that I might be able to shake him off. Then I found the Malibu Club, and the rest you know.'

'But again you didn't call the police,' Sexton Blake said.

'All the time that I was running from him, I was praying that I'd see a policeman,' Paula Dane said. 'But you know how it is. When you really do need one there are never any of them about.'

'And at the Malibu? You could have phoned the police from the Malibu.'

'I was terrified. Shaken up. I needed something to steady me. Well—you might have seen the way I attacked those whiskys, and I don't drink as a rule. I was going to call the police just as soon as I was steady enough to tell them a coherent story. Otherwise, I knew what they'd think. That I was just another hysterical female imagining things. But then Turk caught up with me again, and——'

'Will you go to the police now?'

'I don't know,' Paula said. She twisted her hands in her lap; looked at them. Finally, she looked up at Blake and said: 'Oddly enough, I don't think I'm frightened any more. Not the way that I was. Telling you everything has helped a lot. It's helped me revert to the kind of female I was before all this started. A very stubborn female. The kind who likes to fight her own battles. The kind who likes to know what's going on.'

'You can't fight this battle yourself,' Blake told her. 'You'd lose it if you did. You're up against an organisation. That much is obvious. I don't know what the organisation is, or what it wants from you, but one thing is quite clear. It's not out to do you any good! I think that you should go to the police. I think that you should tell them what you've told me. I——'

He stopped, seeing Paula smiling at him. 'What's so funny?'

'Nothing.'

'Then why are you smiling?'

'No reason.'

She pulled her long legs up beneath her, and smoothed down her skirt.

Blake looked at her without saying anything for a moment, and then reverted to his argument. 'You really can't manage this thing on your own. It's pretty obvious you're in great danger. You need help!'

'I think I'll put the whole thing in the hands of a private detective,' Paula said.

'Not good enough,' Blake told her. 'Private detectives are all right for some things, but for an affair like this——'

'There are private detectives and private detectives,' Paula said firmly.

'And who have you got in mind?' Blake asked sardonically. 'Who's the wonder man you think could sort out this mess?'

'Someone I know.'

'He'd better be good!'

'I think he is,' Paula said. There was a devil of mischief dancing in her eyes.

'And his name?'

Paula smiled at him. 'You know,' she said conversationally. 'I think you're going to be very cross with me. But, some little time back, I remembered something. I knew that I would. I knew that I'd seen you before . . .'

Sexton Blake stared at her.

THREE

Paula Dane looked at her fingers tracing a pattern on the cover of the curved four-seater settee.

She didn't look at Blake.

She said, 'You told me yourself that I needed help, and now I remember where I read about you; you're the one that I want to help me . . .'

She raised her eyes to his, then, and they were very deep, very soft and very appealing.

'There's no one I'd rather have to help me than you,' she said. 'You'd be my first, my last and my only choice.'

Blake didn't say anything and, after a moment, Paula dropped her eyes. She said uncertainly, 'I know I can't pay as much as your other clients, but——'

Blake said quietly: 'The money doesn't matter.'

But Paula had stood up. She reached for her handbag. Blake stopped her. 'I don't want money from you.'

And he meant it.

Paula was no ordinary young woman. Not to him. He could not treat her as an ordinary client.

'But'—she said helplessly—'you said yourself that I can't handle this thing on my own, and if you won't——'

Blake interrupted.

'To every crime there must be a motive,' he said. 'We must

28

uncover the motive in this case, if we are ever to have any answer to creatures like Joe Turk.'

'Then you are going to help me!' Her face lit up.

'You're going to help yourself,' Blake said. 'You're going to help by remembering every little thing which has happened to you during the past few months——'

'Everything?' Paula said, from under an arched eyebrow.

'Yes. Every sordid aspect of your life must be dragged out into the light of day. Everyone you've met recently must be subjected to a close and almost clinical examination.'

Then Blake's voice changed.

'Seriously,' he said, 'that's what we must do. Joe Turk is clearly trying to kidnap you—why? I already know this much about him: he's not the head man in any criminal enterprise. He's obeying orders. But whose? And what is their motive? It must be hidden somewhere in the past. Possibly the immediate past. And we have to find it. So suppose you start taxing your memory.'

'It's not that difficult,' Paula said. 'Four months ago I came to London. Before that—well, before that I was blazing a trail in journalism in the provinces. You know—mornings spent in police courts, and afternoons at bun-fights or Women's Institute Meetings. You know the kind of thing. I think it would be hard to find the motivation for some deep and sinister plot in those surroundings.'

'And after that?' Blake asked. 'After you came to London?'

'Well, I thought that I could get a job in Fleet Street just for the asking. It was the same old story, I'm afraid. I ended up in the job I'm holding down now—copy-writing for an advertising agency.'

She struck an attitude.

'Does your baby drool? Does he go blue in the face or go bump in the night? Try Thompson's Elixir!'

Blake smiled despite himself. Then he said, 'If that's all——'

'Well ...' Paula said doubtfully, '... there is the business about Uncle Roderick ...'

'Oh? And who's he?'

'Who was he, you mean,' Paula said. 'He's dead now.'

'Tell me about him.'

Paula looked more doubtful than ever. 'There's not all that much to tell. And I can't see it's got any bearing at all on what has been happening——'

'Tell me, nevertheless,' Blake insisted.

'Well—well, all right——' Paula leaned back. 'He wasn't my uncle really,' she said. 'His name was Sir Roderick de Courcy. You may have heard of him.' She looked inquiringly at Blake. 'No? Well, he was some distant relative of my mother. A twelfth cousin or something. He died recently, and he left me something in his will—or—rather—I'm hoping he did.'

Blake said quickly, 'What did he leave you, or don't you know?'

'The will isn't being read until next week. I shall have to go north for that. I've had a letter from Sir Roderick's solicitors, so I suppose that I must be a beneficiary. But it won't be much.'

Blake was eyeing her thoughtfully. 'He hadn't much to leave?'

Paula smiled. 'To put it vulgarly, he was loaded. He must have died worth a cool three or four hundred thousand at least. Probably more. Perhaps very much more. I have heard it said he was worth a million.'

Blake drew a sharp breath. 'Well, then . . .' he said.

But Paula shook her head firmly.

'Uh-uh. There is a son. The last of the de Courcys. A wart by the name of Simon. He'll get ninty-nine point nine per cent of the estate. I'd bet on it.'

'But you can't be that sure!'

'Can't I?' said Paula. 'He will. Just you see. And he'll make very good use of it. Why, it might even keep him in wine, women and song for the best part of a year!'

Blake looked at her. 'You don't like Simon.'

'You don't have to be a world-famous detective to deduce that,' she said. 'I admit it freely. I loathe Simon. I've only been in his company for a few days, but, believe me, that was ten years too long!'

Blake was smiling again. 'When was that?'

'When Sir Roderick felt he was about to shuffle off this mortal coil. He thought he would like to cast his fading gaze over the ragged remnants of the family, I suppose. And I was it. My mother died years ago. So he sent me an invitation to go north and spend a few days at Levistone—that's the family seat in Cumberland. I went'—and she sighed—'and I met Simon.'

'The wart.'

'Yes, the wart,' she agreed. 'The old man was dying, but that didn't stop Simon from trying to improve the shining hour, if you see what I mean. He wouldn't leave me alone. Well, when you've got to barricade your bedroom door at night, it's a bit much, don't you think? It wasn't enough to say "No". With his type you've got to beat the word home with a five-foot club.'

'Sounds a really nice fellow,' Blake remarked.

'Oh, yes. All of that. Very,' Paula said sourly. 'Anyway, I stood it for as long as I could, and then I left and came south again. I hadn't used up all my holiday from the Agency, and I just had to fritter it away.'

'I see. And you really don't think your legacy will amount to very much?'

'I know what you're thinking,' Paula said. '*Rich Young Heiress Put Out of Way by Scheming Seventeenth Half-Cousin.* But, frankly, I don't think that will stand up.'

'I'm not sure it will, either,' Blake said thoughtfully. 'But it's an idea one can't just ignore.'

'But, surely, if someone—Simon, for instance—wanted me out of the way so that I couldn't inherit a whole stack of boodle, they'd just stick a knife in my back, or push me under a train, or something. Wouldn't it be far easier for them than attempting to kidnap me? And attempting to kidnap me is what they've been doing.'

'Yes,' Blake said frowning. 'That thought had occurred to me ...'

31

He was silent for a very long moment.

Then he said, 'Can you think of anything else out of the ordinary that's happened to you over the past few weeks?'

'Not a thing.'

'Then,' Blake said slowly, 'we're left with this legacy. It's all we've got—at least for the moment. It might be worth taking the trouble to find out just what your expectations are. You say you had a letter from Sir Roderick's solicitors? Have you got it handy?'

'It's in my bag.'

Paula looked for it, and found it. She handed it to Blake. He took out a notebook and unclipped a fountain pen from his pocket.

'Boddy, Blackman and Boddy,' he said, as he wrote. 'Lincoln's Inn Fields ...' He folded the letter and handed it back to her. He said, 'This will give me something to work on tomorrow.'

'Frankly,' said Paula, 'I don't think it will lead anywhere.'

'Possibly not,' Blake agreed. 'So you can spend your time in contemplation, and if you remember anything else which may be of use please let me know.'

'Of course. Yes, I'll do that.' She frowned unhappily. 'Though I can't think of a thing at the moment. I wish I didn't feel that I'm wasting your time.'

'What do you mean?'

'Well—tomorrow, and Boddy, Blackman and Boddy——'

'We have to start our work of elimination somewhere,' Blake said. 'We might as well begin with your legacy.' He stood up. 'Now I'll leave you.'

'But you can't go yet!' Paula protested. 'You haven't had all of your coffee. In any case, I'm sure that what's left of it is quite cold. Let me make some more.'

'Thank you, but no.' Blake shook his head. 'I'd better not stay. There are still one or two things I have to attend to before I turn in. And there are one or two things for you to attend to, as well.'

'Me?'

'Lock all your windows, and see that your front door is bolted. Don't take any chances.'

'All right . . . if you say so . . .'

Together they walked out into the small hall of the flat. Blake opened the door and turned to say 'Good night.' He was totally unprepared for what happened next.

Paula put an arm around him. She brought his head down. She kissed him on the lips very gently. Then she let him go.

'Good night,' she said softly. 'Good night, and thank you.'

The door closed.

Slowly and thoughtfully, Blake turned around and walked down the thickly carpeted stairs to the street. When he reached it, he quickened his pace and swung up the road into Knightsbridge.

There, by the Tube station, he found himself a phone box, pulled open the door and went inside.

He dialled a number and heard it begin to ring. It rang on and on, and Blake pursed his lips and glanced at his slim, gold wristwatch. He was mildly surprised to see that the time was coming up to half past two.

Then, suddenly, the ringing tone stopped as the receiver was lifted at the other end of the line. *Beep—beep—beep—* went the phone, and Blake fed a coin into the box. 'Tinker?' he said, and was rewarded with a sleepy grunt in reply. 'Blake here,' he said. 'Sorry to wake you.'

'Tha's all ri——' Tinker yawned hugely. 'Haven't been in bed long——'

Blake said, 'And I lost track of the time, I'm afraid.'

Tinker was suddenly wide awake—chuckling.

'You ought to wash it,' Blake said.

'What?'

'That laugh of yours—for a start.'

Tinker chuckled again, unabashed. 'All right, so I'm not so hot on deduction.'

'How did the detective bit go?' Blake wanted to know.

'You mean following up that car number I caught——'

'And Turk,' Sexton Blake said.

'I left a note for you in the usual place in the study,' Tinker said. 'Tracing the car was dead easy. It was a hot one.'

'Stolen ...' Blake did not sound surprised. Paula Dane had been far from sure that the same car had been used in both attempts on her.

'Stolen not too far away from the Malibu Club,' Tinker said.

Yes, Blake thought, it all added up. 'And what about Joe Turk?'

'Nothing on him at all,' Tinker said. 'Not so far. Nothing new or concrete, I mean. He's got a criminal record, of course. But you must have guessed that. You told me he is an enforcer for one of the mobs.'

'But I don't know which one,' Blake said quickly. 'And I want to know.'

'Agreed,' Tinker said. 'But I don't know, either. Not yet. I couldn't get hold of any of our usual sources of such information down at the Yard. They're all off duty, and I didn't think it right to butt in on their beauty sleep. That's why I reckoned I might just as well catch up on my own. Particularly as you seemed to be making a night of it. I'll call in at the Yard again first thing in the morning.'

'All right,' Blake agreed. 'And there's something else. I want you to find out all you can about the late Sir Roderick de Courcy. He died a week or so ago at a place called Levistone, in Cumberland. Got that?'

'Yes. Got it. Am I to look for anything in particular?'

'I don't know what you're to look for,' Blake said truthfully. 'Just dig up anything and everything you can about the old boy. Another thing, too——'

'Yes?'

'Sir Roderick's son, Simon de Courcy. See what you can find out about him. He might have been living beyond his income recently. Ask around.'

'Okay. I'll do that. Is that all?'

Blake smiled into the telephone.

'Isn't it enough?'

Tinker chuckled again. 'It should keep me out of mischief

34

for an hour or two,' he agreed. Then he said, 'And when do I get to hear what this is all about?'

'I'll fill you in just as soon as you've checked with the Yard in the morning,' Blake told him. 'We'd better have a full-blown conference about this one.'

'All right.'

'And now you can go back to sleep.'

'Thanks,' Tinker said laconically. Then he added, 'There's just one more question from me.'

'And what's that?'

'This Turk character. Have you any message for him if I should happen to bump into him?'

'No message, exactly,' Blake said slowly. 'Just thump him before he can carve you up, and everyone will be happy.'

'Everyone except Turk.'

'You're becoming too considerate, Tinker,' Blake said severely. 'Too considerate by far. It's a failing. Just do as I ask you and save your head to rest your hat on.'

He smiled broadly.

'Good night!'

FOUR

It was nine o'clock in the morning when Sexton Blake took his Bentley away from the Baker Street kerb and the tall, rather elderly house where he lived.

He headed south, sliding his way into the traffic stream doing a twentieth-century hesitation waltz towards Oxford Circus. He was bound for Lincoln's Inn, and the offices of the firm of Boddy, Blackman and Boddy, the late Sir Roderick de Courcy's solicitors.

Driving almost automatically as the traffic ahead of him plunged through London's streets at a reckless average speed of seven miles an hour, Blake mentally reviewed the events of the previous evening.

He had gone to the Malibu Club for a quiet, confidential

chat with a snout, just as he had done on innumerable other occasions. It was the ideal place for that sort of thing. And as well as gaining access to some secrets of the underworld, he had also walked head-on into trouble and adventure. He smiled to himself. The Malibu had certainly given him value for money last night.

Sniffy Petersen had been very forthcoming, and the Carfax Case was wrapped up. It was finished. A neat, watertight job, the Director of Public Prosecutions would be delighted to learn when he received the papers Blake had sent him this morning.

And as fast as one case had been closed, another had opened. As a beginning, a very personable young woman had been rescued from something which could only have been a thoroughly unpleasant fate.

Of course, that was just the luck of the game, Sexton Blake thought. The 'very personable' bit. If Paula Dane had been totally unattractive instead of a beautifully curved, well-endowed blonde, he would still have gone to her assistance.

All the same, he had to admit that the fact that Paula was a very desirable young woman had made the world a little brighter on this, the morning after. It had made him feel that little bit younger.

He smiled to himself as he thought about that.

And now, following on what Paula had told him, Tinker was already hard at work elsewhere in London, and he himself was about to begin his own personal series of investigations in her service. Ahead of him lay an interview with some member of the firm of Boddy, Blackman and Boddy.

A singularly unattractive set of names, Blake thought. A singularly dry lot. There was no chance of there being an unexpectedly beautiful blonde among *them*.

He could not have been more right.

Fifteen minutes later, Blake was following a rather dowdy woman who wore squeaking shoes along a very narrow, dusty passage. Immediately after that, he came face to face with the senior partner of this firm of solicitors, Mr Aloysius Boddy himself.

The dowdy woman clerk retired with one last despairing squeak of sad shoes, and Blake allowed himself a quick glance round the room before settling into the chair the senior partner offered him.

It was a tall room. Tall and narrow, with a window which faced out across a street barely wide enough to permit the passage of a very small car. From floor to ceiling were stacked row upon row of heavy steel deed-boxes, all painted a funereal black, and each bearing the name of some honoured and distinguished family.

Cowering under the great cliff of boxes, crouched there as if expecting them to fall at any moment and pound it to matchwood, there was a frail, rather rickety, old oaken desk. And behind the desk sat the senior partner, who now looked at Blake over the top of old-fashioned metal-framed spectacles, coughed wheezily once or twice, sniffed and twitched and rustled some papers, and then inquired: 'You wanted ... hrrmmmph ... to see me?'

'Yes, sir. I think your clerk brought you my card——'

'Your card ...? Oh, yes ... yes ... hrrmmmph ... yes, Sexton Blake. Yes ... I've heard of you ... investigator chap. Never do business of that kind ... hrrmmmph. You're wasting your time, young man.'

He glanced up at Blake again, and this time the detective saw that the eyes behind the spectacles were blue and kindly, if rather remote from worldly things. He said, 'Business of what kind, sir?' .

'Hrrmmmph ...?' The older man blinked. 'Divorce business, what else? Never touch it. Never have, and never will. Don't believe in it. Marriage is a fine institution ... hrrmmmph. No family should be without it.'

'It's not divorce business,' Blake began. 'I don't touch it either. I telephoned earlier. I got your clerk. She said——'

'Not divorce business? Telephoned?'

The old man on the other side of the desk looked rather lost. He spread out palsied fingers and allowed them to quiver over the papers which littered his desk.

'Can never find anything,' he complained querulously. 'That

clerk. Hasn't been here long enough to know about things. Too inexperienced. Always said we should never have had a woman ...'

'Then why did you appoint one?'

'Had to ...' the old man murmured vaguely. '... It's the war, you know. It's the war ...'

He seemed to give up the search for whatever it was he'd been seeking on his impossibly untidy desk. He clasped his wrinkled hands together and began to smooth the skin back on each finger.

He said, 'What was it you wanted to see me about?'

'Sir Roderick de Courcy's estate, sir. I understand that you're handling it.'

'Handling it?' The old man looked brighter. 'Oh, dear me, yes. Yes ... we've handled de Courcy affairs for as long as I can remember ...' The light faded out of his eyes. 'Longer even,' he said.

'Then you can tell me the value of the estate, sir? And there's a will. I understand that it's to be read in the very near future.'

'Yes ...?' The old eyes were vacant. Then life once more shone out through them. 'The value of the estate, you say? No harm in you knowing, Mr Blake. Though why you should want to ...' The voice tailed away, then recovered. 'Half a million pounds sterling, duty paid. That's the value of the estate.'

Sexton Blake drew in a breath. 'And the will, sir? I don't suppose you could tell me its terms, or even give me a hint——? I know this is all very irregular.'

The old man said nothing. To Blake it seemed more than likely that he had not even heard.

'Could you tell me the terms of the will?' he repeated, more loudly. 'Could you give me a hint?'

'What are you shouting for, Mr Blake? I can hear you!' Mr Boddy leaned forward and glared at Blake over the top of his spectacles.

'Look,' Blake said placatingly. 'If it's at all possible ... just

38

a hint would be sufficient. I only need the answers to a few questions . . .'

'What do you want the information for?'

The question came out clearly and strongly. Its directness surprised the detective.

'I have a client,' he said. 'A young woman. There have been two attempts to kidnap her within the last couple of days. Naturally, she is concerned to know why. So am I. It so happens that she has been told Sir Roderick has left her something, and I wondered if this might have some connection with the attempts which have been made on her. Consequently, I thought that if you could give me some idea of the extent of her expectations . . .'

It was as if the old man had not heard a word. 'Are you asking these questions on behalf of a moneylender?' he demanded abruptly.

'I told you, sir——'

'What is the name of your client?'

Blake controlled his mounting impatience by swallowing— hard. He said: 'Paula Dane. Miss Paula Dane.'

'Hrrmmmph. And you say——'

Blake didn't allow him to complete the question, even though he had no idea of what it was to be. He just opened his mouth and said 'Yes' very firmly. He thought it was the only way to save time.

On the other side of the desk, the old man started to chuckle and then to laugh. He laughed until he choked on a bout of coughing. Then he lay gasping face downwards on his desk for a moment, but pushed himself erect before Blake could reach him. He shook out a large white handkerchief, and applied it carefully to the corners of his eyes. Then he slowly wiped his thin-lipped, shrunken mouth.

'Forgive me,' he said. 'I humbly beg your pardon, Mr Blake.'

And then, almost briskly, he added: 'Miss Paula Dane will not have a large inheritance. I repeat: she will not. Does that answer your question?'

'It might,' Blake said doubtfully, 'if all things weren't

relative. But you mentioned half a million pounds a little while back, and——'

The old man said abruptly: 'Miss Paula Dane will receive hardly anything at all under the terms of Sir Roderick's will. What she will receive will only be something in the nature of a simple remembrance. There—does that satisfy you?'

Blake's mouth twisted wryly.

'Satisfy is not a word I would have chosen,' he said. A perfectly feasible motive for everything that had been happening to Paula Dane had just been thrown out of a dusty Lincoln's Inn window. 'However, you've told me what I needed to know, and——'

But the old man wasn't listening. He was going on, his voice climbing querulously. 'And why should Miss Paula Dane have a large inheritance? Tell me that! Why on earth should she expect one?'

'She doesn't,' said Blake. 'She——'

Mr Boddy ignored him. 'She isn't a de Courcy. Not truly. Just an offshoot of the family. And it's the de Courcys themselves that must continue. It's that blood-line which is the one which must thrive. A father's first duty is to his eldest son and to the generations of de Courcys as yet unborn. That is the way it always has been. There isn't enough and to spare to give everyone a piece of the estate—every little snivelling poor relation. Not even out of half a million pounds, duty paid, my dear sir!

'The de Courcys' ancestral home must be maintained. A vast place. Have you any idea of what it costs to maintain that house, Mr Blake? Have you even the glimmerings of an idea?'

'I ...'

The old man swept on.

'Tradition,' he said. 'Tradition—that is what the de Courcys pay for. That's what they spend their money on. It's what they live for. Tradition—and the continuity of an honourable family name. Continuity in an age which lives only for today, and which cannot begin to imagine a tomorrow—nor a yesterday, come to that. But to the de Courcys, the past is every whit as important as the future. For theirs is a great and honourable past. Do you understand me?'

'I ...'

But the old man wasn't really seeking an answer.

'The de Courcy pendant,' he said. 'That's what I mean. And there's continuity for you. Handed down from father to son—father to son. There's history for you.'

The light in his eyes suddenly died. Abruptly, the old man seemed shrunken. He lifted his head on its thin neck. He moved it from side to side. 'What was I saying?'

'The de Courcy pendant ...'

'No heir can inherit without it. You know that? No heir can inherit without it!'

The old man's voice faded. He leant back in his chair and closed his eyes. It seemed to Blake that the interview was over.

He got up to go. At the door, he turned. He thought that the old man was sleeping. He moved forward gently, on the balls of his feet, and reached out a hand to grip the door-knob.

As he did so, a voice rustled out from behind him. 'Never do divorce business,' he said. 'Wasting your time, Mr Blake. Wasting your time.'

And then, very distinctly, the old voice went on: 'I couldn't tell you anything about the will, even if I wanted to. It's against all the ethics of my profession, you know. My partners wouldn't approve, either. Can't tell you a thing. Our duty is to the last of the de Courcys ...'

A sigh.

'... The last of the de Courcys ... that Simon ... a bad one. A bad one.'

There was another deep sigh from the old man as Blake turned and looked at him. The aged eyelids were closed, and lay flat against the shrivelled cheeks.

'Thank you,' Sexton Blake said. He shut the door behind him very quietly.

And, as he walked down the long and dusty passage which led him to the main office, he thought that Mr Aloysius Boddy might be old—he might even be somewhat enfeebled—but his mind and his heart were both in the right place.

FIVE

Blake stepped out into the street and, for a brief instant, he screwed up his eyes. The sunlight hurt him.

It was so clean, so sharp and so bright after the dusty gloom of the offices he had just left.

He began to walk towards Chancery Lane, near where he had left his car, and his steps were slow and laggardly. He was thinking of what Mr Aloysius Boddy had told him: of the words themselves, and of every accent and intonation.

'Miss Paula Dane will not have a large inheritance ... Miss Paula Dane will receive hardly anything at all ...'

That was what the old man had said. Blake had told him of the attempts upon Paula, and he had made that statement. It could only mean that it wouldn't be worth anyone's while to dispose of her in order to lay hands on her legacy.

Paula had been right.

And there went a nice, straightforward motive for the attempts to kidnap her—there it went, down the nearest rat-hole.

Blake thought ruefully that he was now back where he had started.

Then he thought again, and realised that he wasn't. He had advanced a little. But whether it was along a road leading to the solution of his problems only time could tell.

Mr Aloysius Boddy had said something about a de Courcy pendant—whatever that was. It was important, obviously. The old man had insisted that no heir could inherit without it ...

And he had said something else, too. Something which Blake judged to be more important still. He had said—to use his exact words—'The last of the de Courcys ... that Simon ... a bad one ... a bad one ...'

Blake mentally repeated the phrases again and again.

This was the considered opinion of the family solicitor. The old man had bent the ethics of his profession almost to breaking point in order to get the words out. They must be important. The old man was no fool. He had been trying to tell Blake something, and he had made the attempt in the only way that he knew.

He had been trying to tell him something. But what, Blake wondered. But what?

Suppose it was only a considered opinion, Blake thought. Suppose the words meant just what they said. That, and no more?

No! They had to mean more! Boddy, Blackman and Boddy was a reputable firm which had served the de Courcys for generations. The old man had made great play of that fact.

The senior partner of such a firm wouldn't lightly pass judgement on one of his clients. And he would never pass such a judgement in the hearing of a third party!

Back to Simon de Courcy again, Sexton Blake thought.

He had begun his investigations thinking that Simon de Courcy might in some way be responsible for the attacks upon Paula Dane. He had thought of money as being the motive. In talking to Paula, he had described his projected visit to Boddy, Blackman and Boddy as part of a process of elimination.

He had to begin somewhere, he had said. Why not begin with the legacy? Why not eliminate that first?

Well, all right, so he had eliminated it now—with a vengeance. But only a motive had been eliminated, not a man.

If anything, the light of suspicion was now more definitely focused on Simon de Courcy than it had been before.

Blake saw that he was passing a phone box. He stopped and tugged at the door, glancing at his watch as he did so. It was just coming up to ten o'clock. He wondered if he would get Paula Dane at her flat, or if she would have already left for her office. He had to talk to her.

He dialled the number of the block of flats, but she had already gone. However, the porter was able to give him the number of the firm of advertising agents in Knightsbridge that she worked for, and moments later Blake was speaking to her.

'I rather hoped you might like to have lunch with me,' he said.

'I'd love to!' Then she laughed. 'I'd better say that again

43

a little less enthusiastically. A girl shouldn't sound so eager.'

'Anything to report? Any disturbances? Anyone trying to break into your flat?'

'No one trying to break in,' she said, 'and the only thing that I have to report is that I lay awake after you'd gone for hours and hours ...'

A silence came to hang between them. Then she said, a little too brightly: 'Well, I'll see you for lunch then. What time, and where?'

'Half past one?'

She was efficient and impersonal now. She might have been making an appointment for him to see some finished layouts for an advertising campaign. 'Can you make it two o'clock? It's late, I know, but——'

'Fine,' he said. 'At the Berkeley Buttery? You know it?'

'I know it. I'll be there.' And then her voice was suddenly softer again. 'And thank you for inviting me ...'

The line clicked as she put down her phone. Slowly and thoughtfully, Blake hung up in turn.

Why did he feel this way about Paula Dane? Just the sound of her voice on the phone ... He found her oddly disturbing.

Yet he'd had young, and charming, and beautiful clients before, scores of them, and their charm and their youth and their beauty had never affected him. Not in this way.

It must be as he'd thought almost in the first moment of seeing Paula: for him, she was something special.

He went out of the phone box; let the door close behind him. And, as it shut, so he shut Paula out of his mind. He forgot the woman, and concentrated on her problem. He thought it was about time he had a long talk with Tinker: the full-blown conference he had promised himself. But first—before that——

He picked up his car. He drove to Great Russell Street, to the British Museum.

Before going back to Baker Street and a council of war with Tinker, Blake's curiosity prompted him to find out more about the de Courcy pendant.

The door bore a small brass plate which carried the name 'William J. Peard'.

As Blake pushed the door open, a tall, lean man looked up from examining an amulet of intricate design and laid his magnifying glass aside.

He stepped across the room and shook hands with the detective. He said: 'I'm glad to see you, Blake.' And it was as though he had carefully weighed every word that he uttered.

His speech was slow and thoughtful. He pulled a pipe out of his pocket, tapped down the tobacco with a thin, stained finger, and struck a match.

'Sit down,' he said.

He himself leant against a large, solid oak table. His legs were thrust out at an angle. They crossed at the ankles, the one over the other. He bent his head forward, and a quiff of greying brown hair dropped down into his eyes. He brushed it back carefully, drew on his pipe and then removed it from his mouth.

He said: 'Long time no see. What can I do for you?'

Blake looked at him. 'Does the name "The de Courcy Pendant" mean anything to you?'

'It's not a name. It's a description,' Peard said. His eyes were mischievous.

'All right. So a humble detective doesn't know the jargon,' Blake said. Then he added, smiling, 'Would you tell me about it?'

Peard tilted his head back for a moment. He stared at a corner of the ceiling. Then he dropped his gaze to meet that of the detective, and said: 'It's made of gold, crudely worked. It's studded with semi-precious stones. Heaven only knows how old it is, but some authorities put it as being early twelfth century. It was probably made in the Low Countries. Is that the kind of thing you want?'

'Pretty well,' Blake said. 'Has it been in the possession of the de Courcy family all of that time?'

'No ...' Peard shook his head slowly. 'No, the de Courcys got it from Henry Tudor. And no one knows where he got it from.'

He smiled fleetingly. 'He probably stole it. He was that kind of fellow.'

Blake eyed him severely. 'A little more respect, please, for one of the kings of Old England!'

'He was a thief,' Peard said. 'He stole the kingdom from its lawful ruler, didn't he? You can't have a bigger bit of thievery than that. Today's Great Train Robberies pale into insignificance beside it. What are a few million grubby old banknotes? This man pinched a kingdom.'

'Well . . .' Blake said judiciously. 'It's a point of view.'

'He was a murderer, too,' Peard said. 'Killed the Princes in the Tower. No doubt about it. Then blamed their death on the honourable man whose kingdom he had usurped. A man who, needless to say, was dead too, and unable to defend himself.'

'Shakespeare isn't with you,' Blake said.

'Shakespeare,' said Peard, 'was a Tudor playwright who couldn't afford to displease a Tudor monarch.' Then he smiled again. 'But all this has little bearing on the de Courcy pendant.'

'My thoughts precisely,' said Blake. 'You say the family got it from King Henry? How and why?'

'It was given to a member of the family by Henry Tudor,' Peard told him. 'An Edmund de Courcy. I think it was Edmund. Anyway, whoever it was, the yarn is that they received it for services rendered upon the battlefield of Bosworth, where Tudor stole the kingdom from its rightful ruler, Richard the Third.'

He paused, and Blake prompted, 'What services?'

Peard looked at him. 'The story goes that both this Edmund and his father were engaged in the battle on Henry Tudor's side. It's said, I might add, that Edmund was barely fourteen at the time, and he had not yet been blooded in battle. This was his first fight.'

'Go on,' said Blake.

'The battle was fiercely fought right from the outset,' said Peard. 'And, at one time, it looked as if Richard would win— until he was betrayed. But you can read all about that in the history books. To come back to the de Courcys——

'It's said that in the first savage shock of the contending armies, Edmund's father was killed. Cut down and ploughed underfoot, he died in his son's arms. Touching scene. But the lad was made of stern stuff, and he realised that his father's retainers must on no account know that their leader was dead.

'So, hastily brushing away his boyish tears, he nipped behind a convenient thorn bush with his dad's corpse in tow. And there he swiftly put on the old man's armour, and assumed his identity.

'You see, he was afraid that his father's retainers would be demoralised if they knew of the death of their leader. In that event, the battle would have been lost. At this point in time, those who would betray Richard had still to do it, and Henry Tudor's every hope of success was pinned on the de Courcy contingent in the forefront of the fight.'

Sexton Blake nodded.

'So,' Peard continued, 'in his dad's armour, wearing his helm, bearing his shield, and swinging his axe, our young Edmund now proceeded to give that contingent an inspiring example. Wherever the fray was at its fiercest, there he was, bashing away.

'In the end, he led his father's retainers to victory and, after the battle, plundered the dead and the wounded with the zest of a veteran.'

'Charming,' Blake murmured.

And Peard smiled grimly. 'Isn't it, though?'

'A good story,' said Blake.

'Yes,' Peard agreed. 'If it's true. Trouble is with so many of these tall Tudor tales that they're not. Anyway, true or false, Edmund was later rewarded by Henry with a knighthood, a gift of land and the pendant. But whether all this really was for saving the day at Bosworth or not we'll never know. It might have been for performing some other, shadier, service for Henry. Lord knows, there were plenty on offer round about then: dozens to do.

'But whatever the real reason for the award of a knighthood, and the gift of land and the pendant, the de Courcys have

47

always preferred the more valorous story that I've just related. And now it's an integral part of family tradition.

'For instance, I made the point that, in the story, Edmund was barely fourteen at the time that he won his spurs. Consequently, from that day to this, a de Courcy considers that he's attained manhood when he reaches that age. There used to be quite a ceremony to mark the occasion when an eldest son reached the age of fourteen. For all I know, there still is. At fourteen, the eldest son formally assumes responsibility for the de Courcy pendant, following in the steps of young Edmund. That's when it passes into his possession.'

Blake said: 'And isn't there something about an heir being unable to inherit without it?'

'Oh, yes,' Peard agreed. 'Yes, indeed. And Henry Tudor's at the back of that, too. He's reported as saying that as long as the family treasured his gift it would prosper, but that if ever the de Courcys should lose the pendant they would wither away, root and branch, and they would die.'

'Sounds like a witches' curse,' Sexton Blake said.

'Doesn't it?' Peard nodded. 'But—give the devil his due—I don't think Henry Tudor meant it quite like that. He simply wanted to make sure that the de Courcys stayed on his side— as a family. That's my opinion. And the business with the pendant was one way of doing it.

'In those days life was brutish and brief, and families changed sides and allegiances at the drop of a hat. A son might not cheer the same king as his father. Henry Tudor knew all about that. Wasn't this how he'd found it so easy to steal the throne? Well, he certainly wasn't going to have it happen to him?

'So along with the de Courcys' title and their grant of lands, he gave them the pendant, with the proviso that just so long as they kept it, and formally showed that it was still in their possession at times of succession, the title and the lands would remain theirs.

'But, on the other hand, if the pendant should ever be carelessly lost, then that would presumably mean that the family didn't mind incurring royal displeasure and that their allegiance had become shaky. They would forfeit their title to all their honours and all their lands then.'

'And is this proviso still legally valid?' Blake wanted to know.

'That I couldn't tell you,' said Peard. 'You'd need a lawyer to answer that question. A good one. Not an antiquarian. But I should think so. I do know that the de Courcys themselves have always taken the whole thing very seriously.

'For example, there was an eldest son back in the eighties who mislaid the pendant at the crucial moment and, though he found it again, was smartly passed over. It was his younger brother who came into the title and everything that goes with it, and no one contested it then. What would have happened if the pendant had been truly, irrevocably lost we don't know. For it wasn't. But if it had been . . . or, if at some time in the future it were . . .' He paused and he shrugged. 'For the de Courcys that might well be the end. Everything they possess might well revert to the Crown.'

'I see . . .' Sexton Blake said, and he sounded thoughtful. 'Well, thanks. Thanks very much.' He got up to go. He said: 'I won't take up any more of your time. You've been very helpful.'

'I'm always glad to see you, Blake, you know that. And I'm always glad to be of assistance whenever that's possible,' Peard assured him. 'Drop in any time. Do it soon! Don't leave it so long!'

Blake moved towards the door and then, as a thought struck him, he paused. 'Just how much would this pendant be worth?' he inquired. 'By present day values, I mean.'

'Shorn of its history? Simply as a piece of obviously antique jewellery? Is that what you're getting at?'

Blake nodded. 'Could you put a price on it?'

Peard shrugged his thin shoulders. 'It isn't easy to give you an answer. I've never actually seen the pendant, remember. All I have to go on is the published description. I've read that it's very heavy. It's quite large, you know. About the size of one of those municipal coats of arms that adorn a mayor's chain of office. And it's almost pure gold.'

'What do you mean by "almost"?'

Peard shrugged again. 'Say ninety-six or ninety-seven per cent.'

One of Blake's eyebrows quirked upwards. 'Not a thing to be handled, obviously.'

Peard nodded slowly. 'It must be very soft. I should imagine that's one of the reasons the de Courcys have never shown it around. It will have to be treated with care.'

'And its value?'

Peard hesitated. 'Well ... if one was lucky ... selling it simply as an antique ... and taking into account the fact that it's studded with semi-precious stones ... say five thousand pounds.'

'Hm ...' said Blake thoughtfully.

'As a piece of history, though,' Peard said, 'it's value might be very much higher.'

'How much?' Blake wanted to know.

And Peard frowned.

He said: 'None of this is easy for me. You see, what would jack up the pendant's value is an intangible thing. It's the associations the pendant has had. That, combined with its romantic story, and the fact that it is quite unique, would probably mean that it would fetch—well—fifteen or twenty thousand. Maybe more.'

Blake pursed his lips in a soft whistle. 'As much as that!'

'Of course, it would all depend,' Peard said, 'on who was doing the buying, and also on who was doing the selling. The important thing—and the price that it fetched would depend upon this almost entirely—would be the proof offered the purchaser that this *was* the de Courcy pendant. The genuine thing. A collector would have to be pretty sure of that before he would part with fifteen or twenty thousand pounds for it.'

'Yes,' Blake said thoughtfully. 'I can see that. Of course. And you think that without proof of its history—just as an antique—it would fetch about five thousand, eh?'

'It's a guess,' Peard said. 'Nothing more. What you might call a hypothetical answer to a hypothetical question. The de Courcys certainly won't be selling the pendant, now will they?

50

It will never happen. Not while so much depends upon them keeping it safe, and in the family.'

'Mmmm . . .' said Blake. 'I suppose not.' Then he said, 'You don't happen to have a picture of the thing, do you?'

'There's a line-drawing in a book that I have . . .' Peard covered the floor with long, easy strides. He plucked a book from a shelf by the window, and handed it to Blake. 'You'll find it in there. There's also a history of the thing—much the same as I've given you. Let me have the book back some time when you're passing, though. It's rather rare, and I use it fairly frequently.'

'I won't take it then,' Blake said quickly. 'I can arrange to have the picture copied here in the Museum. The book need never leave you.'

'Nonsense! Take it with you! The picture's not much use without the full, formal description. It's all right. I can manage without it for a few weeks. It might even bring you in to see me again soon!'

Blake smiled, and thrust the slim volume into a pocket. He held out his hand. 'Thanks again! You've helped me a lot!'

And it was true.

As he went out of the room and along the corridor, his brain was working overtime.

SIX

The view from Sexton Blake's study was one which was always worth seeing.

It was panoramic.

Through the big picture-window double-glazed in 32-ounce glass, one could range over the multi-coloured rooftops of London and follow the line of the Thames—that river of history—all the way past the bridges of Chelsea, Battersea and Westminster, and on to where the dome of St Paul's broke the sky in the far distance.

Or, closer at hand, one could look down on the thronged pavements far, far below, see the bustling buses and the hustle of Baker Street Station practically opposite, and then lift one's gaze to the formal and green comparative calm of Lord's Cricket Ground, and of Regent's Park.

From Sexton Blake's study window there was always something to see. But, on this morning, neither Tinker nor Blake himself spared the view so much as a glance.

There were too many other things to occupy their attention: all of them concerned with the blonde, beautiful Miss Paula Dane. Blake had promised a full-scale conference with his young partner, and now it began. There was a lot of talking to do and, for the first fifteen minutes, it was Blake who did it.

Tinker listened intently to a carefully concise yet reasonably complete account of everything that had happened the previous night, and also of what Blake had been doing this morning. At the end of it all, he was frowning fiercely. 'What on earth does it all add up to?'

'I've got some ideas.'

Blake helped himself to a cigarette; extended his case. Tinker reached for it, then stopped himself. 'No thanks, chief. I've given 'em up.'

'How many times does that make it?'

Tinker looked hurt. 'Only twice in the past week.'

Blake smiled to himself faintly, and snapped his lighter. Around smoke, he said: 'Obviously someone wants Paula Dane out of the way. And the only possible person I can see with any kind of motive at all is our Mr Simon de Courcy.'

He leaned back.

Tinker was staring at him, and frowning sharply. 'How's that again? I thought you said you'd eliminated Miss Dane's legacy as a motive for everything that's been happening to her.'

'Uh-huh. So I have,' Blake agreed. 'It's not going to be big enough to account for this kind of skulduggery. It's going to be practically nothing at all. That's very clear.'

'Well then ...' said Tinker. He looked somewhat baffled.

'What other motive could Simon de Courcy possibly have for wanting her out of the way?'

'I told you I'd got some ideas,' Blake said, 'and we'll go into all that in a minute. But first fill me in on the ground that you've covered this morning. Did you find anything out about Simon de Courcy I don't already know?'

Tinker gave an expressive shrug. 'Not very much. I went to the Yard first, then down to Fleet Street. To the *Daily Post*. I tackled Splash Kirby about him. But our favourite columnist wasn't much of a help. He told me all that he knew, but it was very little. It practically boils down to this—for what it's worth: I now know where de Courcy's living this week.'

Blake looked at his young partner quickly. 'He moves around?'

'Frequently just ahead of the bailiffs,' said Tinker. 'But sometimes not fast enough. That boy has debts the way some old houses have the death-watch beetle: fairly popping straight out of the woodwork. Small things, but troublesome. Very troublesome. Especially when you're overrun with 'em.'

'But nothing an inheritance of half a million pounds wouldn't take care of,' Blake said.

'Oh, sure,' Tinker agreed. 'His debts all seem to be small, like I said. Though he's got a lot of them. Kirby thought they might add up to six or seven hundred pounds at the most. Simon's always had an allowance of a thousand a year from his father, you see, though invariably he's lived beyond it. And, naturally, never worked to augment it. Not he.

'But there's no doubt at all he'll be able to settle his debts without even thinking about it when he's got his half a million. And I should imagine that the duns will be cooling off round about now: now that he looks all set to inherit.'

He paused, then went on: 'But a few months ago the picture wasn't so rosy. In fact, at one point it was grim. This was before old Sir Roderick kicked the bucket, of course. Back at the time when it must have looked like he'd live for ever. And this was when Simon got himself beaten-up.

'It happened one night. He was knocked about really badly. Though there wasn't much in the papers about it, Kirby told me he was in hospital for the best part of a fortnight. Someone beat the hell out of him. He wouldn't say who. But Kirby said that, at the time, the word was that it was someone Simon owed not just hundreds, but thousands, in gambling debts. Someone who'd got tired of waiting for him to pay. So they put him in hospital to encourage him to hasten things up.'

Blake said sharply, 'And when he came out——?'

Tinker shrugged. 'I suppose he must have settled. He wasn't beaten again, if that's what you mean. And he would have been if he hadn't coughed up.'

'That's likely,' said Blake drily.

'But don't ask me how he managed to settle,' said Tinker. 'Kirby's of the opinion that at that time he hadn't a cent to bless himself with. Maybe Sir Roderick helped out.'

But Blake shook his head briefly. 'Couldn't have. It doesn't jell. Why should Simon's father settle that debt and not all of the others? Particularly when the other debts were all small ones. No, Simon must have got the money from somewhere himself.' He was very thoughtful. 'I think I've a shrewd idea where he got it from.

He was silent for a long, brooding moment, and then nodded slowly. 'You've done very well, Tinker. You've told me a lot. Toss in what I know already, and throw in a deduction or two, and it certainly seems to add up.'

'Thanks very much. But add up to what?' Tinker wanted to know. 'You've got me repeating myself,' he complained. 'This is what I said back at the beginning.'

Blake's mouth slid into a smile.

'I wish you wouldn't be quite so mysterious,' Tinker told him severely. 'You seem pretty sure you've got some kind of a case against Simon de Courcy. So, let me in on it.'

'All in good time,' Blake agreed mildly. 'But you should be able to work it out for yourself.'

'From what you've told me so far?'

'And from what you've told me.'

'I don't get it,' said Tinker. 'I just don't get it. Frankly, I can't see how one begins to tie Simon de Courcy into this thing.'

54

'He's the only man with a motive.'

'Which I haven't been able to work out yet,' said Tinker. 'All right. So you say. But he hasn't shown his hand once. It wasn't Simon who grabbed Paula Dane outside the Malibu Club. It was Joe Turk.'

'And he,' Blake said reasonably, 'was obviously working for somebody.'

'Sure,' Tinker said. 'Too right he was. Ever heard of a man called Jack Dino?'

Blake mulled the name over. 'Can't say I have.'

'That's who Turk works for,' said Tinker. 'Every bit of the time.'

'You got this from the Yard?'

'I got it from Deputy Commander Grimwald. This morning. Before I went to see Kirby. So what does that do to your theory?'

'About Simon de Courcy?' Blake shook his head. 'Nothing at all.'

'You mean that de Courcy and Dino are in this together?'

'Must be,' said Blake, 'if Turk is his boy.'

'It doesn't shake you at all?' Tinker said. 'This Dino is a very rough and tough cookie.'

'It doesn't shake me,' said Blake. 'The motive I'm imputing to Simon de Courcy is very strong. He's a lot of good reasons for wanting Paula Dane out of the way—if I'm right. Half a million good reasons, in fact, at the last count.'

Suddenly Tinker was staring.

'Are you saying,' he demanded incredulously, 'that if he doesn't get her out of the way he won't inherit?'

'That is my guess.' And now Blake leaned forward. 'It's my belief that Simon no longer has the de Courcy pendant in his possession. My guess is that he's sold it. Sold it to pay off those pressing gambling debts you told me about. It all adds up.'

'Blimey!' Tinker breathed.

'It was at a time when—to quote you,' Blake said, 'it must have looked like old Sir Roderick de Courcy would live for ever. And Simon was desperate. He'd already taken one bad beating that had put him in hospital. He wasn't keen on taking another. He needed money, and he needed it quickly. He had to have it at once—if not sooner. How else could he get it but by selling the pendant?'

'Couldn't he have got a loan on his expectations?' Tinker objected.

'Obviously not. If he had been able to, would he have been harried by bailiffs?' Blake said. 'And he must have tried. No doubt he could get a loan now. But now isn't then. In any case, a thing like that takes time to arrange, and there was no time. Whoever it was he owed the gambling debts to was tired of waiting, sick of excuses. And Simon had been hospitalised once to make that quite clear. So he sold the pendant. What else could he do? It was the only thing of any value that he possessed. Presumably he sold it simply for what it would fetch as an antique piece of jewellery. He couldn't say what it was. He couldn't cash in on its history. The sale had to be secret. He probably got five thousand pounds for it—if he was lucky. I'm told that, shorn of its history, that's what it would be worth.'

'And then,' Tinker said, 'he's called home to Cumberland. His father's dying.'

'Yes,' Blake agreed. 'And what a spot Simon's in. He's sold the pendant—for five thousand pounds at the most. Now he needs it back, or he's kissed good-bye to a cool half a million. So what does he do?'

'Tries to buy it back, obviously,' Tinker said, 'if he can raise the money. Tries to snatch it back, if he can't—if, as it seems, he's teamed up with this Jack Dino.'

'Fair enough. But if, for some reason, all attempts to recover it fail, what happens then?'

'Well ...' Tinker said slowly, '... then I suppose he has a facsimile made—if there are accurate pictures of what the thing looks like.'

'There are accurate pictures.'

'Fine. Then that's what he does.'

'Precisely,' said Blake. 'And no one will know—except——'

'——Except Paula Dane?' said Tinker. 'Oh, I follow you,

chief. But why only Paula? What makes her so special? I can see that if she can tell t'other pendant from which Simon's got to get her out of the way—for the will-reading at least. But why only her? Surely old Mr Boddy, the family solicitor you spoke to this morning, would be more likely still to spot the substitution. So why not attempt to snatch him? I'd say he was a natural. Why is Paula the only one who's being got at?'

'That I don't know,' Blake admitted. 'That we have to find out.'

'But Simon's got one hell of a motive, no doubt about it,' said Tinker. 'If it turns out you're right.'

'If——?' Blake cocked an eye at his young partner, then stared at the ceiling. 'What confidence!' he remarked scathingly.

Then he grinned.

'To make sure that I'm right, we'd better start checking. There are several things we can do. But, first, tell me more about this Jack Dino. All that Grimwald told you. I've never heard of him so—for a start—where has he been all my life?'

And Tinker told him.

SEVEN

Jack Dino had not spent all of Sexton Blake's adult life cooped up in prison. Just a large part of it.

As a criminal, he had been a late developer. He'd started early enough—at the age of eleven—but he had learned very slowly. Painfully, too. And the one thing he had never learned as a guest of successive bodies of Prison Commissioners was that crime does not pay.

As thin as a whip, feral-faced, with the pallor of prison perpetually on him, he was an indefatigable trier.

Violence was his métier. He had never been averse to slip-

57

ping on a pair of brass knuckles, wielding a chiv or swinging a length of lead pipe. If anything, he had enjoyed it. And been seen to enjoy it. This was what singled him out. This was what made him dangerous.

Dangerous to society—hence the unfailingly savage prison sentences he had collected in one court after another.

Dangerous to the underworld, too—hence the fact that, from the time he had run through three Approved Schools and finally graduated from Borstal at the age of nineteen, he'd never been a free man for very long.

With the figures for detected indictable crime running at less than forty per cent in the average year, Jack Dino, in his innocence, might have been pardoned for wondering why it was he saw the inside of a cell with such regularity. Right from the first, he'd been one of a mob—never the same mob for very long, but also never a loner—and the favourable odds against detection invariably seemed to operate successfully for his companions in crime. Why not for him, too?

On paper, the chances were better than evens that, like his fellow mobsters, he'd never be caught—or—at worst—only very infrequently. Yet the heavy hand of the Law fell on his shoulder, and his shoulder alone, with sickening regularity, time after time.

Late developer that he was, it took him several long prison sentences to arrive at the truth of the matter. In fact, he'd only just arrived at it. Yet it was shocking in its simplicity.

The truth was that he terrified the other criminals that he worked with. None wanted to work with him twice. They were scared of his sadism; appalled at his brutality. They went in fear of the fact that, at any moment, he might well drag them over the brink into murder—then a capital crime.

Dino hadn't killed yet, but this was just luck. It wasn't for want of trying. There was always a first time, and they wanted no part of it. And they weren't only shivering at the thought of the rope.

So as soon as one or another of them conveniently could, an anonymous phone call—a tip-off about Dino—was put through to the police.

For, by and large, the British professional criminal will use violence on occasion, but only within strictly defined limits. Its insensate use frightens him as much as—if not more than—the next man, even when he's not directly involved as a participant.

He has more to lose.

He knows that violence breeds violence, and it does more. Criminal violence angers the British public: slow to wrath, easy-going, mild and usually permissive where crime is concerned, but implacable when aroused.

The professional criminal exists because the public at large allows him a living. If every man's hand was turned against him, at best it would be very bad for his business.

And this was the basic reason why, time after time, Dino was shopped: put inside.

Everyone would be better off, the underworld thought—and judges agreed—if he lived out his life behind bars.

It was years before Dino realised what had been happening, and during all of that time he kept his own counsel: he never coughed. He didn't cough afterwards, either. He just thought about things, slowly added them up. And the sum total he reached didn't make a reformed man of him, but it did make a changed one.

He stopped running around with a mob. He became his own boss, and hand-picked two other men to work with him: men he judged almost as ruthless and bloody-minded as he was himself.

They came to him gladly, for they were pariahs, as he was: potential killers, dangerous men no one in the underworld really wanted to know.

There was 'Babe' Jenkins, who could handle a sawn-off shotgun—few better—and who was the best man in all London to have behind the wheel of your motor if you had to go anywhere in one hell of a hurry. 'Babe' Jenkins, so called on account of his smooth, chubby and cherubic face which, in a tight spot and when the chips were all down, masked a cold, soulless indifference to the fate of anyone, man, woman or child, who got in his way.

There was 'Babe' Jenkins. And there was Joe Turk, top of his class as an enforcer, a callous bully. And there was Dino himself.

The three of them made a small, but highly formidable, team.

And they went into 'Protection'. It suited their talents. Have a club proprietor pay up—or else. Or else his club was smashed up. And it didn't end there. But Joe had only to nail one man to the floor through the knees.

The word flashed around. No trouble at all after that. Payments were made as soon as demanded. Sometimes before.

They started in Stepney, not poaching at first, just taking the new clubs as they opened, preparing the ground, getting ready. And then they struck.

Without any warning, and without any kind of formal declaration of war, they hit the principal mob taking tribute from club owners in Stepney. And they hit them hard.

The blitzkrieg started at six o'clock on a Sunday morning. The better the day, the better the deed.

By five minutes past six, three of the other gang's protected clubs were on fire, and by ten minutes past the other gang's leader was swimming in blood in his bed, his face and chest blasted by buckshot at very short range. It was Bloody Sunday.

Just two minutes later, his second-in-command lost a hand when the telephone he grabbed for to silence its insistent summons blew up with a roar.

'Babe' Jenkins not only knew everything there was to know about motors and shotguns, he was by way of being an explosives expert as well, and he looked even more harmless than usual in GPO Telephone Engineer's overalls.

Turk and Dino together worked over the rest of the gang with deadly precision, catching most of them in their beds—or in someone else's. Only two men escaped unmarked and unharmed—but not to fight back.

There was no fighting to do—not after twenty minutes to seven on that Sunday morning. Half the gang was in hospital, in a severe state of shock. The gang leader would live, but had lost both of his eyes. Three clubs were still burning merrily. And the war was over.

It was at twenty minutes to seven that all tribute in Stepney was unconditionally surrendered to Dino, and Jenkins, and Joe Turk. The King was blind, and who wanted to be a maimed hero?

Long live the King!

One week after that, Dino extended the sphere of his operations, and he moved West. He'd given the Soho boys plenty to think about. They'd heard the good word, and he didn't anticipate having any trouble. Certainly not with the small fry.

Which was why he chose a small club in the West End as the first to be 'protected'. Not a large one, where he'd have to deal with large-scale opposition. A small club: currently being milked by small men who swiftly faded away when he appeared.

The bad news from Stepney had travelled.

The good news about this small West End club, Dino discovered, was that it had a gaming-room he'd known nothing of.

And that was how he met Simon de Courcy. Through this gaming-room, or, rather, its book of bad debts.

And they met in an alley behind the club, whither a pretty girl with a high split skirt had decoyed De Courcy.

Dino, and 'Babe' Jenkins, and Joe Turk—and Simon de Courcy backing up fast against a wall.

They met there. Three against one.

They put Simon de Courcy in hospital for the best part of a fortnight.

EIGHT

As the taxi swung left off the Cromwell Road and entered Emperors' Close, S.W.7, Tinker saw that it was a cul-de-sac lined with tall, Victorian houses.

He swivelled round in his seat, looking for Number 62, the house where, Kirby had told him, Simon de Courcy currently had a maisonette.

He didn't see it at once, nor did his driver. The taxi slowed to a crawl, the cabbie peering out, counting the numbers. Many of the houses were in very poor shape, Tinker saw. Most of their faces were weather-beaten and unpainted. Some still showed pock-marks and scars left over from the war.

And here and there along the Close, the stones of which the houses were built had begun to crumble. Railings sagged, and the roadway itself was a patchwork of indifferent repair.

In the centre of the Close there was a grove of fourteen thin-trunked and soot-stained trees. They were fenced off from the roadway, and the grass around them was lank and long.

Seeing the grove, and looking beyond it to the houses, Tinker had an impression of Victorian respectability struggling to live within its means—and always failing.

The Close was drab and grim and colourless. It would be an address in winter, and an oven in summer; and, in the autumn, the trees within the tiny grove would send their leaves to crackle like parchment before the winds which swept the bare, cracked paving-stones until—and it looked as if it might be soon—the whole place was pulled down.

The taxi lost even more speed, edged up in front of a house which bore the number 62 in flaking black paint above a battery of bell-pushes, and came to a halt. Tinker got out. As he paid off the driver, he looked up at the windows of the house where Simon de Courcy currently lived. He saw they were not clean. The curtains seemed to hang moistly, in deep folds, like curtains which have been left hanging too long. Over the house was settled a slight odour of decay and indifference.

The taxi swung around and headed back to Cromwell Road, and Tinker mounted three yellow stone steps from the pavement and rang one of the bells. It was a bell below a rusting card-holder into which had been thrust a roughly torn piece of paper bearing the name of De Courcy. Other decayed cardholders above and below framed other names: Tsao, Abongyeh, Salim-Saleh. The last of the De Courcys was keeping company with the League of Nations. No one answered the bell.

Tinker rang it again. Still silence ensued. A child came out from one of the houses on the other side of the Close and regarded him with round, saucer-like eyes. Why was it piccaninnies always looked frightened? Tinker wondered. Or did they? Was it, perhaps, him?

Tinker rang the bell a third time and, because he could hear nothing from inside the house, he then raised his hand in a fist to knock upon the flaking paint of the door.

It was at this moment that the door opened.

Tinker felt rather foolish. It was as though he had been caught in the Communist salute. He coughed, and let the clenched fist fall down by his side. He said 'Mr de Courcy?' and he looked at the man who stood in the doorway.

The man was tall. He had a long, lean face, and he was unshaven. His dark hair was untidy. He was wearing a rumpled silk scarf at his throat, and had on a dark-red silk dressing-gown over grey trousers. His bare feet had been thrust into scuffed and scratched brown leather mules.

He looked as though he had only just got out of bed.

'Mr de Courcy?' Tinker said again. 'Mr Simon de Courcy?' And the man stared at him.

His eyes were of a bright and intense blue, and they blazed in deep, shadowed sockets. Tinker had the impression that, all the while, they were trying to crawl forward and peer around the thin, aristocratically hooked nose which separated them.

The man was staring at him with savage suspicion. Then— 'Yes, I'm Simon de Courcy,' he admitted unwillingly. He added roughly, 'Who're you? What do you want?'

Tinker reached into an inside pocket, and saw de Courcy

visibly stiffen. He brought out a card-case, selected a card, and extended it. 'My name is Latimer, Mr de Courcy. John Latimer. I am a fine-art dealer by profession. What you might call an antiquarian, and——'

De Courcy allowed himself to relax.

What had he been expecting? Tinker wondered. Who had he been expecting? He looked beyond the other man, and into the hall. He saw shabbiness everywhere. Another bailiff? Another writ?

'What do you want?' de Courcy demanded again.

And now Tinker shifted from one foot to the other, apparently ill-at-ease. He and Blake had been over this ground—thoroughly. 'I'm here on a matter concerning the de Courcy pendant,' he said.

The other man took his hands out of the pockets of his dressing-gown. Tinker saw that the hands were a trifle unsteady. De Courcy accepted the card which Tinker still offered him, and glanced at it briefly. Handing it back, but not meeting Tinker's eyes with his own, he growled out, 'And what about the de Courcy pendant?'

Tinker seemed to hesitate.

Then he said, 'The firm that I represent is always getting inquiries about such *objet d'art* from across the Atlantic——'

De Courcy said roughly, 'The de Courcy pendant is not for sale.'

Tinker coughed. It was a nervous sound. 'That is what we —that is to say, my firm—understood.' He seemed to be searching for a way in which to continue. He sighed. He said, 'It's very difficult, Mr de Courcy ...'

The other man looked at him. He didn't say anything. Tinker went on: 'The fact is that someone has approached us with a firm offer of the pendant. And we could place it, of course. No difficulty about that, at all. These rich American collectors ...'

He gestured vaguely.

'But, naturally,' he said, 'we ... er ... well—we have to be sure ...'

His voice tailed away. He looked at the tall man helplessly.

64

Abruptly, Simon de Courcy said, 'You'd better come in.'

He swung around and stalked off down the hall, leaving Tinker to close the outer door and to follow.

To the left of a flight of bare stairs which climbed steeply to the upper floors of the house, a plywood partition cut off the end of the hall. A partition with another door in it.

Simon de Courcy led the way through into a short passageway beyond, and skirted the head of more bare stairs, stone ones, going down into dank darkness. He ushered Tinker into a rear ground-floor room which smelled of damp and decay. 'Now, Mr . . .'

'Latimer,' Tinker said, taking a swift look around him.

The room was as poorly appointed as most places in London let furnished at seven or eight pounds a week. An old-fashioned table complete with scratches and woodworm and ring-marks stood in front of tall windows facing out on a ruined garden. Overhead, a stained ceiling gazed yellowly down. On the floor was a patched carpet and, around the walls, several rickety chairs, none of them matching. In front of an ancient gas-fire which blocked out the grate of a fireplace equally antedeluvian were ranged two easy-chairs in faded loose covers and a lumpy, uncomfortable-looking settee.

Tinker's swift-travelling gaze jumped from the settee to the room's second door, opposite the tall windows, and then jerked back abruptly. From the depths of the settee, half-hidden by one of the misshapen cushions, a pair of frilly black nylon panties peeped at him coyly.

'Mr Latimer'—abruptly Simon de Courcy reclaimed his attention—'suppose you begin at the beginning and tell me what this is all about.'

'Well, sir . . .' Out of the corner of his eye, Tinker could still see the black nylon panties. Resolutely, he turned his back on them. 'Well, sir, the fact is that a few days ago——'

But there Tinker was interrupted.

Abruptly, the room's second door was jerked open. 'Simon —Simon, have you seen——'

A very young woman was framed in the doorway. A very young attractive redhead. She was wearing a black nylon bra, a thin black nylon suspender belt, sheer black nylon stockings. Nothing else.

It was quite plain that she hadn't known Simon de Courcy had a visitor. In the instant that she saw Tinker she gave a strangled squeak; whipped around; fled. The door slammed behind her, but not before Tinker had seen that it gave on to a disordered bedroom.

He returned his eyes to Simon de Courcy. He cleared his throat. 'Herrumph ... yes, sir ...'

He began again.

'A few days ago, sir, my firm was contacted by a gentleman who told us that he had the de Courcy pendant in his possession, and wished to sell it. As you will know, sir, my firm has had several offers for the pendant over the years, chiefly from the other side of the Atlantic. On each occasion we contacted the late Sir Roderick—hoping against hope, as it were——'

'Which firm did you say you represented?'

If Simon de Courcy had looked somewhat ill-at-ease immediately after the pretty redhead's startling entrance and exit, he was completely in control of himself now.

'Which firm did you say?' he repeated.

Tinker hadn't said. Nor was a firm's name on the business card he had proferred.

'I didn't, sir. It's Maxwell's, of Kensington Church Street.'

'Maxwell's?' Simon grunted. 'I don't know it.'

'Of course, sir,' Tinker said deprecatingly, 'ours is not a general business. We're not a big firm, you see, and we don't deal over the counter. We buy discriminately, and then sell to our own small circle of wealthy customers.'

'And this man who offered you the pendant——?'

Tinker looked lost for a moment. 'I don't understand, sir.'

'Aren't you going to give me his name?' Simon de Courcy demanded.

'Well, er ...' Tinker took refuge in a conventional phrase. 'Well, sir, I don't think I could do that. Not at this stage. My employers ...'

'But I possess the pendant,' Simon said forcefully, 'and it's not for sale. This man—this crook who approached your firm

—is obviously trying to defraud. The real de Courcy pendant will never be for sale, you dealers must understand that! I believe that I am correct in saying that there are no photographs of the pendant in general circulation——'

'There *are* one or two line-drawings, sir——'

'Line-drawings? Very bad ones! And I should know! I tell you, this man is a crook! The fact that you dealers never take no for an answer is an encouragement to men like this, and because there are no photographs of the pendant in general circulation a fraud would be all too easy——'

'Well, not easy, sir——'

'I think that this man, whoever he is, should be prosecuted,' Simon de Courcy said fiercely. 'Give me his name, and I'll take proceedings against him myself!'

'I'm afraid I couldn't do that, sir, not without consulting Mr Maxwell.' Tinker tried to look unhappy and harrassed. It was not difficult. The cover story he and Blake had concocted to get him into this house seemed to be running away with him.

'Well, consult your Mr Maxwell,' Simon said. 'There's a telephone out in the passage. Ring him up and consult him.'

Tinker smiled nervously. 'I couldn't do that, either, I'm afraid. Mr Maxwell is away in Scotland on a business trip, and——'

'It was another dealer who tried to sell you this spurious pendant, wasn't it?' Simon shot at him.

'A dealer? Why——'

'I knew it!' Simon fixed angry eyes on Tinker's face. 'It wouldn't have been a Mr Montford, or Williams, or Jones——'

He paused, still watching Tinker intently.

'—Or Lewis——?' he said.

Tinker cleared his throat, but said nothing.

Simon de Courcy said heavily, 'You're not going to tell me?'

'I can't, sir.'

'Perhaps you think I'm exaggerating the case when I call this man—whoever he is—a swindler, and a crook? Perhaps he's a dealer known to your employer, or to yourself, in a personal way? Perhaps you think he wouldn't attempt to swindle you? Is that it?' His voice had risen. 'Perhaps you think that he really does possess the pendant!'

'Oh, no, sir——'

'Then what do you think? Have you ever seen the pendant yourself?'

'No, sir.'

'Then I'll show it to you. Perhaps that will convince you!'

Simon de Courcy swung around and strode swiftly out of the room, almost cannoning into the young redheaded girl on the way. He barged on without apology, and slammed the bedroom door after him. The young redhead came farther into the room.

She wore a dress now. A figure-hugging short evening dress, Tinker saw—and drew his own conclusions. She had a pert face: extremely pretty in a bright, babyish kind of way.

She gave Tinker a swift, sidelong glance out of china-blue eyes as she crossed to the settee. It was a look of considerable calculation.

She had a trim little figure, and from the way that she moved it was clear that she knew it.

'Sorry to barge in just now,' she said. Her glance travelled swiftly along the settee; came to rest for a moment. Then she moved around the settee, looking at him sidelong again. 'I didn't know you were here.'

'Think nothing of it,' said Tinker, and added, after a second's reflection: 'My pleasure.'

The girl giggled.

'I'm Roxie,' she said. 'Roxie Marlowe. What's your name?'

'Latimer,' Tinker said untruthfully. 'John Latimer.'

'You're a friend of Simon's?'

'No,' Tinker said. 'But you are.' He regarded her innocently. 'I can tell.'

She made a face at him, and then sat down on the settee and pushed her feet into high-heeled shoes which had been hidden from his view on the floor. From the same place, she lifted a black evening bag, opened it, and with one smooth, unhurried movement, took the black nylon briefs out from behind their cushion and popped them inside it.

Tinker watched fascinated.

She looked back at him. 'Now you know.'

'I know what?'

She giggled again. 'The state of my defences.' Then she looked more serious, and jerked her head in the direction of the bedroom door. 'What's got into him? Do you know?'

'Mr de Courcy? I'm afraid,' Tinker said, 'I've rather upset him.'

She looked at him sharply. 'What are you after? Money?' There was sudden contempt in her voice now. 'You'll get paid!'

Tinker stared at her blankly. 'I don't understand.'

'You don't, eh?' She regarded him thoughtfully. 'Maybe it's true . . .' Then she said flippantly, 'All right, forget it!'

'I came to see Mr de Courcy about the pendant.'

'Which pendant? Oh, I see . . .' The girl stood up and moved around the settee in Tinker's direction. She leaned far over him. 'Got a cigarette?'

'Sure.'

He lit it for her.

She blew smoke. 'And that made him mad? Simon mad over that old thing?'

She might have said more but, at that moment, Simon de Courcy came back into the room.

He carried a large, flat jewel-case in his hand. Clearly, it was very old. The red leather which covered it was worn and beginning to peel away from one corner. He laid it down upon the table, opened it and motioned to Tinker. 'Here you are!' There was a note of suppressed excitement in his voice.

Tinker moved. He gazed down on the pendant cushioned in time-worn, nearly threadbare black velvet. Gold gleamed back at him dully. The semi-precious stones which studded the pendant had had their fires dimmed by age.

Tinker recalled the line-drawings in the book which Blake had brought back with him from the British Museum and insisted he study very carefully indeed. As far as he could see, the drawings corresponded in every detail with the pendant in front of him.

He nodded to himself, and looked up into the eyes of Simon de Courcy. 'Magnificent!' he said, and he meant it.

Simon regarded him closely for a moment. He seemed to be about to say something, but the girl cut in on him. She had been looking at the pendant disinterestedly, and now she said to Simon: 'I must go. I have a modelling job to do in less than an hour, and I've got to change.'

'I'll come with you to the door.'

'When am I going to see you again, Simon?'

'I'll ring you.'

'Are you sure?'

'Yes, Roxie, I'm sure.'

''Cos, if you're not, I may take time out to have supper tonight with a producer I know. He's asked me to his flat . . .'

Her eyes rested on Tinker for the briefest of instants—speculatively.

Simon de Courcy said irritably, 'You know how that will finish up, Roxie. And you'll have nothing to show for it except a hang-over!'

He urged her forward, out of the room.

Left alone, Tinker slipped a magnifying glass out of his pocket, and glanced towards the door. Then he carefully lifted the pendant from its case, and crossed the room to the window. In the light, he gave the pendant a swift but very thorough examination, and frowned.

It was perfect. There was nothing at all wrong with it. It was very heavy and it looked very old. Front and back there were no blemishes, no pock-marks, nothing at all to suggest that this pendant was a twentieth-century casting, or that it had been made up from drawings—or photographs, even.

There was nothing at all to suggest that it was not the real thing.

Then, as Simon and Roxie Marlowe argued in the outer hall and the low murmur of their voices came into the room where Tinker was, he replaced the pendant in its case and sat down in one of the easy-chairs. He sat down and extended his legs

70

and began to think—hard. And his thoughts weren't at all pleasant.

It looked as if Blake's theories were totally wrong.

If this was the real pendant, bang went every motive imputed to Simon de Courcy.

It looked as if they would have to go right back to the beginning again in their search for a reason for what had been happening to Paula Dane. And, meanwhile . . .

It was vital they know the real reason for everything that had been happening to Paula in order to identify the people responsible, and speedily neutralise the danger that she was in. No reason, no identification and no hope of reducing the danger to Paula, nor of averting it. No hope, either, of anticipating the next blow which would be aimed at her, or even of knowing from which direction the unknown enemy would choose to strike.

This whole case, Tinker thought broodingly, was one hell of a mess. And he was still thinking it when Simon returned a few moments later.

'Well, Mr Latimer, now that you're satisfied, what about giving me the name of the dealer who tried to defraud your firm?'

'I'm sorry,' Tinker said. 'I would if I could. And I mean that, Mr de Courcy. But I can't tell you anything until I get Mr Maxwell's approval. I'll wire him right away, though, and as soon as he gives me permission I'll contact you again.'

He paused, and then repeated, 'I really am sorry.'

'So am I,' Simon grunted, and hesitated for a long moment. Then shrugged.

'All right, then.' His voice was ungracious. He turned away. 'You can see yourself out?'

Tinker could, and he did. He was glad to go. He had a lot to think about.

NINE

Blake leant against the bar in the Berkeley Buttery, sipping his drink and waiting for Paula Dane.

The time by the clock over the bar was five minutes to two. He was that much early. As he savoured his drink lingering over it, taking it down a sip at a time, he wondered how Tinker was getting on with Simon de Courcy, what he'd found out.

Across the way, a very attractive brunette in her middle thirties looked at him with unaffected admiration in her eyes. She asked herself what this tall, lean and undoubtedly masculine man did for a living.

She saw the strong line of his jaw, his determined mouth and his clear grey eyes, and she thought it was probably something dangerous.

She could make a fool of herself over a man who lived dangerously.

Then, as he turned his head, she saw the fine lines which radiated from the corners of his eyes. He was obviously a man who could laugh at himself and at the world.

She liked her men to have a sense of humour, and she looked hard at Blake, willing him to see her. But he didn't.

He was looking towards the Moorish arch which separated the hall from the bar. He finished his drink unhurriedly, and put down his glass. He turned and walked easily and unaffectedly to meet the tall blonde who was just entering the room.

Two eyes bored into his back as he did so, but Blake didn't feel them. He said to Paula, 'It's good to see you.'

Paula looked past him. She caught the full glance of the other woman in the bar. For a moment they looked at each other, and there was unashamed speculation in their eyes.

Then, still looking at the other woman, she made to lay her hand on Blake's arm—a proprietary gesture. But, suddenly, she was aware that he was watching her amusedly. Her hand fell to her side. The colour rose in her cheeks.

He saw everything. He knew everything. What could you do with a man like that?

The brunette sitting in the bar, older than Paula Dane and more worldly-wise, had her own ideas of what she might do with a man like that. It was just a wish, and she knew it. Her worldly wisdom told her that this was one man no woman would ever be able to have on a string. But there was no harm in thinking about it. She felt her breath quicken.

Meanwhile, Paula was covering her confusion by saying, 'Shall we eat?' Still Blake watched her amusedly. She was very glad to be able to turn and walk ahead of him into the dining-room.

She was wearing a powder-blue suit of light gaberdine with a pencil-slim skirt which moulded itself to the gentle curves of her figure. The seams of her nylons were very straight. She wore a tiny, pert, navy-blue hat, and high-heeled court shoes of navy-blue leather. She carried a small leather envelope bag.

She accepted the chair which the waiter drew out for her, and sat down, smiling at Blake across the table. Beneath the suit she wore a white blouse which grew up into a ruffle of white lace around her throat; and on the left lapel of her suit, in honour of the occasion, she wore a tiny posy of gaily coloured flowers.

Blake ordered, and the waiter left them, and, for a while, they talked of inconsequential things. Paula found that Blake had a fund of amusing experiences to recount, and that his wit was dry and incisive without being in the least malicious. Lunch progressed, and Paula told herself that never had she enjoyed a meal so much. The food was good, and the company excellent. Her eyes sparkled.

Then, over coffee and Strega, Blake became much more serious. He said, 'I've had rather a busy morning.' He went on to tell her of his visit to Sir Roderick de Courcy's solicitors, and gave her the gist of his conversation with Peard at the British Museum.

He continued, 'My partner, Edward Carter, hasn't been dragging his feet on this business either.'

He told her what Tinker had found out at New Scotland

73

Yard and down in Fleet Street that morning, and added, 'Here's what I deduce from all this——'

And Paula listened intently, her eyes very wide now, as he outlined his theories.

He concluded: 'My partner's with Simon now. The object of that little exercise is to try and see if I'm right in thinking that Simon's sold the real pendant and had a facsimile made.'

Paula said quickly: 'But how will Mr Carter know? I mean——'

'Call him "Tinker",' said Blake. 'Everyone does.'

'How will he know?' Paula repeated. 'How will he tell a facsimile from the real thing?'

'Unless it's a very good one,' Blake said, 'he'll spot it easily. Tinker's no slouch where antique jewellery's concerned. Which is one of the reasons why I asked him to call on Simon de Courcy: why I didn't do it myself. Besides, he'll be watching Simon's reactions very closely. They might tell him a lot.

'On the other hand'—and he shrugged—'if Simon has had a facsimile made, it might even be good enough to fool Tinker. Frankly, that's what I expect. It ties in with my theories. Which brings me to the half a million pound question, Miss Dane . . .'

'Yes, Mr Blake?' She smiled back at him, though his face was serious.

'How would *you* tell t'other from which?' He put the question bluntly.

'How would I know the real pendant, you mean?'

Blake nodded tautly.

A lot depended on the answer she gave him and, indeed, whether she could give him any kind of answer at all.

But——

'Simple!' she told him. And Blake was surprised at just how simple it was—and very relieved.

'I'd know the real thing anywhere. I literally cut my teeth on it!' she said.

*   *   *

'I'd better explain . . .'

74

Paula accepted a cigarette, and Blake lit it for her. She went on:

'When I was just four months old my father had the offer of a very, very good job. There was only one snag. The job was in West Africa: that part of the world then known as "the White Man's Grave".

'However, beggars couldn't be choosers. And that's what we were round about then. This was in nineteen-thirty-six, and the Depression was far from being over. So my father decided to take the job and, since the first tour of duty was going to last for four years, my mother made up her mind that she'd go with him. Four years is a very long time.

'But what to do with me? That was the question. Everyone was appalled at the idea of an infant of my tender age fighting the good fight with mosquitoes and all the rest. It was predicted I'd be dead in a month. And that was when Sir Roderick de Courcy's wife, Ellen, piped up.'

She drew on her cigarette.

'I've already told you,' she said, 'that Sir Roderick and my mother were distantly related. They used to correspond fitfully. And, in the course of a letter, my mother mentioned her problem. Aunt Ellen immediately came up with an offer.

'She was crazy about children. Wanted one desperately. Simon had not yet been born. Not even conceived. And Ellen said she would take me, look after me until my father and mother came back at the end of the first four-year tour. And that is what happened. Except that my father and mother came back earlier than expected, of course. They returned to this country after only three years—on the outbreak of war.'

'Meantime,' said Blake, 'you actually cut your teeth on the fabulous de Courcy pendant.'

She smiled at him. 'Yes, I actually did. But don't ask me how I happened to get hold of it. I just wouldn't know. But the proof's still there to be seen—on the real pendant, I mean. It's very soft.'

'Yes, I know. Almost pure gold.'

'Turn it over,' said Paula, 'and there you are. Infant teethmarks on the back.'

75

'But would you have looked for them at the will-reading?' Blake wanted to know. 'I mean, if there'd been no thought of a possible substitution of a facsimile pendant for the real thing —would you have looked?'

'Oh, I think so,' said Paula swiftly.

And she went on: 'You see, from the time that my parents came back to England in nineteen-thirty-nine I saw nothing at all of Sir Roderick until he sent for me six weeks ago, when he was dying. My own father was killed in the war, and my mother—well—I think she still wrote to Sir Roderick from time to time—in fact, I know that she did—but that was all. We never went visiting. We weren't very well off, you see, and Sir Roderick was inclined to be generous. My mother was a proud woman and—well—maybe you can guess the rest.'

'What about when your mother died?'

'Her daughter's proud, too,' Paula said. 'No charity, thanks. But I haven't yet made my point: why I'd certainly have been keen to inspect the pendant. What I was going to say was that, naturally enough, I have no personal recollection at all of literally cutting my teeth on it. I didn't know that I had—until I went to see Sir Roderick six weeks ago. And he told me. He was talking about the pendant, relating all of its history, and he told me this. Naturally, that made me keen to see it again.'

'It wasn't there at the time?'

'At Levistone, when Sir Roderick was dying? No, he'd invested Simon with it at the age of fourteen—you know all about that. And Simon said he'd got it tucked away in a safe deposit down here, in London.'

'I see . . .'

'But Sir Roderick did give me a couple of photographs of the pendant on which you can see the tiny teeth-marks—if you know what you're looking for.'

'He *what*——?' Blake drew a sharp breath.

'He gave me a couple of——'

'That's what I thought you said. And you've still got them?'

'Of course. Back at the flat. If I'd known they were going to be important, I'd have brought them with me.'

'They're going to be important, all right!' Blake said forcefully. 'Very important indeed, unless I miss my guess! I think I'd better have them. I'll come back to the flat with you when we leave here and pick them up.'

'All right,' Paula agreed. 'But I'll have to ring the office first. I don't get all that long for my lunch, you know.'

'I'm not so sure that you should be going to the office at all,' Blake said. 'Not with things as they are. But we'll come back to that later. Now, was Simon there at the time Sir Roderick gave you these photographs?'

'Yes.' Paula nodded. She stubbed out her cigarette. 'Yes, he was. And this was the first he'd heard about my cutting my teeth on the pendant, too.'

'Are you sure? How could that be?'

Paula shrugged. 'I gathered that Simon had always found his father a bit of a bore on the subject of the pendant and de Courcy traditions. He might well have been on the receiving end of the story before, and simply not listened.'

'And he hadn't noticed the teeth-marks——?'

'On the pendant itself? Apparently not. But, as I said, they're pretty tiny. You can see that in the photographs.'

'Yes, the photographs ... well, what about those? Hadn't Simon seen them before?'

'Again,' Paula said, 'apparently not. He seemed uncommonly interested in them.'

'I've no doubt that he was,' Blake said grimly. 'Oh, yes, I'll wager they gave him a bit of a shock!

'Just think about it—if I'm right.

'He's disposed of the real pendant some months before, when in a tight spot. As soon as he hears his father is dying, he tries to get it back somehow—anyhow—but he can't, and he has a facsimile made. We'll assume it's a very good one. He's delighted with it.

'And then'—Blake's mouth twisted—'just when he thinks everything's been taken care of, he discovers that the facsimile's too damn good by a long chalk! What irony! I should imagine it was made up from drawings and a detailed description prepared years ago. Perhaps the very same drawings and the self-same description I've got in a book I borrowed down at the British Museum this morning. A book which, I might add, was printed and published fifty years before you cut your milk teeth! There's a thought for you!'

He leaned back in his chair. He said: 'Another thing that I'll wager is that the facsimile isn't ninety-six or ninety-seven per cent gold. Gold of that purity isn't easily come by these days. So the facsimile isn't as soft as the original pendant, and getting another infant to have a chew at it would just be a sheer waste of time.'

He stretched his long legs luxuriantly. 'It all adds up. This lunch has certainly been very good value! You've told me a lot!'

Paula pouted. 'Only very good value that way?'

Blake smiled at her. Then his smile died. 'But don't let's forget what this is all about. It's about someone who's out to get you, and between now and the will-reading you're going to give them no opportunity. If you still go in to the office each day—and I seriously think you should have second thoughts about that—you're going to go straight home at night, and you're going to lock yourself into your flat. You're not going to go out at all!'

'You're making me into a prisoner. It was bad enough feeling a fugitive!' Paula protested.

'Rather that than something worse.'

'You do make it sound all very dreadful and terribly serious ...'

'It is, Paula! You have a very short memory. Only yester-day——'

'Oh, yes. But that was before you came along.'

'My being in on this thing isn't going to make it any better,' Blake said incisively. 'In fact, until we've advanced out of the realms of theory and established some facts to clobber the enemy with things can only get worse! Never forget that—if I'm right—you're standing in the way of a man coming to grips with half a million pounds. There's no telling what he might do if he gets to know that you're not alone with this thing any more: that I'm with you. I'd say he'd want to finish it—and finish you—and for keeps—very fast. Before we finish him!'

'You're trying to frighten me to make a stay-at-home of me,' Paula declared.

'I'm trying to get you to face up to the facts, nothing more,' Blake insisted. 'But I'll certainly feel very much happier if I do make a stay-at-home of you. I'll know that you're safe.'

She said: 'All right. I'll do just as you say. I'll be good—even if it does take a terrific effort.'

Blake was signalling the waiter; calling for his bill.

'But I still think you've been trying to frighten me, and exaggerating the danger,' Paula said.

At that precise moment she was just one hundred and eighty seconds away from the terrifying discovery that she could not have been more wrong.

TEN

'Kill the bitch!' Jack Dino's voice came out venomously. 'Why mess about any longer? Let's be done with her!'

And Joe Turk and 'Babe' Jenkins, in the car with him, both nodded bleakly.

From every point of view it seemed like a first-class idea—though not one which would commend itself to Simon de Courcy.

All that de Courcy had ever wanted was that the Dane woman should be removed from the scene temporarily. Nothing more. And they all knew it. De Courcy was afraid of the consequences of more precipitate action.

As well he might be, Jack Dino thought grimly. For the quick killing of Miss Paula Dane would butcher more than one desirable bird with the same stone.

The killing of Miss Paula Dane would put Simon de Courcy at their mercy for the rest of his natural life. Both him and his dead father's half million. Afraid of the consequences of murder as he so patently was, he'd blackmail very nicely.

They'd be able to take him for everything he was going to possess.

So—— 'Kill the bitch!' Dino repeated. 'Kill her as soon as she comes out! We've tried it de Co...y's way, and it hasn't worked. We've wasted too much time ... this thing. Now we'll try it my way.'

And the thought of violence to come, with profit to follow, was very warming.

Violence to come, and profit to follow ... it's the story of my life, Dino thought. And his mouth twisted into a thin-lipped grin as he recalled how he had first met Simon de Courcy. And where.

He recalled de Courcy's blood slickering the cobblestones of the alley. Bad blood. Bad debtor's blood. How he had bled.

And how quickly he had paid off his outstanding gambling debts afterwards.

No doubt about it, a savage beating invariably got swift results.

Violence and profit ... how they went together. Though he'd never dreamt as he'd laid Simon de Courcy's face open with his brass knuckles that this act of violence would eventually put him in line to net a cool half a million.

All he'd been concerned about were de Courcy's unpaid gambling debts then. De Courcy had been just another name to him. Just one more welsher. The one selected at random to be given the treatment which would 'encourage the others'. The one picked out haphazardly to be taught a lesson.

The totally unexpected thing had happened some weeks later when de Courcy had actually sought him out to ask for his help.

What a situation!

You beat a man up. You make him bleed. You put the boot in—deep in the crutch. You hospitalise him for the best part of a fortnight. You put the fear of God into him—so much so that he can hardly wait to leave hospital to pay what he owes. You don't expect to have him looking you up after that with a proposition.

But it had happened.

And, in a way, maybe it wasn't so strange after all, Dino thought. De Courcy had needed a bunch of right villains with his precious pendant gone beyond hope of recovery, and with a young woman to remove from the scene—at least temporarily —because the first-class facsimile that he'd had made had turned out to be too damn good by far.

In these circumstances, who better for the job he'd had in mind than the villains who'd actually introduced themselves to him, as you might say, and given him a fair sample of their standard of work?

Yet this was far from being the only reason that de Courcy had to come looking for him, Dino was certain of that.

He knew, none better, that de Courcy hated his guts and yet, in some peculiar way, felt drawn to him compulsively. Dino had had experience of such strange love–hate relationships often before, particularly in the hot-house atmosphere of Her Majesty's Prisons. The weak fawned on the strong.

And Simon de Courcy was weak. No doubt about it. A weak man with a compulsive need to be dominated. Hating himself for his weakness, trying to prove himself to be one hundred and one per cent masculine by an off-hand, frequently callous treatment of women, Simon de Courcy still couldn't stop himself yearning for the ultimate in pseudo-sexual excitement: the sting of the whip.

Well, Dino thought, it's a love–hate relationship which can now last a little longer. It can last for just as long as it takes to skin him of every penny of his inheritance. Why, he'll even half want me to bleed him white, in his weird way. It'll give him a vicarious thrill.

The thought amused Dino, and his thin, bitter mouth quirked up at the corners as he stared out of the car through the windscreen: stared straight ahead.

The car was pulled in close to the kerb just one hundred and fifty yards short of the entrance to the Berkeley Buttery, its engine running, ready to go. It was a big car, powerful and heavy, a lethal weapon. And it was ready and waiting. Waiting to kill.

Then its appointed victim emerged from the Buttery: came out and down on to the pavement.

'Go!' Dino snapped.

And, like a rocket homing straight on to its target, the car went.

* * *

Paula Dane had no warning at all.

She had no premonition of danger.

She hesitated on the pavement outside the Buttery and half-turned towards Blake just behind her. She was about to ask him if he had his car, or whether they would be taking a cab back to Lowndes Square to pick up the photographs that he wanted.

But the question was never uttered.

Less—much less—than a hundred yards away from her now, the big, heavy car was coming straight at her, and she didn't know it. Travelling at ninety miles an hour, one and a half miles a minute, forty-five yards a second, the moment of impact, of death, of utter oblivion, was only an instant away. And Paula remained unaware.

But, in that same split second, Blake knew what was happening.

He saw the car hurtling towards them, wheels already half on the pavement. There was no time to bellow a warning.

Paula opened her mouth to ask her question and, in the same moment, was jerked off her feet as Blake grabbed her, swung around and literally threw her away from him before leaping back to safety himself.

Paula fell awkwardly on the marble steps of the Buttery, legs kicking wildly. And the car was upon her. She saw it then; screamed. It was a sound completely lost in the savage snarl of a powerful engine. It seemed that she was done for.

But, in fact, Blake's prompt action had saved her life.

For a brass handrail bisected the flight of shallow marble steps which led down from the revolving doors of the Buttery. A brass handrail which projected beyond the last step and on ιͻ the pavement.

82

The lower end of this handrail now smashed against the grille of the car as it came for Paula. The entire handrail was uprooted. It ploughed the car's bonnet with a screech of metal. It took out the windscreen in an explosion of glass. Behind the wheel, 'Babe' Jenkins was momentarily blinded. He had to swerve.

The car missed Paula by a hairsbreadth. No more. The rear wraparound bumper ripped one of her shoes off. The brass handrail, loose from its moorings, whipped round like a flail.

And then the car was roaring on and away, bucking madly down from the pavement, leaving ruin behind it. And Paula was dimly aware of Blake standing over her, slapping her face.

She didn't know that she was still screaming.

There was blood on her legs, her skirt was torn.

Blake gripped her fiercely. 'Stop it! Stop it!'

He slapped her again.

Only then was she aware of what she was doing, and her screams ended on a ragged gasp.

People were running up, crowding in from every point of the compass, and now Blake held her very gently, and lifted her to her feet.

And that was when reaction hit Paula, and hit her hard. She burst into tears.

*　　　*　　　*

Three-quarters of an hour later, Paula was still apologising.

'I don't know how you'll ever forgive me for making such an exhibition of myself. I've never been such a ninny before.'

'You've never been so close to being ploughed into the pavement before,' Blake told her grimly, and held the door for her. She led the way into the hall of the block of flats in Lowndes Square where she lived.

'And that's another thing,' she said. 'I didn't believe you. I accused you of exaggerating. I——'

But there she broke off. She had just caught sight of herself in a full-length mirror. 'Lord,' she said, 'what a mess!'

She had taken time out in the last forty-five minutes to

effect urgent running repairs, but had been able to do little or nothing to salvage the wreckage of nylons and shoes.

'You were lucky to get off so lightly,' said Blake.

'Lucky? Huh! It wasn't luck. It was you. And you know what these shoes cost? And I've only had them a week. And my skirt—oh, my poor skirt.'

She had just spotted a split seam she had overlooked earlier —pardonably. The police had kept interrupting her running repairs with insistent questions.

Had they got the car's number? They hadn't, of course. Its plates had been obscured. But Blake had described it.

Had they seen who was driving? Yes, they both had, and both could describe the man at the wheel, but that was all. They couldn't put a name to him.

Had there been anyone else in the car? Paula said one other man. Blake had thought two, but couldn't be sure. He had seen the third man—if there had been a third man—only dimly. Which was a pity. For the third man was the only one of the trio he could be expected to recognise, and would have done— instantly.

Joe Turk.

Not that it mattered.

For Paula was still unwilling to involve the police, and Blake had to respect her decision, at least for the moment. After all, what could they tell the police that was cold, cast-iron certainty? What could they prove?

Nothing at all. Nothing—yet.

So the police had gone away with some descriptions and the belief that they were looking for a drunken driver, not a coldly murderous one. And Paula and Blake had come on here to Lowndes Square, to be intercepted by the hall porter now as they made for the lift.

'Oh, Miss Dane——'

The porter was a round little man with wispy black hair slicked thinly across a fine head of skin. He was a smug little man with plenty of bounce, and an eminently self-satisfied expression.

'Unctuous busybody,' Paula growled under her breath.

'Oh, Miss Dane——' The porter had reached them now, and his bright beady eyes were very active, darting up, darting down, taking in Paula's dishevelled appearance, poking and prying, and then flicking sideways to get a good look at Blake. 'Had an accident, Miss Dane——?'

She was short with him. 'What does it look like?'

'Um ... yes ... I am sorry ..' He wasn't, of course. He was just making conventional noises. He waited hopefully for a moment for details, but then, when none were forthcoming, went smugly on, 'I just wanted to tell you that everything's all right.'

'All right——?' Paula echoed. She didn't know what he was talking about.

In any case, whatever it was, she was sure it was just an excuse. Just something to make her pause long enough for him to run his inquisitive little eyes over her and her companion.

Come in here three times in a row with the same man, she thought, and—though it was none of his damned business—this character would be hinting it was high time for a marriage licence.

Come in three times in a row with three different men, and he'd be suggesting he made a fourth.

'What do you mean, everything's all right?' she demanded.

'The electric fire in your bedroom ...' The way that he spoke suggested all kinds of shared intimacies, and Paula squirmed inwardly.

'Well, what about it?'

'It's been attended to. The man came this morning.'

'Man——?' Paula said. She looked blank.

'The electric fire in your bedroom,' the porter repeated. 'The man came and fixed it. But really, Miss Dane, really, you know'—and a playful note of rebuke entered his voice—'you should have let us know he was coming. It isn't good enough to simply give him your key, and——'

'Wait a minute,' said Paula. 'What man is this? I've given no one a key.'

'Oh, come, Miss Dane ... this was the electrician you sent for.'

'But,' Paula said tensely, 'there's never been anything wrong with my electric fire. And I certainly didn't send for an electrician. I——'

Blake interrupted. He fixed the hall porter with a hard eye. 'He let himself in?'

'But of course. Miss Dane had given him her keys, and——'

'I tell you,' Paula said grimly, 'I've given no one any keys.'

'Naturally,' the porter said, 'I stopped him down here in the hall. But then he told me what Miss Dane had asked him to do, and—well—as I said—he had her keys——'

'So you let him go up on his own.'

Something in Blake's tone put the hall porter on the defensive. 'He did have Miss Dane's keys. He told me so. He——'

'He had some keys, I don't doubt,' Blake said bleakly. 'But they weren't Miss Dane's.'

'But——'

'To get into her flat,' Blake said, 'he wouldn't need keys. Only picklocks.'

'What——?'

'Come on, Paula.' Blake swung round on her tersely. 'Let's get up there. Let's see what's been going on.'

It didn't take them long to find out. Paula opened the door and then took a pace backwards. 'Oh, no!'

The flat was a shambles.

Behind them, the hall porter peered in around them and swallowed noisily. 'But he told me——'

'The photographs,' Blake said sharply to Paula. 'The photographs of the pendant. Where are they?'

'In this chest of drawers ...' And now she was looking for them. 'I put them in here ... I know that I did.'

But they weren't there any more.

*   *   *

At about the same time that Paula was making this unhappy discovery, Simon de Courcy was dialling Jack Dino's phone number.

On the table in front of him, the counterfeit pendant

gleamed dully against the worn black satin interior of its old and scuffed leather case.

'Dino?' Simon said. His voice was high, and it shook ever so slightly. 'Dino? This is de Courcy. Where the hell have you been all afternoon? I've been trying to get you.'

Dino didn't tell him.

Jack Dino was not a man to advertise failure, only success. 'Babe got those photographs that you wanted,' he grunted.

'Photographs——? Oh ... oh, yes, those ...' De Courcy hesitated, and then it came out with a rush. 'Well, it looks like you needn't have bothered.'

'Well, well ...' Dino said softly, dangerously. 'So now you tell me.'

'The thing is,' de Courcy said quickly, 'this lunchtime I had a visitor. You remember I told you that the pawnbroker Barny Lewis said he'd sold the pendant, and that was why I couldn't get it back? He'd sold it for cash over the counter to an American—an anonymous American. Just sold it as an antique without a history——'

'What about it?' Dino growled.

'He was lying. That's what about it. He was lying when he told me he hadn't got it any more. He was holding out on me. Look—he's trying to sell it for a top price, that's how I know. He's selling it as the de Courcy pendant.

'He's offered it to at least one firm in the rare *objet d'art* business—Maxwell's, of Kensington Church Street. They sent a man round here to see me. Naturally, they wanted to know what was going on, and if I had sold the thing. Obviously, Lewis is out to get all he can, and if the papers pick up the story——'

'Yes ...' Dino said. 'Yes, indeed ...'

'I had to show this fellow from Maxwell's the fake,' de Courcy blurted. 'He seemed satisfied, but——'

'You don't have to spell it out,' Dino interrupted. 'I know what you're driving at.'

'I want that pendant back, Dino. Just get it back and everything's fine. We can forget all about those photographs and the Dane woman——'

87

'I said you don't have to spell it out!' Dino snarled. 'You act like there's no such thing as wire-tapping. Where have you been all your life?' he sounded jumpy. 'You run off at the mouth like a garden hose!'

'I'm sorry, Dino. I——'

'You want the real pendant. Okay. I'll get it for you,' Dino said curtly. 'I'll see you some time.'

He hung up abruptly.

Simon de Courcy took out a cigarette, and lit it. He was not surprised to see that his hand was shaking.

He dropped the lid of the large, flat jewel-case which held the facsimile pendant.

The case shut with a snap.

ELEVEN

At six that night, Blake left Paula Dane's flat in Lowndes Square. He had helped her tidy up, despite her objections, and had stayed with her until the lock on her front door had been replaced by one which could neither be picked nor be forced.

He was alarmed at the ease with which the enemy had penetrated the apartment.

So he told her to lock and bolt the door after him, and to secure every window, and he left her with the assurance that he would call again later that evening. Then he headed back to Baker Street quickly, and another conference with Tinker: a council of war.

At seven that night, Tinker was in a car on the Cromwell Road, driving towards Emperors' Close.

At eight o'clock, Paradise Street, way over on the other side of London, was quiet and deserted.

Paradise Street was within a stone's throw of the Mile End Road, but it might just as well have been half of the world away. Paradise Street was a backwater. The pulsing, sprawling life of The Road never touched it. The tailors and café proprietors with their boisterous clientele had passed it by. At eight o'clock at night, Paradise Street was as good as dead.

There was only one shop in the street—a jeweller's. It had thick glass windows protected by bent, rusting bars of iron separated from each other by a distance no greater than the width of a man's hand.

Above the shop there was a flaking fascia. Begrimed letters spelled out the name of Bernard Lewis. Next to the name was a wrought-iron fixture from which hung suspended three grubby brass balls.

Below this sign, beyond the cheap glass pitted and marred by a million tiny bubbles, two windows carried a display of rings, bracelets and old-fashioned pocket-watches. To the forefront of each display there were cards which proclaimed that these goods were being sold at bargain prices. They were unredeemed pledges.

A light burned in the shop beyond. A single electric bulb, placed high, threw brilliant, hard rays down upon the completely bald head of a small man who bent over account books and ledgers. The man was Bernard Lewis—known as Barny to his intimates. And they were many.

He was sixty-three years of age, bald as a billiard ball and sallow skinned. His eyes were by nature melancholy, and they seemed to suggest that he found life to be a hard, unremitting labour from one day to another. A wearisome, profitless burden.

He had lived in Paradise Street all of his life, and, from the age of fourteen, had been connected with the pawnbroking and cheap jewellery business, first on behalf of his father, who had owned this same shop, and then on his own account. And, from the age of fourteen, he had done 'favours for friends' on the side.

He always referred to them as 'favours for friends'—these furtive transactions which took place after his shop was officially closed for the night. Men with hard faces would sidle up to the shop and be admitted; they would leave pieces of jewellery, scrap gold, trinkets and precious stones. They would accept money—a few pounds—and they would depart.

If they saw a policeman as they entered or left the shop they would hesitate. They might even hide in the shelter of some convenient doorway until the officer of the law had passed them by. Barny's friends didn't like policemen, nor did Barny himself.

This was the key to his popularity with the shifty-eyed, hard-faced men he did his 'favours' for. This, and the fact that he was a fence.

Now—this night—Barny Lewis bent over his books, and the shop was quiet all around him. From somewhere overhead there came the ticking of a clock, and, from next door, through the thin walls, there filtered the muffled sound of somebody screaming. Barny Lewis wasn't alarmed. He knew his television programmes. Thursday night, eight o'clock, BBC One, Doctor Kildare.

In Paradise Street itself, nothing moved.

Then, at four minutes past eight, two men entered the street from the direction of the Mile End Road. They were walking quickly. Both were short men. One, thin as a whip and feral-faced, the other squat in a black belted overcoat which seemed to emphasise the immense width of his shoulders.

A car came up behind them, creeping slowly along the kerb. Neither of the two men looked at the car. It was big, black and powerful, and shone in the dim light of the street-lamps. Its windscreen sparkled. Its radiator grille looked brand new. The whole car looked as if it had only recently been given a respray.

Presently the car swung out from the kerb and did a slow U-turn. It came to rest at the pavement's edge, facing back the way it had come. The driver cut his lights, but left his engine running. The two men walked on.

They reached Barny Lewis's shop, and the thin one—whose face showed a totally unnatural pallor—extended a hand to rap upon the glass of the door. The other man, the one in the black overcoat, stepped back into the shadows and turned his head first this way, then that, to look up and down the street carefully.

Barny Lewis shuffled to the door. He tried to peer out

90

through the glass. He could see only one man, and him but dimly. He grunted to himself and unbolted the door. He let it swing inwards on its safety-chain.

'Who is it?'

'Open up, Barny!'

'What do you want?'

Lewis didn't recognise the man that he saw. To the best of his knowledge he had never seen him before.

'Who sent you? What do you want?' he demanded. 'I'm closed. What do you want with me?'

'I've got something. It's hot. You want we should do business in the street?'

The man's voice was urgent. Barny Lewis had heard that urgency in men's voices before. That he recognised. And he recognised the pallor of the man's face at the same time.

Prison pallor. It was a passport. Grumbling to himself—more for effect than out of bad humour—he tugged at the chain, pushed the door shut, then opened it.

'All right,' he said. 'All right. You come in. We talk business. But I never keep too much money by me. So, what you got, it'll have to be cheap. What is it, heh?'

The thin man came in. So did the other. He came in quickly, moving at an amazing speed for a man of his bulk. He was standing before Lewis before the pawnbroker even realised there had been two men outside, not just one.

'Take it easy, Joe,' the thin man said. He closed the door, heard the latch snap, leaned against it. 'Just make him talk.'

'What is this?' Barny Lewis was alarmed. 'What are you doing in my shop? You get out of here, you understand?'

The man in the black overcoat moved. He was fast. Out of nowhere, an open razor appeared in his hand.

'You're going to talk!' His voice was thick; guttural. 'You're going to talk and talk fast. Otherwise . . .'

The razor sang thinly as it sped through the air. It missed Barny Lewis's cheek by thousandths of an inch. He felt the wind of it. He fell back, and he was shaking.

'What do you want with me?' His voice rose shrilly. 'What do you want?'

91

'The de Courcy pendant.' The thin man who leaned against the door answered Barny's frenzied question. 'You've got it. We want it. Make it quick. Just produce it.'

'Pendant! I don't know what you're talking about.'

'You can do better than that!'

'A Mr de Courcy I know—yes'—Barney quavered—'and he did bring something in, but that was—that was months ago.'

'And it was a pendant. Right? The de Courcy pendant. Now stop wasting time. Get it.'

'But—but I can't. It isn't here. I haven't got it any more.'

Barny Lewis was very frightened. The words came out of him in something akin to a sob.

'How can I give you what I haven't got?'

'You're lying!' The thin man by the door spoke the words decisively. 'Sure it was just a pendant when Mr de Courcy brought it in. A piece of old junk. Valuable—certainly—but nothing special ... until you started putting two and two together. Then you knew exactly what it was, and you started putting out feelers in the right quarters. You've been trying to sell it for a top price. We know that. You can't trick us—not if you want to live a little longer.'

'I sold it months ago,' Barny Lewis said. 'Months, you hear? I sold it over the counter here, in this shop. I told Mr de Courcy all this.'

'We don't believe you.'

'But it's true! What should I do? Hang on to something I bought legitimately? Keep it for ever?'

'You haven't sold it. You're lying. You're still trying to sell. You can't fool us.'

'On my life, I am telling the truth!'

The squat man moved forward and his open razor glittered in the light. 'Come on, come on, Dino,' he said. 'Why do we waste time? Still he lies. Let me carve him a little bit.'

'I tell you, it's true! It's true! The pendant's sold. I haven't got it! It's true!' Barny Lewis gabbled the words in terror. 'Why don't you believe me,' he sobbed, 'when I tell the truth?'

'Give it to him, Joe,' Dino said suddenly.

Lewis began to back away. 'No—no—please——'

92

'Give it to him, Joe. But not with the razor. That could be your trade-mark. Give it to him some other way.'

'Please—I——'

'Go on, Joe. What are you waiting for? Beat the truth out of him!'

'No! No! *No!*'

The last word was a frenzied scream. It was cut short as Joe Turk chopped Lewis down. He hit him on the side of the head, and brass knuckles glinted as the blow struck home.

Lewis staggered. He groaned out loud. He clutched for his desk as if to steady himself. His legs bent beneath him.

Turk's face split in an awful smile. He went towards Lewis. He reached out for him.

Then he froze.

Lewis had a gun in his hand.

'You want trouble?' the old man quavered. 'You get out of my shop or I put a bullet in both of you. It'll be self-defence. Go on, get out! Get out, or I shoot the both of you. Get out! Get out!'

'Mr Lewis doesn't want our company,' Dino said. His face wore a dreamy expression, but in their deep sockets his eyes were blazing. 'I don't think he likes us, Joe.'

'You get out! I call the police!'

Lewis pulled himself upright. He held on to his desk with one hand. He needed the support. The other hand—trembling —held the gun.

'All right, we'll go,' Dino said. 'Ready, Joe?'

He pushed himself up from the door. He made as if to turn round. In that moment Turk made a movement, and Lewis's gun jerked sideways to cover him. Lewis never had the time to pull the trigger. Dino had jumped for him; smashed him viciously across the side of the neck with a hand as rigid and as hard as iron.

Lewis's fingers opened. He staggered. Dino hit him again; again hard; again on the side of the neck. Lewis's gun fell out of his nerveless fingers. Turk caught it before it hit the floor.

There was a rasping sound as Lewis's fingernails slid over

the wood of his desk. Then he slumped down. His head struck the top of the counter as he fell.

Dino bent over him, kicking, kicking, kicking, savagely, determinedly and breathing hard.

Then he stopped, straightened up and he was smiling.

'Has he gone?' Turk wanted to know. 'Has he——'

Dino extended a finger. He thrust it callously into one of Lewis's wide-open eyes.

'He's gone.'

'We should get out of here!'

'We're not going empty-handed. You grab some stuff while I take a look around.'

Dino went swiftly through Lewis's pockets, but found no keys. He left the shop; entered the room beyond and flipped the light switch. He saw an old safe which stood in one corner of the room; tried it. It was locked.

'It'll take gelignite. Gelignite. Nothing less.' And he swore.

Then his eyes fell on Lewis's stock-book, a big leather-bound ledger which lay on a shelf. He dragged it down, opened it and turned its pages quickly, urgently scanning column after column of entries in Lewis's spidery, semi-literate hand.

It should be here . . . it had been a legitimate deal. It——

Suddenly, Dino dragged in a breath. There it was.

Lewis had been telling the truth. Pendant bought, pendant sold, dates, prices, the lot.

Dino started to laugh. Merriment bubbled up out of him. He slammed the big, heavy book shut and hefted it back on to its shelf.

He went out of the back room and re-entered the shop. He felt good. He felt fine. Violence acted on him like a tonic. Good humouredly, he kicked Lewis's body as he passed it. There was blood on the floor.

'You all set, Joe?'

'I'm okay, Dino. I've got some stuff.'

'All right then.' Dino sounded gay and light-hearted. 'Let's get out of here.'

His gloved hand caught at the door, thumbed back the latch,

pulled the door open. He stepped out into the street, hesitated on the pavement and then as the Turk joined him he moved off across the road.

He looked at his watch in the light of the nearest street-lamp. It was twenty-five minutes past eight. The rear door of the waiting car was thrust open just a split second before he and Turk reached it.

Four seconds after that, the car was rolling down Paradise Street, gathering speed as it went. Half a minute later, it was lost in the traffic on the Mile End Road.

Back in the pawnbroker's shop, Barny Lewis stirred. His fingers clenched themselves. He tried to get to his feet, and couldn't. His dying brain told his muscles and nerves to make one final effort. He must call the police. He must tell——

He moved perhaps three millimetres. Not more. Then, as his brain screamed out its instructions, his body found itself unable to carry them out.

Blood came from his mouth and out of his nose. On the floor, in the dust, at eight twenty-seven precisely, Barny Lewis died.

And there, just fifteen minutes later, a man called Nick Reuter, who was a self-employed private inquiry agent and an occasional operative for Sexton Blake, found Lewis's body. Then he spent ten minutes looking around.

At eight fifty-two, he first rang Sexton Blake's Baker Street number and held a brief conversation with the detective. Then he called the police.

TWELVE

At ten minutes past nine the door-bell rang stridently in Simon de Courcy's maisonette in Emperors' Close.

It rang in the passageway outside the dark and deserted, ill-furnished living-room. In the bedroom beyond, harsh, urgent breathing was checked, but only for a moment. The bell rang again.

The sound of the breathing became more urgent still, savage, with small slapping sounds. Still it went on; on; and then was suddenly stilled on a shuddering gasp. The bell was ringing continuously now out on the landing.

Simon de Courcy came out of the bedroom, wrapping his dressing-gown around his thin, lank frame. His eyes were bright and feverish, but his loose-lipped weak mouth hung slackly.

Behind him, Roxie Marlowe lay motionless, breathing shallowly. The little redhead's eyes were closed, legs and arms rigid, hands tightly clenched.

She stayed there for a long moment, breath held, expression tense, then suddenly a sob caught in her throat, and she flung herself over on to her face.

'Damn!' she said. 'Damn!'

Simon de Courcy did not hear her above the noise the bell was still making.

He had paused in the dark outer room to thrust his bare feet into mules. Now he gathered up skirt, blouse, jacket, handbag, and threw them all into the bedroom, slamming the door behind them.

He went out, down the passage and into the hall, and approached the front door.

In the bedroom, Roxie Marlowe glared at her things sprawled on the floor and ground out distinctly, 'You swine!'

Then her shoulders started to droop as if in defeat. Her hard-pointed breasts sagged. She sighed a long, weary sigh. She pushed herself up and started to dress. She moved very slowly.

*　　　*　　　*

Out in the hall, Simon de Courcy was moving back—fast.

No sooner had he got the front door open than three men had shouldered their way in.

Three men in a hurry. Three men that he recognised. Dino, 'Babe' Jenkins and Joe Turk.

'What's going on?' he wanted to know. He sounded alarmed.

96

'Back up, friend,' Dino said curtly. 'Save it until we're inside.'

The three men crowded through the passageway from the hall and into the living-room, hustling Simon de Courcy ahead of them. Dino firmly shut all doors behind them as they went.

In the dark and cold living-room, Turk stopped Simon de Courcy as he reached for the light switch. 'Wait a minute!'

He crossed the room to the windows overlooking the ruined garden, gently eased back a curtain and stood looking out for the best part of a minute, motionless and tense.

'I wish someone would tell me——' Simon de Courcy began.

'Shut up!' 'Babe' Jenkins snarled.

Joe Turk stood rigidly, looking out of the window into the night, for another long moment, then slowly allowed himself to relax. He moved the curtains carefully back into place.

'All right,' he growled. 'Now you can put the light on.'

Simon did so, and then exploded: 'What is all this? What the hell's going on?'

'You know someone's watching this place?' Dino demanded.

'Watching . . .?' Simon de Courcy's jaw had dropped slackly. He swallowed. 'But—but that's ridiculous.'

'It's a fact. Tell him, Joe.'

Joe Turk's face was expressionless. 'Character over the other side of the Close. Thought there might be more than one. But it looks like he's on his own.'

'But,' Simon de Courcy said helplessly, 'but—but who——?'

'We know who,' Dino said. 'And we know why. Only question is—what's to be done about it. And I think I've got the answer to that, too. You're going to do some travelling.'

Simon de Courcy stared. 'What are you talking about?'

'You. You're going to do some travelling, like I said.'

'But——' Simon de Courcy broke off. He said accusingly, 'You didn't get the pendant!'

'No.' And Dino grinned. His eyes burned maliciously. 'It seems that Barny Lewis didn't have it after all. You were misinformed. He sold it months ago, like he told you.'

'I don't believe it!'

'I was convinced,' Dino said.

'You believed him?' Simon swore. He tried hard to control himself. He said: 'He's led you straight up the garden! You ought to go back there—force the truth out of him somehow!'

'No need,' said Jack Dino. 'He was telling the truth. Besides, it's impossible.'

'What do you mean?'

Dino said softly, 'Lewis is dead.'

'Dead?' Simon echoed stupidly. He felt icy fingers clamp down round his heart. 'How can he be dead?'

'Joe started to rough him up,' Dino said. His voice was pitched in a reasoning tone. He was explaining a perfectly natural reaction to an everyday situation. 'Lewis had a gun. He had it hidden. When Joe slammed into him he got his hand on it. He told us to get out, and his finger was trembling on the trigger.'

'And you killed him! My God! You killed him!'

'We could have gone out,' Dino said. 'We could have done as he told us. But, like as not, he would have shot us in the back.'

It wasn't true, but that didn't matter.

'Like as not he'd have shot us in the back,' Dino repeated. 'He could have called the police then. A clear case of self-defence. And then where would you have been?'

'Me——? What are you talking about?' Simon's voice had risen shrilly.

'Naturally,' Dino said, 'the police would have wanted to know what we had been doing there. And Lewis would have told them. Then you'd have been in a fine mess, wouldn't you? In real trouble with the police on top of everything else.'

He grinned suddenly, savagely, and he said sweetly, 'We only did it for you.'

'Leave me out of it!'

'Not on your life,' Dino said softly. 'We're all in this together. Blood brothers now, you might say. You'll remember that when you come into that half a million. We'll take good care that you don't ever forget it.'

'I didn't want Lewis dead!'

'Maybe you could have done better, eh, de Courcy?' Dino's voice was like ice. 'Well, why didn't you try? Or maybe you wouldn't have done so well.'

'I wanted the pendant. The real pendant. I would never have killed the one man who knew where it is!'

'The *one* man?' Dino said silkily. 'Aren't you forgetting the visitor you had this lunchtime—the man from Maxwell's? Maybe he'll tell you.' Dino laughed, and it was an ugly sound. 'Yes, why don't you ask him?'

'What are you driving at?'

'You didn't even check, did you? You didn't find out that the firm that man claimed to represent simply doesn't exist.'

'I don't believe you. I——'

'I checked,' Dino said flatly. 'When I knew for a certain fact that Lewis didn't have the real pendant any more—that's when I checked. I thought we might break into Maxwell's offices and examine their files—just to see who really did offer the pendant to them. But they're not in the book, d'you hear? I asked round. There is no Maxwell's in Kensington Church Street. There never has been.'

'You're mistaken! You must be!'

'Why must it always be me who's mistaken? Why can it never be you? This character came to you by taxi. Right? You see—I've asked around. And I know a few drivers. I protect one or two. And this character who came to see you, he was tall, wasn't he? Young? About twenty-five, or less, blue eyes, blond hair? That's right, isn't it? I got a good description. You want me to tell you the colour of the suit he was wearing, or describe the pattern on his tie?'

'What do you mean?'

'That's the man, isn't it? Well—isn't it? And he was no antique dealer. Take it from me. That man's name is Carter. And you want to know where he is right at this moment? Because I can tell you. He's over the other side of the Close. He's the man who's watching this house. He's a detective.'

'What——?'

'You heard me,' Dino said brutally. 'And I'll tell you more.

99

This Carter, he's Sexton Blake's junior partner. And Blake is working for Paula Dane. They had lunch together. They were laughing. They seemed to be enjoying a joke together. Well— at least until I wiped the grins off their faces. But I have the feeling that that joke was on you.'

'Blake——' Simon de Courcy said. He felt sick in the stomach. 'Sexton Blake!'

'Now tell me you've never heard of him,' Dino said bitingly.

'Oh, God!' Simon de Courcy put his head in his hands.

Dino regarded him pityingly.

Then he said: 'Listen to me. We can still come out of this laughing. You can still grab that half a million. Just do what I tell you, and everything will be fine.'

De Courcy lifted his head and stared at him.

Dino said: 'Basically nothing has changed—if we act fast. All we've got to do is get the Dane woman out of the way— but it must be tonight!—and the situation is back under control. With her out of the way, what does it matter what she's told Blake? There is no proof. We've got those photographs that your father gave her. There's no proof at all.'

'Oh, sure!' De Courcy laughed harshly. 'No proof at all ... everything is so easy. All we have to do is get the Dane woman out of the way.'

Then the words ripped out of him shrilly.

'But how in hell do we do that? You've tried, haven't you? Or maybe you haven't been trying at all. Is that what you're telling me?'

On the other side of the room, Turk moved menacingly.

'Hold it, Joe!' Jack Dino's voice was hard. He turned back to de Courcy. 'We've tried all right, and—okay—we've failed. In the beginning the Dane bitch had all the luck, and now she's got Sexton Blake helping her. It seems like it's just impossible to get her, doesn't it? Especially now ...' And he paused. Then he said tautly, 'But if you think that—especially now—you'll be wrong!'

'You're talking in riddles,' de Courcy said wearily.

'Then get this. Simply by making one telephone call I can get Paula Dane over here.'

'Here———? Over here? You're out of your mind!'

'You want me to prove it? Where's your phone?'

'Out in the passage. But———'

'The number, Babe,' Dino said, cutting him short. 'You got it this morning when you were in her flat.'

'Sure ...'

'Babe' Jenkins gave it to him.

Dino went out into the passage, picked up the phone and dialled.

He said, 'Miss Paula Dane, please.' And he waited until the porter at the block of flats in Lowndes Square put him through.

He folded a handkerchief across the mouthpiece. He made his voice crisp and efficient. 'Miss Dane—is that you? Fine. This is Mr Carter. Sexton Blake's assistant. Yes ... yes ... everything all right in your part of the world? Good ...'

And he listened.

Then he said: 'He was going to call in on you, was he? Uh-huh. That's what I'm ringing about. There's been a change of plan. Mr Blake would like you to come over here right away. Yes. Tonight. Right away. Can you manage that? It's very, very important.

'Where?

'Number sixty-two Emperors' Close. Yes. The maisonette there. Simon de Courcy's place———'

He listened again, briefly.

Then he spoke rapidly into the phone. 'There's not a lot of time to explain, but de Courcy has broken down. He's telling Mr Blake all kinds of things. He's cracked up completely. Those attacks on you the other day—and that business with the car this afternoon—he's confessed to responsibility. Yes ... yes. There are other things, too, and Mr Blake thinks that you should be here. You do see how important it is, don't you? Will you get here as soon as you can? You will? Good. Good. Make it as soon as you possibly can, Miss Dane—if not sooner.'

Smiling broadly, he replaced the phone, and turned to look over his shoulder at Simon de Courcy. 'There you are. Easy. Especially now that Blake's working for her.'

Then he moved.

He said: 'But you're not going to be here when she arrives. Nor is that character over the road. If you go, he will. You're the one that he's interested in. He'll follow you wherever you lead him. And I suggest you make that the ancient home of the de Courcys—right up in Cumberland.'

'But—but you're not serious!'

'Get moving,' said Dino. 'And don't worry, I'll get in touch' —he grinned—'after the will-reading. Until then, no news is good news, eh? And don't forget to take that fake pendant with you.'

De Courcy hesitated, then shrugged. He said lamely, 'All right.'

'Babe' Jenkins and Turk both stood behind him in the living-room doorway. He had to push past them. Everything he needed was in the bedroom. Turk looked at him. 'Doesn't seem very keen, does he, Dino?'

'I was wondering,' de Courcy said, 'what you lot were going to get out of all this.'

'Babe' Jenkins laughed. 'Don't worry about us. We'll do all right.'

'That,' said Simon de Courcy, 'is what I'm afraid of. Maybe I——'

'Maybe nothing,' Dino interrupted him roughly, 'you're going!'

Then came another interruption. A startling one.

A voice asked pointedly, 'Going where?'

The four men jerked around.

*   *   *

Roxie Marlowe was framed in the doorway of the bedroom, looking a little the worse for wear but fully dressed.

Turk swore. 'How long has she been here?'

De Courcy swallowed and rubbed his hand up over his face. 'I forgot all about her. She's been here all the time.'

'And she'll have heard everything.' Turk looked alarmingly in Dino's direction.

But all Dino did was to laugh.

102

'You haven't heard her screaming for help, have you, Joe?'
His eyes lingered over Roxie's excellent legs, then started
climbing. 'She's your bit of tail, is she, de Courcy?'

'Yes.'

'She *was* your bit of tail,' Jack Dino said, and still his eyes
lingered. 'All right, de Courcy, get dressed and get moving.
And make it fast.'

Simon de Courcy moved awkwardly. 'I'm going up to
Cumberland, Roxie. You're coming with me.'

'She's staying,' said Jack Dino. 'She knows too damn
much.'

'Roxie, are you coming with me?' de Courcy persisted.

The redhead had been staring at Dino. Now she shifted her
gaze. Shook her auburn head. 'You heard the man. You can't
give me a thing any more, Simon. Maybe you never could. I
know too damn much—particularly how spineless and kinky
you are. I'll stay with the big boys.'

She moved away from the bedroom door.

On the other side of the room, Dino laughed.

'Okay, kiddo,' he told her. 'That suits me fine.'

He motioned to the room Roxie had just left

'Go back in there,' he said. 'I'll join you in a minute. Then
we'll start getting better acquainted ...'

He turned to Simon de Courcy. 'I told you to get moving,'
he said menacingly. 'On your way, buster! And don't stop till
you get to Cumberland.'

THIRTEEN

It was nine forty-five when Paula Dane entered Emperors'
Close.

She came around the corner from the direction of the
Cromwell Road, and she was walking quickly. Sexton Blake
had wanted her to be at the rendezvous as soon as she could.

She had tried for a cab, but without success. At this time of night, Paula thought bitterly, they were all probably cruising around the West End. Trust it to be like that when she was in a hurry—when Sexton Blake urgently wanted to see her. She could have reached Emperors' Close much more quickly if she'd made up her mind to take a bus in the first place: if she hadn't wasted her time looking for an elusive taxi.

As her heels beat out a tattoo on the paving-stones, Paula's eyes sped over the tall houses which flanked either side of the road. The curtains were drawn across the windows, and here and there light showed thinly. Paula looked for the numbers on the houses. Sixty-two—that was where Simon de Courcy lived. Sixty-two . . .

Loose, filmy wreaths of mist, as delicate as cobwebs, floated in front of the street-lamps as Paula hurried along. She was alone in the echoing street; alone with her shadow which grew and wavered and melted as she moved between one lamp and the next. There was no other human being in sight.

A sudden, sighing waft of wind caught at a sheet of newspaper, picked it up from a gutter and sent it cart-wheeling across the road. The wreaths of mist quivered and danced. An old tom-cat, black as a witch, sat within the magic circle of light thrown by one of the street-lamps, stared tiredly at the newspaper, and watched it go.

Then Paula saw, straight ahead, a small grove, a clump of spindly trees. Directly opposite the grove she saw a painted number on the front of a house. The number was sixty. Simon's house must be the next one. She quickened her pace.

She reached the house, climbed the three steps from the pavement, and rang the bell of the maisonette.

To her left, a curtain flickered back into place at the window of the ground floor front room. Paula caught the movement out of the corner of an eye. That would be Sexton Blake, or perhaps Edward Carter. Again Paula cursed the shortage of taxis. She had kept Blake waiting.

Then the door started to open, and Paula had a smile on her face. She began to say, 'I'm sorry I'm so la——'

And then she stopped.

Instead, she gasped: 'You!'

She didn't say anything more after that. She didn't because she couldn't. Two huge hands had reached out for her. One fastened over her mouth. The other gripped her neck and pulled her brutally into the house.

It was Joe Turk behind the hands. So much her mind told her as she struggled uselessly.

Where was Blake? What was happening? Where was Blake?

She tried to kick, but Turk held her. He dragged her down the hall and into darkness.

Joe Turk!

This man had made her a fugitive, and now he had her!

The great, hairy hands!

No, her mind whimpered. No ...

But she couldn't escape.

Joe Turk could do whatever he liked with her. She was helpless.

The hands were remorseless.

*   *   *

Sexton Blake drove towards Lowndes Square and Paula Dane's flat, and his mouth was set grimly.

The pace of this case was certainly hotting up, just as he'd predicted. The killing had started.

He had just left Paradise Street and the body of a very dead Barny Lewis. He had gone there as soon as Nick Reuter had called him.

If only Lewis had been the first name on the list he had given Nick.

If he had, would he still be alive?

Possibly ...

Maybe ...

But it was useless to speculate.

The fact was that Lewis had not been the first name on Nick's list. He had been the last. Tinker had put the names down on paper immediately after his interview with Simon de

Courcy, and he had put them down in precisely the same order that de Courcy had uttered them.

Mountford. Williams. Jones.

And then—and only then—Lewis.

One of these people possibly knew something about the de Courcy pendant. But which one—if any? Blake had called in an old friend, the best free-lance private inquiry agent he knew, to find out.

And Nick Reuter had had to start somewhere. With any list of names to work through you had to start somewhere. Why not at the top?

With the advantage of hindsight, it was easy to say that the last should have been first. The first one to set about tracing, the first one to visit, the first one to show Simon's photograph to. That print Tinker had culled from the picture library of the *Daily Post*.

'*Know this man, sir? Take your time. Have a good look. What I want to know is: have you done any business with him in the last six or seven months?*'

That was the routine, and it seemed very simple, and if you knew nothing about what it really involved it was also easy to say that with only four names on his list Nick Reuter should have reached Lewis sooner. But Sexton Blake didn't say that. Not at all.

For the truth was—and Blake knew it—that Nick had had a damned difficult job.

Nothing was simple, nothing straightforward, about tracing anyone in a city the size of London, especially when you only had a surname to go on. Sure, you could also hazard a guess that every one of the people named on the list was some kind of a dealer—if they existed at all. But did that help very much?

To particularise: what kind of a dealer? There were only about nine hundred and ninety-nine different varieties in the London area.

No, even though he'd arrived in Paradise Street too late to save Lewis, Nick Reuter had done very well. In little more than three hours he'd found the one man in all London he'd

106

been looking for: the one man on his list who'd bought an ancient gold pendant from Simon de Courcy. Lewis's stock-book confirmed it. And this wasn't all.

Lewis's stock-book showed he'd later sold the pendant for cash over the counter. The purchaser's name wasn't given but, despite this, Blake knew how to trace him. And Reuter would do it first thing in the morning.

Blake intended to recover the pendant de Courcy had sold, and use it to blow this whole case sky-high. He intended to recover the pendant, and he knew just how to do it. The stock-book had told him.

For Lewis had entered the amount realised on the sale of the pendant as dollars, with its sterling equivalent in brackets below. So the pendant must have been sold to an American, or to a Canadian. Blake had done some very fast mental arithmetic to reach this quite definite conclusion. No other kind of dollars would do.

And this conclusion led on to another.

It didn't matter that the man who had bought the pendant from Lewis was so far anonymous. He could still be traced. The pendant was an antique, and a Board of Trade export licence would be needed to take it out of the country. All Reuter would have to do first thing in the morning would be to go round to the Board of Trade and find out the name and address of the man who had applied for such a licence. And having a good idea of the man's nationality, American or Canadian, should cut the time this inquiry would take to the very minimum possible.

By noon tomorrow, Blake now told himself grimly, I'll have Simon de Courcy just where I want him.

He cornered into Lowndes Square, and slowed his big car to a crawl.

Just as soon as he'd seen Paula Dane and made sure she was obeying his orders and not taking chances, he'd go on to Emperors' Close and compare notes with Tinker. This was his plan.

But a few minutes later it became obvious that something had gone very wrong with the first half of it.

Paula Dane wasn't at home, the night porter told Blake. She had gone out.

*   *   *

'Out ...?' Blake heard himself echo. He had an uneasy feeling in the pit of his stomach. 'When did she go out?'

'Oh.... well over an hour ago, it was, sir.'

Well over an hour. Out in the dark night for well over an hour. Anything could have happened to her, Blake thought. Anything, good or bad.

'You wouldn't know where she went?' he asked, and his voice was tight. The uneasy feeling in the pit of his stomach had swelled into a sour, burning sickness.

'Well, sir, she did ask me to get her a cab. But I couldn't. She did tell me the address, though. Let me think.'

The porter's voice tailed away. He said into the silence made electric by Blake's mounting unease and tension: 'You know how it is, sir. You hear so many addresses ... It was Emperors' Gate ... No ... no, I'm telling a lie ... that wasn't it ...'

'Emperors' Close?' Blake said swiftly.

'Yes, sir.' The porter both looked and sounded relieved. 'Yes, that was it. Emperors' Close. Sixty something, Emperors' Close. Fancy you guessing that!'

'And what time was this? Can you give me a time?'

'Well'—the porter was doubtful—'well, I don't know to the minute, but it wouldn't be long after I came on duty. There was this telephone call ...'

'Which telephone call?'

'Why, the one Miss Dane had, sir. She had this phone call, and a few minutes after that she was down here in the hall asking me to get her a cab. But I couldn't, sir. You know how it is, sometimes ...'

'You took the call? Can you remember the time? It could be important.'

'I took the call all right, sir. It came through my box. And time—well—say around twenty past nine. Though it might have been earlier.'

108

'Was it a man or a woman calling? Can you remember?'

'Well——'

Blake fought to control his mounting impatience. He waited.

'Well—a man—I think.'

'And did he, she or it give a name?'

'Name, sir? Oh, no, sir. We don't ask names. Not when we're just putting a call through, like. Unless we get special instructions of course. You see——'

'Thanks,' Blake said abruptly, and spun round on his heel. He went out to his car fast. What was going on? Paula had disregarded his express instructions. She had not only gone out, she had gone straight to Simon de Courcy. Why, for Pete's sake? What had happened?

Could it be that there'd been all kinds of developments he was not yet aware of, and that Tinker had attempted to reach him while he was with Nick Reuter down in Paradise Street?

Yes, that must be it.

And then, having tried to get him, and failed, Tinker had for some reason rung Paula and called her out.

But·for what reason Blake couldn't think.

Yet something like this must have happened, for why else would Paula have gone to Emperors' Close?

Clearly, Blake thought, the sooner he himself got there the better.

So he wasted no time. He took all the short cuts he knew, and soon—very soon—he was pulling in to a side turning off the Cromwell Road. He'd walk the rest of the way. It wasn't far. Barely two hundred yards. And until he knew for certain what was going on, it might be better not to advertise his arrival.

He got out of the car swiftly. He came to the Close. He looked for Tinker, and didn't see him. Come to that, he hadn't seen his car either. What on earth had been happening here?

He moved down the Close. He made little noise. He came abreast of Simon's house, paused, then approached it more closely. Near enough to read the names over the bells. Then he backed off again. There were no lights in Simon's part of the house. None that he could see. He thought that very strange.

Where had Paula and Tinker gone?

Back to Baker Street, perhaps? Blake left the Close quickly, found a telephone box, and rang his own number. But it wasn't his partner who answered the phone, it was his motherly old housekeeper, Mrs Bardell.

'Mr Tinker, sir? Lor' love you, no, sir, he hasn't been back here. Nor any young lady, either. He did call you though, on the tellyphone, about an hour ago. He said to tell you he was in Saint Neots.'

'What did you say?' Blake's voice had risen sharply. 'Said to tell me that he was where?'

'In Saint Neots, sir. You know, the home of them quads, sir. Or was it quins?'

Blake wondered if he was going mad.

'But what on earth is he doing there?'

'Following Mr de Courcy, sir. That's what he said. He's done a bunk, he said. His very words.'

'And did he mention Miss Dane?'

'Not at all, sir. But I gathered, sir—you know how you do—that Mr Tinker was on his own, and that Mr de Courcy was on his own, too.'

Then where was Paula Dane?

'Oh, and he did say something else, sir. Asked me to give you the message. He told me to tell you that before he chased off after Mr de Courcy he saw someone called Joe Turk arrive at the house with two other men. He said he reckernised Joe Turk from his picture in the Rogues Gallery, and that he thought he had someone called Dino with him. Would that be right, sir?'

Would it be right!

Blake now knew that he had to get back to the house in Emperors' Close fast. If Paula had gone there, and Joe Turk had been waiting . . .

He felt himself shiver.

'I'll be in touch again, Mrs Bardell,' he said quickly. He pressed the cradle down on the phone to break the connection; dialled again. This time, Paula's home number.

No, the night porter told him, she still hadn't returned . . .

110

Blake left the telephone box and retraced his steps swiftly. He went back to the Close. But this time he went around the back of the houses, and along the cobbled mews which lay there. He found the back door of the de Courcy house next to a garage in the process of being converted into a cottage. Builders' materials were everywhere.

The back door was rotten, and hung on its hinges. Blake tried it gently, then firmly. And it moved. Seconds later, he was standing at the end of a small wildly overgrown garden. Quickly, but quietly, he made his way to the house.

He reached it. The ground floor windows were dark. An eerie stillness lay over the ruined garden. Behind him, an Underground train pounded its way through one of the District Line culverts, then all was quiet again. Deathly quiet. No sound came out of the house. Moving very carefully, making no noise, Blake sought a way in.

He found a door which opened on to the garden. A door heavy and oaken and studded with nails. He tried it. Locked. But wherever Blake went he was fully equipped to deal with a situation like this. Just as long as the door wasn't bolted on the inside ...

A bare sixty second later, he was telling himself that he was lucky, and he was slipping tempered steel picklocks back into his pocket: sliding them in on the end of his keychain, doing it gently, so that even this brief manoeuvre gave birth to no sound.

In front of him, the door lay open.

He slipped through, and found himself in a narrow passage smelling of damp. It was very dark in there; very still. He moved forward carefully, walking on the balls of his feet, and came out of the passage into something he supposed was a small kitchen. All around him lay heavy, stifling silence.

Yet perhaps Paula was somewhere in this house. This was the thought that drove him on. What had happened to her? Why had she come to this place at all?

He moved on out of the kitchen, and skirted the head of some stairs leading down into stygian blackness. He could now

111

see another door on his right. A door leading into the living-room of this maisonette? He turned towards it.

And that was when he heard a noise. It was a sharp sound, and it came from behind him.

The hairs along his spine jerked up on end. He tried to swing round, but was not quick enough. Something struck him on the head, and the surrounding darkness exploded into a million shining stars.

He felt his legs begin to crumple beneath him, and a great black pit—the chasm of unconsciousness—opened up in front of him as he pitched forward.

From that same instant, he knew no more.

FOURTEEN

Blake opened his eyes on inky blackness. The back of his head throbbed painfully. There was a gritty taste in his mouth. When he tried to raise a hand to touch his head, he found that he couldn't. He was lying on his back on a hard, cold, uneven surface, and his hands were bound behind him.

He tried to move his feet then. They felt numb and useless. Immediately after trying to move them he knew that they were bound, too.

He made his unwilling body relax. He passed his tongue over dried and cracked lips and considered the situation. He didn't know where he was, nor who had attacked and bound him. The last thing he remembered was pitching head-first into unconsciousness after receiving a vicious blow across the back of his skull. He wished he knew more.

He sighed, and the slight sound produced an immediate response. A voice came out of the darkness. 'Are you all right?'

It was a woman's voice, and it was anxious. It spoke urgently. Blake recognised it instantly. 'Paula!' he said.

112

Then: 'Paula, where are you?'

'I'm over here, in the corner . . .'

Blake strained forward. He could see nothing.

'They tied me up,' Paula said. 'I can't move.'

'That makes two of us. Who are "they"?'

'Joe Turk. Isn't that what that man's called? You remember —you told me. Well, he dragged you down here. He's one of them. There's someone called Jack Dino as well, and we're in a cellar beneath Simon's house, and——'

'You'll have to go a little more slowly,' Blake interrupted. 'My head feels like an echo chamber. One of the Beatles' best. I can't take this all at once. So just tell me everything slowly. Particularly everything that happened to you. Start from the time that I left your flat.'

'Well,' Paula said, 'I locked and bolted the door behind you. I was going to be a very good girl and stay home all evening. I was planning to wash a few things and—oh, I don't know— read a bit. And I did. Until at quarter past, or twenty past nine the telephone rang.'

'And?'

'The caller was a man. Your Mr Carter—I mean Tinker— he said. He told me that you wanted to see me here, at this house. He said it was urgent, and that I'd better come over at once. I wouldn't have questioned it, anyway, since I thought I was speaking to a friend, and that you—well—that you wanted me. But, in any case, he explained why you wanted to see me. Apparently, you were here, and Simon de Courcy's nerve had cracked. He was telling all he knew about everything that's been happening to me. He was telling you all kinds of things. About that car this afternoon—everything. That was why you wanted me over here. That was why I came . . .'

Her voice grew quiet. The words came out in short sentences. They were easy for Blake to grasp. She told him everything that she knew.

And the things that she told him entered his throbbing brain, and stayed there.

* * *

113

While Paula Dane talked quietly to Blake in the blackness of the cellar, two men argued vehemently in the living-room of the house overhead.

The men were Jack Dino and Joe Turk, and the subject of their argument was the problem of what to do with their captives.

In the next room, Roxie Marlowe slept the sleep of the truly exhausted. 'Not to worry about her,' Dino had assured his henchman. 'That broad won't wake for hours. When I left her just now she was dead to the world. Besides, even if she did wake up it wouldn't matter. She's one of my girls now and she'll do what she's told.' He laughed coarsely. 'Never saw such a bird for doing what she's told. She and de Courcy are two of a kind.'

'All right, all right,' growled Joe. 'But what about Blake and the woman downstairs?'

*   *   *

'Get rid of both of them,' Dino said bluntly, 'that's what. Babe's on his way down to Southcliffe right at this moment. Correct? And he's going to fix up a boat and come back here. He's due any minute. You know all about that. So what's the trouble? While it's still dark, Babe takes us all down to Southcliffe, and we load Blake and the girl on to the boat and we head out to sea. A mile out we tie weights on to them and drop them over the side. A splash or two, a few bubbles and it's all over. So what's wrong with that?'

'I don't like it,' Turk said, and his hard eyes were shadowed with doubt. 'I don't like it, Dino.'

'What's the matter with you? Turning soft, or something?'

'Up you, Dino,' Turk said dangerously.

'Then what?'

'I don't like that character Blake being a part of all this.'

'You mean'—Dino stared at his companion incredulously—'you don't think we ought to get rid of him?'

'Dino,' Turk said, 'you know what this man is, and you know who he is—and I don't mean just his name. It's——' He struggled for the right words with which to express himself.

114

'Look, Dino,' he said, 'look, killing this character'll be just like killing a copper. All right, so we did for Lewis, and, okay, we get rid of the girl, that seems sense. But Blake—well—that's a different thing altogether. Kill him, and it'll be just like killing a copper. They'll never rest to get us, Dino, you know that.'

'But'—and now Dino both looked and sounded somewhat exasperated—'who'll even know that he's dead? Only the fishes. And if and when—eventually—whatever's left of him surfaces, all right, what then? What's to connect him with us?'

'I don't know, Dino. I——'

'Look, Joe,' Dino said earnestly, 'you're seeing ghosts. There's nothing to worry about. Nothing at all. For a start, who knows that Blake's here? No one, that's who. He's been here for three hours, and who's beating the door down? His partner's tailing de Courcy all the way up to Cumberland. No one knows that we've got him down in the cellar. And no one but Blake even so much as guesses that we've got the Dane bird either. Look, Joe, we've got this thing made. For God's sake don't start having second thoughts now.'

'All I'm saying is, Dino, that——'

'I know what you're saying, Joe. I know. But, believe me, do it my way and there's no risk at all with this thing. Look, I've worked out all the chances. We need the Dane woman dead so as to put the maximum squeeze on de Courcy as soon as he inherits his father's half million, and we can't have her dead and leave Blake alive. You know that we can't. Think about it.'

'But, Dino, it's just——'

'I tell you, there's no real risk at all. Okay, imagine the very worst thing that could possibly happen. We're stopped on the way down to Southcliffe. Or have an accident, maybe, something like that. Though I should mention that "Babe" Jenkins has never had one single accident in his whole goddamned life, let's suppose that this is the time that it happens. So, all right, is Blake dead? Have we killed him? We have not. He's just sleeping peacefully in the back of the car. Sleeping, you hear me? And breathing. And so is the Dane woman.

115

'We don't make a kill until we're a mile or more out to sea, and even then we don't harm a hair of their heads. Just slip 'em over the side when nobody's near us or watching. What's wrong with that?'

Dino's face and voice were animated. 'And just think of what happens afterwards, Joe. Afterwards, when we put the bite on de Courcy. Half a million pounds, and that de Courcy's as soft as—well—are you thinking? A few choice threats will melt him. We can take him for everything he's got! Think of what you could do with your share!'

Dino stopped talking. He eyed Turk. The squat man didn't say anything. He seemed to be turning something over and over in his mind.

Finally, Dino said, 'Joe?' And his cold and bitter blue eyes were fixed on his companion. His voice was questioning. 'Well, what do you think now, Joe?'

And there was silence again.

Then——

'Okay,' Turk grunted at last. 'Okay. But we play it just as you said it. For a hundred and fifty thousand smackers—okay!'

*   *   *

'. . . And that was the way it was,' Paula said simply. 'Turk grabbed me and tied me up, and left me down here.'

'And "here" is a cellar,' Blake said.

'It looks as if it was used as an air-raid shelter during the war,' Paula told him. 'There are steel girders reinforcing the roof, and lots of rough concrete.'

'Not much hope of being heard then,' Blake said. 'If we shouted, I mean.'

'No chance at all, I should think. I'm sure that if Turk had thought that we could be heard he would have gagged us. He wouldn't abstain on account of any olde-worlde courtesy.'

She was silent for a long moment, and then she sighed a little tremulously. 'What happens now? What will they do to us?'

'What indeed?' Blake's mind echoed. 'What indeed?'

They were not left wondering for very long. Suddenly, with

a grating of metal on stone, a square of light appeared out of nowhere. The door of the cellar opened. The lights were switched on. Bare bulbs beat down on the captives as Dino and Turk came in through the door.

Turk came first, and he bent over Paula, and swung her—none too gently—over on to her face.

Blake shouted out a protest, and Dino eyed him malevolently. 'Shut up! Save your breath!'

'What are you doing to her?'

'You'll find out soon enough!'

Dino bent down by Paula's side. She tried to struggle. It was useless. She strained against her bonds to no avail.

A hypodermic syringe was in Dino's hand. He bared Paula's arm, and thrust the needle home. While Blake twisted impotently, Dino pumped the contents of the syringe into a vein. Finally, he straightened up. Paula's body was slack and inert.

'What have you given her?' Blake demanded.

'She's just having a little nap, that's all.' Dino grinned at him without humour. 'She's tired—just as you are. A little sleep will do you the world of good. Are you going to struggle, too? Or are you going to accept the inevitable? Just a little sleep, and a short sea voyage. A very short one!'

Turk's hands were hard as he threw the detective over on to his face.

'Resistance is useless,' Dino said, and the needle plunged home. 'Resistance is worse than useless.'

Those words, spinning round and round into the vortex of oblivion, were the last that Blake heard.

FIFTEEN

The slow-moving Thames was cloaked with fog all the way from Greenwich to beyond Sheerness.

It was a thick fog, wet, grey and heavy, like a rain-soaked

blanket. Out upon the broad surface of the river it clung close to the oily water, and built itself up into an impenetrable wall. Visibility was down to less than fifty feet.

Inching its way through the fog, engines throbbing gently, there was a long, low motor-cruiser. It was almost invisible. It was painted grey, and it merged into the surrounding banks of moisture. Its name was *Sea Wolf*.

Behind its wheel stood Jack Dino. Together with Turk and his captives, he had been driven to Southcliffe by 'Babe' Jenkins shortly before five o'clock that morning. There, after appropriating some lead weights from a nearby fishing vessel, Dino with Turk and their prisoners had put out from the quay.

'Babe' Jenkins had been left behind: left with the car. This remained a sure and certain means of escape in the unlikely event of anything going wrong.

Dino was quite sure that nothing at all could go wrong, but he had not forgotten his impassioned argument with Turk back at the house in Emperors' Close. Consequently—and for the sake of Joe's peace of mind more than anything else—he was going through the motions of being very careful indeed.

Now the *Sea Wolf* crept down the river, and, behind the wheel, Jack Dino applauded the Fates who had made things easy for him.

His captives had given him no trouble, and he expected none. They were stowed away in the fore-cabin, and they were still sleeping peacefully under the influence of the narcotic drug with which he had injected them.

With any luck, Dino thought, they would never wake up at all.

The fog suddenly became thicker, cutting visibility down to a matter of inches. Moisture beaded Dino's face. Then, as his eyes strained ahead, the fog rolled back a little and he was once more able to see the squat shape of Joe Turk as he stood up in the bows of the *Sea Wolf*, serving as look-out.

'How is it, Joe?' he called, and his voice echoed back off the walls of moisture. 'Are we all clear ahead?'

'Okay . . . okay . . .' came in surly grunts from Joe.

Jack Dino grimaced. He knew that Turk was annoyed at the late time of their arrival at Southcliffe. And Turk was right, Dino admitted to himself ruefully.

Dino had dallied overlong with the redhead back at Emperors' Close. Foolishly unnecessarily, because, after all, Roxie would keep, as Turk had pointed out. She'd be there, ready and waiting, when they got back. But the fact remained that he had overstayed the time in the arms of his new mistress—and now dawn was breaking slowly to the eastwards. Turk was right. The job should have been over by now.

Around them on the river, life went on. Tugs slid forward gently pulling laden barges and hooting dismally. Big ships crept upstream, radar antennae sweeping the channel ahead, and masters praying for an early landfall.

From Her Majesty's Coast-guard Station at Rochester, four coast-guard cutters—twice the usual number because of the fog—crept down the Medway on the early morning tide.

Now the sun was up, but it had not yet attained any degree of heat, and the fog persisted. Jack Dino hoped that it would continue to persist until they were well clear of the Estuary. He hoped that it would cover them like a blanket while the cruiser hove-to, and while his victims were dropped over the side.

Then, a few muffled splashes later, they would be able to restart their engines and return to where 'Babe' Jenkins awaited them. After that—a comfortable ride back to London. The fog, if it lasted, would cover everything. It was providential.

For his victims it would serve as a shroud.

Still, Turk was right. They should have started out sooner. That damn redheaded broad . . .

He pulled back his lips from his teeth and smiled a mirthless smile. Then he called out again, peering ahead: 'How is it, Joe?' And with the swiftness of an echo the grunt of Turk came back to him, 'Okay . . . okay . . .'

Beneath Turk's feet, below a steel deck, the fore-cabin was a tiny prison for Blake and Paula. It was a place not more than eight feet square, and at some time during the life of the *Sea*

119

Wolf it had been converted from passenger accommodation to a store for cordage, fuel and the like.

It reeked of paint and oil. Its walls and floor were stained and unscrubbed. Piled here and there were loose coils of rope, cans of oil and tins of paint, together with some other representative items from the thousand and one things required to keep a craft in sea-worthy condition.

The fore-cabin was the store of the ship, and the stores had been deposited roughly.

The prisoners which the cabin contained had been dealt with unkindly, too. They had been dropped down in a heap, the one next to the other. They lay there, unconscious and unknowing, with their heads rolling slackly with every movement of the craft.

Paula's lips were parted. She seemed to be in a dreamless sleep. Her face was calm and remote.

Beside her lay Blake.

Paula slept soundly, as though she would never wake. But Blake's eyelids were twitching.

Due to the time lost through Jack Dino's ill-considered dalliance with Roxie Marlowe the effects of the narcotic were wearing off. Though unknown to him, Blake had the immoral little redhead to thank for that.

Quite suddenly, the eyelids came apart and the eyes beneath looked out blankly.

They gazed at the roof of the cabin for a full minute without moving and without blinking. They registered no emotion at all.

Then the eyelids flickered three times in swift succession, and a tongue poked out of Blake's mouth to explore the surface of his lips. He made an involuntary movement as though to sit up.

Then his eyes showed that he had remembered. His arms ceased to strain futilely at the bonds which held them fast. He turned his head and began to look about him.

He looked at Paula first. His eyes found her, rested on her face for a moment, as though seeking some reassurance, and then moved on. They fastened on the lead weights which lay beyond her.

He knew then why they were making this trip—this short sea trip, as Dino had described it. It would be short indeed. And one-way.

He closed his eyes for a moment and shut in the thought. He considered it, and decided that he was not afraid to die. But— he further decided—he was not going to die if he had any say in the matter. The position was grim, but it was not impossible. Nothing was impossible while life persisted.

Once more he opened his eyes, and this time he saw the handbag.

Paula's handbag lay on the floor of the cabin where Dino had tossed it down. At first its presence aboard puzzled Blake. Then, such was the speed at which his intelligence returned, then he knew.

Dino intended to make a clean sweep of both of them. There were to be no mistakes, and no loose ends. Nothing was to be forgotten to become an embarrassment later.

That was why the handbag had been brought along. It was to be weighted and dropped into the sea after its owner. It was to have its part in the 'clean sweep' Dino planned.

From overhead there suddenly came a voice grunting, 'Okay ... okay ...'

Blake made a face as he heard it. He recognised the voice. Turk had come along, too.

That meant that there were at least two of the enemy— Dino and Turk. Two of the enemy against two bound and helpless prisoners, of whom one was a woman.

The equation could be reduced even further. In a tight spot of this sort, Paula was as yet untried and unproved.

She might be useful. On the other hand, she might not ... Then she moved.

She moved only fractionally, and she moaned softly. Blake looked at her anxiously. He saw her eyelids jerk back. He said: 'How are you feeling? Are you all right?'

Her eyes moved towards him, fixed on his face and consciousness entered them.

121

She said slowly and distinctly, and with obvious effort, 'I feel fine!'

It wasn't true, and both of them knew it, but it helped Blake to know that Paula wasn't going to lie back and bemoan their lot.

She said, 'What's going to happen to us?' And although she had just demonstrated her resilience, Blake felt he couldn't portray their future faithfully.

He thought that he had better cushion the blow.

So he said, 'Dino and Turk think that they are going to get us both out of the way for a while, I suppose . . .'

He smiled at her, and then added, 'Of course we won't let them.'

It was an absurd thing to say, bound and helpless as they were, but Paula accepted it at its face value.

'Of course,' she said gravely. Then, 'What do we do?'

An idea came into Blake's mind. It was an impossible idea, but it might work. It all depended upon how much time was left to them before Dino decided to throw them overboard.

'You have a mirror in your handbag?' he asked. 'Not a compact. A plain, strong mirror?'

She nodded swiftly. 'Do you want it?' She didn't ask him why.

'Just tell me where it is.'

'No. I'll get it. I can manage.'

Already, as she spoke, she was dragging her body over the floor. She reached the bag and bent forward over it. Her back was arched. Her body shook with strain. She said, 'It's easy when you know how.' But Blake knew the effort it took.

She hit the catch of the bag sharply with her chin several times, and then leant upon it. 'It's open,' she said suddenly. 'It won't be long now.'

She pushed the handbag from her. She caught at the straps with her teeth, and spilled the contents of the bag out over the floor.

There was a tinkle as the mirror fell.

She noted where it was, and pushed herself against it. She inched it over the floor towards Blake. 'Can you reach it?'

He turned his back, strained downwards and took it into his hands.

He moved to face her. He said: 'I don't know how long this will take. I don't know how much time we have . . .'

He didn't want her to build up her hopes, and then have them all destroyed.

'I can pray,' Paula said calmly. She saw him wince, and heard the snapping sound the mirror made as it broke.

In the same moment, Blake felt the warmth and stickiness of blood.

*   *   *

He had snapped the mirror into three jagged pieces. So much his fingers told him. He dropped two of the pieces down on the floor, and began to work on his bonds with the other.

Grimly, he forced his fingers to grip the glass. They skidded and slipped on the polished, blood-smeared surface.

Careless of pain, heedless of hurt, he worked on: sawing at the rope which bound his wrists, until his fingers were too numb and the glass was too slippery to work any more.

Paula looked at him and didn't say anything. There was nothing to be said. All of her spirit went into her eyes to urge him on.

He rubbed his fingers against the floor. He picked up one of the other pieces of glass and attacked the ropes afresh.

Now sweat stood out upon his forehead in fine beads. His shoulders shook in the unnatural position he was compelled to adopt.

It seemed like an age since he had commenced work on his bonds. It seemed to be longer than an age—an eternity. Still he struggled on, and then, around him, the boat began to rock a little more strongly.

That told Blake something. That made him work like a man possessed of a demon. The boat had left the Estuary behind. It had entered the waters of the sea.

It couldn't be long now. Time was running out. Another ten or fifteen minutes at the most, and they would be overboard. Another ten or fifteen minutes. It was nothing!

He jabbed at the cords with the sharp edge of the mirror, and felt the glass go all the way through. It dug into his wrist. He thought: *Now! It must be now!*

He couldn't wait to saw clear through the ropes which bound him. There wasn't the time. Brute strength would have to be put to use.

He had done something to his bonds. He had weakened them in some way and to some degree. Now he would discover if he had weakened them sufficiently.

He rolled over on to his back, and he lay there for a moment, trembling. Then he put forth all of his strength.

He bunched up the muscles in his arms, and clenched his fists tight. He thrust outwards—ever outwards—and felt the ropes bite into the torn flesh of his wrists.

He thought that he would scream aloud from pain. He thought that he would have to give in and acknowledge defeat. But then he shut down that part of his mind. He blanked the agony out.

He thrust outward yet again—throwing his last few ounces of strength into the battle. He did that, and the rope snapped.

*　　*　　*

His hands skidded, out of control, across the floor. When he raised them, shaking, above his face, the knuckles were skinned and bleeding. More blood dripped from his lacerated wrists. He sat up. He could do that now. He was no longer hog-tied.

He turned his attention to the ropes binding his legs and he worked as quickly as he could.

Time was slipping away fast. He didn't dare think about it. Time was flying away, and there was still a lot to be done.

His feet were free. He stood up, and every bone within his body cried aloud. He moved forward across the rolling floor and reached Paula Dane. Swiftly, he set her free.

She said quietly, 'And now?'

As if to answer her, the engines stopped.

The boat plunged and rocked. The floor slipped up at a crazy angle, and then came down again. Blake fell heavily. He didn't attempt to get up. There were footsteps on the deck overhead. At any moment, Turk or Dino, or both of them, were due to appear.

Swiftly, Blake reached out for the ragged pieces of rope. He wound them around his ankles loosely. His hands he thrust behind him. Out of the corner of his eye he could see that Paula was following his example.

The cabin door opened.

It came open swiftly and snapped back against the bulkhead, carried there by the motion of the sea.

Joe Turk stood in the doorway, peering into the cabin.

Blake's eyes were very nearly closed. His mouth was slack.

Turk came on into the cabin, and stood for a moment as though considering something. Then he moved forward.

He bent down over Blake. He reached out his hands, and took hold of the detective's shoulders. He set his legs to haul Blake roughly to his feet.

And, while he did so, the detective watched him covertly. Watched, and bided his time, and waited for the best moment to strike.

Then it came. Turk was ready to lift him up. His guard was down.

Blake said a short and silent prayer, and then he went into action.

SIXTEEN

Blake came up off the floor with a rush. He came up from underneath Turk. The squat man's defences were down. They didn't exist.

Blake hit him. He slammed a short, jolting blow above Turk's heart. He saw the squat man's face. It was close to his own.

Turk didn't know what was happening. He rocked back on his heels, and his eyes were wide open and staring.

In the second that it took his dazed mind to evaluate the situation, Blake hit him again.

The sound made by the blow was that of a hammer being driven into mud. Blake buried his fist in Turk's solar plexus.

The squat man gagged and gaped and bent double. He folded up slowly. He gasped for air. His hands went wide, and unclenched themselves in his agony.

Blake hit him a third time.

He put all his weight behind the blow. He snapped Turk's head back with an uppercut which exploded on his heavy, fleshy jaw.

Turk was carried backwards across the cabin. He was carried back as though by some furious wind. He crashed against the far wall and his legs splayed out from beneath him. He slid down the wall and jolted into a sitting position. His head was loose on his neck.

Blake didn't wait to see any more. He leapt for the cabin door, and threw it open.

He went up the short companionway on to the deck, and he was travelling fast. He had to surprise Dino. He had to get to him before Dino realised what had happened.

He burst out on to the deck, and he had to pause for an instant. He had to glance rakingly round to see where Dino was.

It was time wasted. Dino saw Blake first and, astounded though he must have been, reacted immediately. As the detective threw himself across the plunging deck, Dino grabbed for a gun. It came up in his hand, and its snout was unwavering.

The gun exploded almost in Blake's face. He felt the searing heat of the explosion, and smelled the acrid scent of flame and powder. Then he was grappling with Dino, trying to force the gun out of his hand.

He slammed him back against a bulkhead. He slammed him back once, twice, three times, and he heard Dino gasp with pain.

Then, somehow, Dino got an arm free. The hand which held the gun travelled backwards.

Blake slammed Dino against the bulkhead once again. The hand which held the gun came round in a wide arc.

126

Dino used the revolver like a club. He caught Blake's cheek with the foresight and ripped at the flesh. Blake felt blood begin to run down his face.

He shook his head, and drove for Dino's chin. The thin, feral-faced man was as slippery as an eel. He went down beneath the blow, and bobbed up inside it. The gun was still in his hand, and its snout was within inches of Blake's stomach. The detective chopped him down—hard—and prayed.

The gun exploded. Something white hot raked Blake's side. He had been hit, but Dino's hand could no longer hold the weapon. His fingers were paralysed by the force of Blake's chopping blow. They had to open.

The gun described a short arc through the air and fell on the deck. Again it roared. A bullet ploughed its way through the woodwork of the wheelhouse, and splinters flew.

Blake hadn't time to sit down and nurse his injury. He hadn't time to wonder whether he would live or die of his wound. Dino was on him, and from nowhere a long knife had appeared in his hand.

He gripped it blade uppermost. His thumb came over the haft. He lunged with it, and its point darted for Blake's stomach.

The detective went back. He had to move to give himself more room. White fire stabbed him as he moved. His side burned with a fierce, hot flame.

Dino came on. His lips were drawn back from his teeth in a ghastly grin. His eyes blazed deep in their sockets.

Still Blake went back. Suddenly, Dino lunged again.

He went in to rip and to tear, but Blake was ready for him. He jumped sideways, felt his feet slide on the deck, but—somehow—stayed upright. He kept his balance.

And Dino lunged forward against an enemy who just wasn't there any more. For an instant, he was off-balance.

Blake brought his hands up high. They were laced together. He brought them down—hard and fast—on Dino's neck. It was the rabbit-punch to end all rabbit-punches.

Dino collapsed. His body slammed down on the deck. The knife skidded free, and he didn't go after it.

127

Breathing hard, Blake straightened up.

Then someone cried out. It was Paula. Blake swung around and made for the fore-cabin. His side ached, throbbed and burned. He touched it with gentle fingers and they came away wet with blood.

Then there was another cry from the fore-cabin. Just before Blake reached the companionway, Joe Turk came up it. He got to the deck, and he had a razor in his hand. An open razor. There were no more cries from the cabin. There was silence.

Turk had his back to a bulkhead. He was watching Blake, and his eyes were very cold; very hard. He waited for Blake to come on. He waited and watched, and the hand which held the open razor trembled ever so slightly.

Then Blake went in. He went in fast. He knew that he had to. He had to finish Turk, or be finished by him. He struck forward with the lightning speed of a rattlesnake. And yet he didn't strike. Just before the instant of impact, he recoiled. He went back as if jerked by a spring.

And Turk reacted to the feint just as Blake had prayed he would do. He slashed wildly with his open razor, but only cut air. And, instantly, Blake was on him. He had caught him by the throat in a vicious grip. The squat man's eyes bulged.

The razor tinkled to the deck. Blake lashed out at it, and it slid over the metal plating and fell into the heaving sea.

Blake used all of his strength. He threw Turk from him. The squat man went back and fell against the deck. He fell awkwardly. The air left him in a rush.

Blake went after him, and Turk saw salvation in a belaying pin. He reached for it. It was a little too far away for him to grasp. As the detective came on, he extended himself. He grabbed for the pin. To do it, he had to lean against the short rail which ran round the deck.

The rail was hinged. The hinge was rusted. It couldn't take Turk's weight. It collapsed, and Turk grabbed wildly for some other support. But there was none. His fingers skidded through space. He went out backwards into the sea.

In that moment, a bullet snarled across the deck and buried itself in the wood of the companionway beyond him.

Another shot followed to ricochet off the metal plates of the deck.

Blake swung around and, in that instant, Turk's bubbling scream came up to him from out of the water.

'I can't swim! I can't swim!'

Then Dino was facing him, the gun in his hand.

Something moved to one side of Blake. He caught the movement out of the corner of his eye as he started towards Dino. He saw it was Paula.

She was looking badly bruised and badly beaten. So much Blake saw in the fraction of time it took her to flash across his field of vision.

Then, in the next instant, he had thrown himself upon Dino, and Paula had made a clean dive from the rolling deck into the sea. She struck out in the direction of Joe Turk.

Meanwhile, Blake grappled with Dino for possession of the revolver. He wrenched and he twisted, and Dino's fingers were trapped by the trigger-guard. He had to let go, or have his fingers break.

He released the weapon, and Blake tried to throw it into the sea. But it fell short. And there was no time to go after it. Dino had not relied upon the revolver as his only weapon. He grabbed for and held a machete with a cruel blade. He swung with it.

The blow went wide. Blake went back, panting, exhausted. Dino slashed again, and Blake went back even farther. Inch by inch, he retreated across the deck, conserving his failing strength, waiting for his opportunity. He reached the side of the boat, and Dino made as though to rush him.

In that moment, Paula came up over the side, climbing a short rope-ladder, dragging herself up, hand-over-hand. She was some distance away from Dino, but the movement distracted him. He flicked his eyes in her direction.

As they moved, so did Blake. He went in under the machete which Dino swung too late. He slammed out an arm and checked the sweep of the weapon. He grabbed Dino's wrist and forced it backwards. He had Dino spread wide. The weapon fell free.

Blake put all that he still had in the way of strength into the blow which followed.

He slammed Dino on the point of the jaw, and he went back across the deck. He fell, and one leg was beneath him. He cried out as a bone cracked.

Blake went towards him and, as he did so, both he and Dino saw the revolver in the same instant. It was only inches away from Dino's outflung hand.

Blake leapt for it, and Dino lunged for it. Dino got his hand on it a fraction of a second before Blake reached him.

They struggled again, but these were the weary contortions of exhausted men. The wound in Blake's side blazed agonisingly.

Dino tried to gouge out his eyes and then, failing, bit him in the wrist. Blake grunted, and tried to prise the revolver loose. Dino held on, and attempted to bring the weapon up.

Both men were panting. Every movement was sluggish.

Suddenly, the gun exploded.

Dino jumped convulsively. A strange, lost look came into his eyes. He ceased to struggle.

The hand which held the revolver fell open, and the weapon dropped a few inches to clatter against the deck.

SEVENTEEN

There was blood pulsing out through a jagged hole in Dino's suit. It was a hole just above his stomach. He looked down dazedly, and tried to stop the flow of blood with his fingers.

He looked at Blake, and there was a swift recognition of his fate in his eyes. They were dark with unspoken fears. He licked his lips and, in the sudden quiet, his tongue made a tiny rasping sound.

Blake bent over him. He touched him very gently. He raised

is head, cradling it in his hands. There was nothing he could ɔ to save Jack Dino, and he knew it.

The man was bleeding too much and too quickly. He would ɛ dead in ten minutes. If, indeed, he lasted that long.

Paula came to stand beside Blake. She didn't say anything, ɪt she produced a small flask of brandy which Blake un-ɔrked and put to the lips of the dying man.

Then, suddenly, Paula looked up. 'Watch out!'

Her voice was frenzied. She twisted away from Blake and ɪade for the wheel-house. Blake looked up, and saw, bearing ɔwn silently upon them, a long, dark shape, cutting its way ɪrough the fog.

'Ahoy there!'

The sound echoed around the tall walls of moisture. It re-ɔunded from one side to the other.

'Ahoy!'

The vessel came closer. Now Blake could make out the ɪape of her, and see men in uniform crowding the narrow ɪidge. In front of the bridge there was a searchlight which ɪddenly, blindingly, was brought into play. It swept the deck f the *Sea Wolf* and fixed on Blake as he bent over Jack Dino. ɪ cut through the fog as a knife cuts through butter.

The searchlight went out.

In the next moment, the long, low vessel was alongside. ɪen leapt the gap between the ships. Two of them, tall figures ɪ blue, stepped swiftly to where Dino lay.

'There were shots. What's going on?'

They spoke with authority. They were the police of the ɪrritorial waters; members of Her Majesty's Coast-Guard ɪatrol.

Blake began to explain. But Dino cut him short. He put up ɪ hand and gripped Blake's own. He tugged very gently to ɪtract attention.

He said, 'Man called Lewis . . . in London . . . a jeweller . . .'

Even the effort of speaking seemed to be too much for him ɔw. He stopped, and Blake and the coast-guards bent closer.

Then Dino made another effort. This time his voice came ɪearly. He put forth the last shreds of his strength. 'I'm

131

dying,' he said. 'I know it. I want to tell you. Lewis dead . . .'

'I know,' said Blake.

'You know . . .?' The fading eyes blinked. Then Jack Din said: 'And I killed him. Joe Turk had nothing to do with i He wasn't even there. I killed him, d'you hear?'

'Turk is dead,' Paula said. She stood above Blake, and he dress clung to her. It was soaked with sea-water. 'He drowned she said. 'I tried to save him, but he couldn't swim, and I fought me off—you know, the way that they do. He'd just ha a shot at knocking me unconscious in the cabin. I hadn't th strength left to bring him in.'

'Dead?' Dino echoed. 'Dead? Joe?' His eyelids close Tiny blood bubbles formed at the corners of his mouth. The with an effort, he opened his eyes again. He said slowly an distinctly: 'Joe being dead makes no difference. I kille Lewis. All on my own. You ask de Courcy, he'll tell you. H was behind the whole thing.'

He gasped suddenly, and the breath rattled in his throat.

'De Courcy was behind it all,' he said. 'But he didn't allo for Lewis's death. That was my idea, and mine alone. D Courcy wanted the Dane woman out of the way. He hadn't g the de Courcy pendant . . . sold it . . .' His voice trailed away rallied, '. . . He couldn't inherit without it. He had a penda made. A fake. A good one. Too damned good. It would hav fooled everyone. But not the Dane woman. He had to get h out of the way, so that she couldn't say the pendant was fake . . .'

He was breathing with difficulty now.

'And Lewis?' Blake prompted.

'Lewis?' The deep-set, burning eyes had lost all their fire they looked up at the detective. 'I killed Barny Lewis. D Courcy had sold him the real pendant. Now he wanted it bac He went to Lewis and asked for it. Lewis told him he hadn got it. Sold it . . . sold it to an American. He told that to d Courcy, but de Courcy didn't believe him. I went to Lewis shop . . . shake Lewis down . . . to get the pendant . . .'

Dino smiled wearily. 'Didn't get it . . . Lewis dead.'

132

He looked up at Blake imploringly. 'That's all ... all you eed ... isn't it? Nothing else ...?'

Then, suddenly, his body twisted. He tried to sit up. He ouldn't. He flopped back, gasping, and then swiftly the gasp-ng noise changed to a rattle in the back of his throat.

Paula turned her head away.

Jack Dino lay still. Blood had spilled from his mouth. Blake ot slowly to his feet. One of the two coast-guards looked own at Dino, and then up at Blake.

'There'll be questions ...'

Blake didn't hear what the coast-guard said after that. He asn't listening to him. He was living again the past, hurtling ours. Suddenly his side stabbed at him, and he went white ith the shock of the pain.

Paula went to him. She moved swiftly.

Blake looked into her eyes. He touched her hand.

'It's all over.'

And suddenly she smiled at him; gripped his hand tightly. 'Bar the shouting,' she said.

*   *   *

The fog over the Estuary had lifted now. Time had passed. nd still 'Babe' Jenkins sat behind the wheel of the big car, nd waited, staring out over the water through high-powered eld-glasses.

He waited for the return of Jack Dino and Turk. But he uessed, as one quarter of an hour followed another, that some-hing must have gone wrong, and that they'd never come back. Ie remembered Turk saying they were cutting it fine; that hey had wasted too much time at the house ...

Still he watched, and he waited. This was his job. Watching nd waiting, and keeping a line of swift escape open until the ery last possible moment.

Then he saw the *Sea Wolf*.

She was coming back up the Estuary, and coast-guard utters were with her, flanking her as she ploughed on through he changing tide.

And the man at the wheel of the *Sea Wolf*? 'Babe' Jenkins

narrowed his eyes, and peered out through the powerful lenses.

The man at the wheel of the *Sea Wolf* was Blake. And Paula Dane was there with him. Of Jack Dino and Joe Tur there was no sign.

Then 'Babe' Jenkins considered what he ought to do. Get the hell out of here? He had the car. But he still didn't know what had happened to Dino and Joe. Deep in his bones, he had a feeling ... But this was one man who never relied upon feelings. Only facts.

And the fact was that Dino and Joe weren't anywhere to be seen on the *Sea Wolf*. The fact was that they might have escaped.

So, still, he waited. Dino and Joe might have need of him in a hurry. He waited while messages flashed between the coast guard cutters and their shore station, and between the shore station and New Scotland Yard.

He waited for another forty-five minutes after he'd seen the *Sea Wolf*, giving Dino and Joe every chance to rejoin him.

Then the police found him there.

EIGHTEEN

Roxie Marlowe read all about the death of Jack Dino in the late lunch edition of the *Evening Standard*.

The news did nothing to make her day.

True, she knew Jack Dino hardly at all, despite their brief but hectic period of getting acquainted, as Dino had put it, the previous night. Getting acquainted—so that was the name for it.

Her mouth tugged down wryly, and her back ached.

But, for all his faults, and he must have had many to get himself killed, Roxie thought, Jack Dino had had every appearance of being a promising meal-ticket; a way to make sure that

134

one still got one's corn between jobs. And now he was dead.

Good thing she'd left the house in Emperors' Close early: as soon as she'd awakened, in fact. Good thing, too, she'd awakened when she did.

After her hard day's night, she might have slept for very much longer, and awoken not only to find Dino gone but police thick as bluebottles all round the bed.

Well, she couldn't go back there. They'd be there now.

So what to do? She owed a month's rent on her room, and though she'd had a modelling job the previous day the money from that hadn't gone very far. She had no more modelling jobs in the offing. She phoned her film producer friend and was told he was out of town. She sighed heavily. It looked as if she would have to make a determined effort to get some regular work ...

Consequently, in the late afternoon, she presented herself at the Jason Model Agency in Tottenham Court Road.

'You remember me, Mr Jason,' she said brightly, sitting down in the broad interview chair, the one with the patent, adjustable reclining back, and crossing her excellent legs in the most provocative way that she knew. And she knew three.

'Of course, I've been out of touch for ages,' she said. 'But I thought that you might have something that I could do. Regularly, I mean ...'

Mr Jason was a very small man, olive-eyed, black-haired and as round as a barrel. He sat behind a large desk, nattily-suited, the stub of a cigar jammed into one corner of his thick-lipped mouth.

'Regularly, eh? Hmmm ...' He looked at her speculatively. The cigar travelled across his mouth. He chewed on it. 'Yes ... I think something could be arranged, on much the same basis as before ...'

Roxie hitched her skirt higher and looked at him blandly.

Mr Jason coughed. He glanced at his watch. 'Oops! Nearly five o'clock! Time my staff were off home.'

He padded across to the communicating door.

'Good night, Miss Williams. Good night, Miss Forsyth,' he breezed.

'Er——' There was a flutter of feminine consternation. 'Only five o'clock? But——'

Never look a gift-horse in the mouth, especially when it's sitting in the patent, adjustable, reclinable interview chair.

'Good night, Mr Jason,' chorused the voices from the room beyond.

The outer door closed with a thud of finality. Feet pounded the stairs, going down and away. Mr Jason turned to Roxie Marlowe with a wide, sharp-toothed smile.

'Yes, Roxie,' he said. 'As I was saying there could well be a regular job for you at Jason's. Now, let me see . . .'

He touched a catch on the interview chair, and the reclining back sank down slowly.

'Oh, well . . .' thought Roxie as she sank down with it, 'Here we go again . . .'

*   *   *

At about the same time, and a bare mile away across London, a taxi came around the corner from Mount Street and entered Berkeley Square.

It drew in to the kerb before an imposing modern building, and disgorged two passengers: a tall, slim man with wide shoulders, and a smartly dressed woman.

The man thrust his left hand into his trouser pocket, and drew out some silver coins. His right hand was bandaged, and he moved very stiffly. He paid off the driver, and guided his companion across the pavement.

'This way,' he said.

The man was Sexton Blake. His attractive companion was Paula Dane.

A commissionaire in a dazzling, gold-braided uniform which wouldn't have disgraced a Peruvian admiral sprang forward swiftly to open heavily chromed doors for them. He saluted smartly.

'Good afternoon, Mr Blake. Good afternoon, Madam.'

Together they entered a wide, expensively carpeted lobby, and approached a low flight of stairs.

And at that moment, as always, with his shoes sinking deep

136

into the luxuriantly thick pile underfoot, and all the trappings of this new material success abundantly obvious on every side, Blake felt a sudden twinge of nostalgia for the old days: for the days when Baker Street had been his headquarters as well as his home.

In those days there had been himself, Tinker and Pedro— the great brindled bloodhound, often seemingly asleep at his master's feet in the study yet ever alert for the slightest move on the part of the man who filled his whole life.

Nowadays there was still himself, Pedro and Tinker. But as well there was building up the whole high-pressure organisation known as SEXTON BLAKE INVESTIGATIONS with its new headquarters in these excessively plush Berkeley Square offices and its tentacles stretching out all over the globe.

The success and the growth of the organisation had been almost frightening for a man who had never had any great financial ambitions. Sometimes Blake wondered just how it had all come about.

At one moment, it sometimes seemed to him, he had been cosily ensconced in his Baker Street niche, handling problems and solving mysteries in his own quietly efficient way. The next moment the whole thing seemed to have escalated into Big Business. And now this: receptionists, and private wire circuits, and agents in other capitals—and endless reams of paper work.

It had all started with the insurance companies. The moment he took his first retainer for fraudulent claims investigation from his first insurance company he was doomed. He could see that now, though at the time it had seemed a very pleasant way of being subsidised.

The trouble had been that he was not content to take the retainer and do little for it. He had started to make suggestions to the companies as to how they might cut down future losses. And he had pointed out what were, to him, obvious flaws in the security methods of many of the insurance companies' clients.

'Right!' said the insurance men in effect. 'You've shown us what's wrong. Now show us how to rectify it.'

That, Blake thought, was the time when he should have said 'No'. He should have confined himself to his basic suggestions. On the other hand—who was better qualified than himself to lay out plans for guarding the halls of commerce against the scourges of villainy?

Blake was fond of remarking: 'The first essential of a good detective is a criminal mind. He must see illegal possibilities which are not obvious to the ordinary mind. Of course, he must resist them too!'

Or, as No-Nose Charlie Hoskisson, the peterman, had once sighed: 'You're a great loss to the profession, Mr Blake—a great loss.'

Blake could walk into almost any organisation and see possibilities of villainy. And having seen them he could devise means to thwart them.

It was valuable work; there was no doubt about that. In the course of a year Blake's proposals saved the community many millions of pounds. Now it had come to this—an extra office, the Berkeley Square suite, and staff to go with it.

But it was tedious work, too. Of that there was even less doubt. Often, he longed for the old days, the simple, uncomplicated days. And he was always willing—just give him the opportunity!—to divorce himself from the Sexton Blake Organisation, capital 'O', and personally tackle some rich piece of devilry in the private sector. Hence the help he had so unstintingly given Paula Dane.

As they now climbed the steps together, she looked at him questioningly, and then let her eyes drop until they focused on his side.

He smiled at her. 'Don't worry,' he said. 'I'm fit enough. Another seven days—that's what they said at the London Clinic—and I'll be as good as new.'

Paula said, 'I'm sure the doctor mentioned something about taking it easy . . .'

Blake lifted an eyebrow at her. It was a humorous eyebrow. He didn't say anything.

They reached a broad landing, and facing them there was a door which was flat-painted in a light shade of grey. It was lettered with the words: SEXTON BLAKE INVESTIGATIONS. Blake pushed it gently, and stood to one side. 'Come and meet my new staff,' he said.

Paula passed through the doorway into the room beyond.

As they entered, a girl got up from behind a mahogany desk by a window. She said a little breathlessly: 'I hope you're all right, Mr Blake.'

'I'm fine, Marion, thank you. Paula—I want you to meet my receptionist, Marion Lang. Marion—this is Paula Dane. We've been helping her.'

The two women shook hands.

Then Marion said, 'Mr Carter has been trying to reach you.'

'Tinker? Where is he?'

'He said to tell you that he trailed Simon de Courcy all the way to Cumberland.'

'He's gone to Levistone?' Paula said.

'Yes. He arrived there this morning, after driving all night. Mr Carter is going to phone back again in an hour.'

'So Simon has finally gone to earth,' Blake said. 'Well, now we know where he is, we can tell the police. They'll be glad to know. They've been trying to trace him since this morning— ever since they took our statements, and those of the coast-guards, in fact. Good old Tinker! Marion—will you get me Inspector Coutts at Scotland Yard? Put the call through to my office. Paula——'

She followed him across the room. Just before they reached the door of Blake's office, another woman entered.

She was an attractive woman in her early forties, and she carried a tea-tray. On the tray were two delicate china cups with golden rims.

'I'm very glad you're back,' she said to Blake, and her smile was for him. 'I thought you might like a cup of tea. It's freshly made.'

'Louise, you're a life-saver! Paula—meet Louise Pringle, company secretary and maker of wonderful tea.'

The woman smiled and passed by Blake. She went ahead of them into Blake's office, set down the tea-tray and went out again.

'Added to that,' Blake said quietly, 'she's a rather wonderful person. I must tell you about her some day.'

'Your call to the Yard, Mr Blake,' Marion Lang sang out.

'Thank you!' Blake moved swiftly forward, made a face and slowed down to an easy walk.

'I told you so!' Paula said.

'All right,' Blake told her. 'All right. You win. For seven days I'll do things slowly.'

He crossed the office and scooped up the phone. 'Hallo, Coutts! How are you?'

He listened, then grinned. 'You old fraud!' he said. 'You don't get rid of me that easily!'

He nodded to Paula, and she moved into the office away from the door, which she closed gently behind her. While Blake talked, Paula wandered round the room—just looking.

She thought that the room and Blake went together. It was a part, a reflection, of his personality. It was comfort and utility combined. It was a place which had been furnished with taste and affection—a place which a wanderer like Blake might feel at home in.

It was quite, quite different to all the rest of the building.

She touched the mellowed wood of a bookcase. It was soft and smooth and silky beneath her fingertips. She thought of what she was going to say to Blake—of how she was going to explain this desire that she had to be a part of all this; as much a part as Louise Pringle, who obviously adored Blake; as much a part as Marion Lang, who might even—in a young woman's way—think that she was a little in love with him.

Suddenly it came to her that Blake had stopped speaking. She looked up to see that he had put down the phone and was watching her.

His eyes were a blue-grey, she thought. They were kind eyes. There were little wrinkles at the corners of them. He smiled often. He was smiling now.

'A penny for them,' he said.

She smiled back, and moved towards his desk. She said, 'I was just thinking how empty and pointless life is going to be after today ...'

140

He began to say something, but she stopped him.

'I'd like to do something with my life,' she said. 'I'd like to feel that it was leading somewhere—that I was helping people—you know? Now all I do is write copy, and persuade people to buy things they don't need with money they haven't got. I'd like to do something useful—and I'd like to be with you.'

She wasn't looking at him. She was hurrying on.

'I can type,' she said quickly. 'I can do shorthand. Very good shorthand. I'm reasonably self-reliant. I get on well with people. I ...'

She stopped. She said: 'Perhaps I ought to learn a little more about copy-writing. I can't even sell myself, can I?'

Blake lifted his head and looked at her. 'You're doing fine,' he said. 'But it's very largely wasted effort.'

'Oh ... I see ...'

She was disappointed. Terribly disappointed. But she managed a smile.

'Look at this,' Blake said. He crossed his office and opened a door. There was another office beyond; a room with a long window which looked out over the Square. It was carpeted with midnight-blue carpet. There was a long, polished desk. There was even an electric typewriter. Paula could see that the room was ready and waiting. It was for Blake's personal secretary.

He told her that much. Then he said, 'But I probably won't get the girl that I want.'

'You've someone in mind, then?'

'Oh, yes. Of course.' And he shrugged. 'But working here means long hours, and it calls for complete identification with the job in hand. Something most people tend to avoid in these palmy days. So I don't know. I don't know whether she really will leave her present job and come to me.'

'She's working for somebody else as a personal secretary?' Paula asked.

'No. But I think she's just the person I need. She's a good typist. She's self-reliant. She does shorthand—very good shorthand, I know ...'

141

'I hope you get her,' Paula said. And she meant it sincerely. 'Has she seen the office?'

'Yes. And I hope I get her, too. What do you say?'

'Who?' Paula looked helplessly round her. 'Who? Me? But I thought——'

Then the light dawned.

'You meant me all the time!' Paula said.

'And will you take it?'

Paula didn't answer. Slowly, she took off her coat. She draped it over a chair. She crossed the room, looked down at the polished desk, and stroked it with her fingers. Then she slipped behind it, and flicked a switch.

The electric typewriter hummed gently.

'Can I start now?' she said.

THE END

FIRE OVER INDIA

W. Howard Baker

CHAPTER ONE

The year was nineteen forty-two, the month March, the day Friday.

Friday the thirteenth.

Unlucky thirteen. Black Friday.

Night came quickly to Calcutta. Light was blue—the colour of thin smoke—along the fringes of Chowringhee. Then grey. Then mauve.

Neons branded the deepening dusk.

Only six hundred miles away to the east, the British Burma Army was fighting a hopeless, losing battle against the Japanese invader. Rangoon had fallen to the enemy five days before. Now Prome was threatened and Mandalay would be taken soon. The Imperial Armies of Japan were advancing towards the very gates of India. And advancing rapidly.

Desperate men fought desperate rearguard actions and tried, in vain, to stem the yellow tide. They fought, retreated and turned to fight again. They died in their thousands, swiftly by bullet or slowly by bayonet. The Japanese took prisoners, but few survived.

But here, in the Empire's Second City, the conflict still seemed remote. It might have been six thousand miles away, not a bare six hundred. Here, in Calcutta, it was very much 'business as usual'.

The pavements were restless with a motley passing parade. Fastidious Brahmins, immaculately garbed, frowned with distaste as they rubbed shoulders with British soldiers from the front, green-clad, heavy-booted, clumsy and sweating. Tall, bearded and turbaned Sikhs slid by, as graceful as girls. Chinese airmen were bland in uniforms tailored in America.

G.I.s with fatly-naked Glen-Miller faces and rimless spectacles took advantage of every opportunity to use their Leica cameras. Like slippery, silvered eels, worming and squirming, the Hindu watch-sellers, the brothel touts and the vendors of picture postcards insinuated themselves through the human tide.

Across the broad, wide bustle of the road, emerald-green taxis passed and repassed endlessly. Heavily laden bullock carts lurched by as if trundling on square wheels. Rickshaw coolies died a thousand deaths a second, and lived to saw the air with their bicycle bells, clamorous for custom. In the gutters, emaciated, self-mutilated or deformed, the beggars whined insistently for alms.

This was Calcutta in the third year of war.

The Howrah Bridge flung arches stark and black and skeletal across the silvery, sludgy River Hooghly. In a sky which darkened perceptibly with every passing second, bannered clouds were brilliant with green and gold, and a single star shone brightly.

In the Hindu quarter of the city, Redcaps and civil policemen were just beginning an intensive, hovel-to-hovel search for a man called Blake.

* * *

Blake came up out of the dank, dark pit of unconsciousness to the wailing of women and the clash of cymbals.

The sound was frighteningly loud; all around him. This was the first thing that he knew.

Then his mouth hurt him. He was gagged. His eyes jerked open. Cloth was drawn tight over his face. A hood. He could barely breathe and he couldn't see.

The gag. The hood. He tried to move his head and failed. His hands—his feet——

Ropes bound him, biting into his flesh as he strained against them. Sweat ran into his eyes. He was a prisoner and all around him the wailing women's voices and the clashing metal mounted in frenzy.

Then he became conscious of the fact that he was lying on a *charpoy*—a string bed. He was bound to it and being borne along. Dimly, through the hood which covered his face, he saw the fluttering light and shade of the flaring tongues of torches. In the same moment he smelt the sour river smell. The Hooghly. The stench of twice-rotten filth. And then he smelt something else—and trembled.

It was the sickeningly sweet scent of roasting flesh. Human

146

esh. It was borne on the wind off the burning ghats where the Hindus cremated their dead.

With incredulous horror he realised what was happening to him, and where he was.

He tried to cry out, but the thick gag choked him. He was frantic now. He squared his mouth and the veins stood out in knots on his forehead. He put forth every ounce of the strength he still possessed in a wild attempt to burst free of his bonds. It was useless. Blood from his torn lips ran into his throat.

With every clash of the cymbals, his doom came nearer. 'Hari bolo,' chanted the unseen coolies who bore him inexorably on. 'Hari bolo,' wailed the women, consigning the years of his age and the extremity of his torment to the gods.

On the street, Redcaps paused between searching one squalid dwelling and the next to watch the procession go by. They saw the shapeless figure sheeted from sight atop a *charpoy* strewn with *champa* blossoms. Torches flared and guttered and shadows whirled upwards. Cymbals clashed and women wailed. The Redcaps turned away. Blake had to be found.

They did not know until much later how near their quarry had been to them then. The funeral procession went on its way unmolested down to the banks of the Hooghly. There the *charpoy* was set down on stacked, oiled kindling. The bearers retired to a safe distance.

Blake heard them go.

It was then he knew, with fear, that his time had come. Again he tried, frantically, to struggle free.

The flaming, flaring torches wheeled in the wind. Blake's body was arched beneath its shroud as still he strained and struggled. The torches blazed through the air and fell like golden rain upon him.

The kindling caught fire. The sour-sweet stench of burning flesh arose once more above the Hooghly. For one last, terrible time Blake smelt it. His own flesh burning.

He screamed behind the gag. And he went on screaming. And then, in agony, he died.

CHAPTER TWO

The fire burned bright and Blake was dead. His corpse w
burning. A chill wind blew.

The funeral party broke up. It had served its purpose. It d
integrated before the wind. And Mahdu Nath, the man who h
called it into being, who had organised it and led it, we
quickly through the maze of mean streets beyond the Hoogh
thinly, bitterly triumphant—and alone.

From a gutter greasy with filth and ordure, a blind cripp
whined for alms. Mahdu Nath did not heed his plea. He stro
on swiftly, stoop-shouldered and vulpine in a black alpaca froc
coat and tight white trousers, a white Gandhi cap on his he
and a malacca lawyer-cane in his hand. He was a man apart.

Glimpsed through the open doorway of a wayside temp
yellow light burnished the oiled hair of a gaggle of coolie-wom
prostrate before the obscene enormity of Ganesh, the Elepha
God. Nath's thin lips curled.

He had nothing but contempt for this people—*his* peop
Nothing but scorn, he thought bitterly, for these supplian
and beggars.

Ever since leaving Law School he had publicly worked f
their advancement; ceaselessly he had agitated for their ind
pendence. But secretly he despised them. They lived on the
knees and for all he truly cared, they could die on them. I
regarded them only as creatures to be used—as he had us
them tonight and would use them again.

They were but pawns in his master-plan and their drear
and aspirations merely stepping-stones to the fulfilment of h
own ambitions. He sought personal power—real power—a
he would get it. The mobs he could summon into being woul
all unwittingly, give it to him.

Fools—they believed every passionate, spell-binding wo
that came out of his mouth, and when he promised the
liberty they thought he meant it. They could see no furth
than the end of the British Raj. They thought that *was* t

d, whereas in reality it would be but the beginning. It would
the time when he, Mahdu Nath, would at last come into his
n and have the power he craved for. He would take it. For
the chill wind, a warm feeling spread through his chest as
held a little holiday in his heart.

Sexton Blake was dead. Blake, who could have ruined every-
ng. He could have upset the master-plan; could have des-
yed it utterly. He had found out too much too soon.

But, instead of the plan, it was the famous Sexton Blake
nself who had been destroyed—betrayed by his own clever-
ss. He had made his own bed and had been made to lie on it.

Mahdu Nath smiled bleakly to himself as he remembered.

*   *   *

He remembered a hotel room in the Hindu quarter of the
y. A sleazy place. A fly-trap. But safe, he'd thought. He
d his lieutenants had met there before.

He was back eight hours in time. Behind closed shutters, in
e oppressive, still, stale heat of noonday, he talked final
ategy with the men who would clothe his master-plan with
tion, and transform his dream of power into reality.

They were all there—Chandra Sen, big and bald, loud-
outhed and loud-dressed in gaudy European clothes, and
er Lal in a *dhoti*, as thin and grey and furtive as a rat;
opal, the young impetuous one, with black moustaches like
in cavalry sabres, and Dil the old impetous one, and Gupta,
e crafty-eyed careerist agitator. All there—all listening.

And then his eyes, wandering briefly from their faces as he
ked, touched upon a picture set crookedly on the wall.

It was a small thing to notice, but on such small things the
te of nations sometimes rests. Still talking, he stood up to
aighten the picture. He had a passion for order. And then——

Something made him glance behind the picture as he set it
aight.

There was a microphone behind it!

There was a microphone behind it, and momentarily his
art seemed to contract. It was a tight knot in his chest and
s world lurched sickeningly. But his voice didn't falter.

Somehow he managed to go on speaking as if nothing were

amiss. He had to. He had to have time to think. And all th
while his eyes darted this way and that, like mice.

He saw that the microphone was wired to the picture-hoo
The hook was firmly embedded in the wall. There was no tra
of any other connection. His mind raced on. This meant th
the hook must go through the wall to an amplifier and hea
phones—where? In the adjoining room?

This was the first thing he had to find out.

The second was: who was listening-in to the final briefin
and how much had he overheard? A third question which flashe
into his mind was answered as soon as asked. Of course, th
Hindu hotel-keeper must know that the room had been wir
for sound. He was a traitor and must be dealt with according!

Mahdu Nath motioned to the other men in the room.

They came around him quickly—silently—as still he carrie
on speaking as if nothing had happened. They saw what I
had seen and they understood. They left him then—still tall
ing, talking to an empty room—and for five long seconds the
was no other sound but this.

Then everything happened at once.

There was a sudden crash from outside in the corridor. Th
sound of splintering wood. Another crash. Two shots in quic
succession. Breaking glass. Shouting voices. Another shot fro
deep in the bowels of the ramshackle building. A bubblin
scream.

Then all was confusion.

Mahdu Nath ran out into the corridor. Along its length th
doors of other rooms were jarring open. Voices were raised i
alarm. Somewhere a woman began to laugh hysterically.
European woman.

Sher Lal came up the stairs from the hall two at a time wi
sweat on his face, his lips twisted back from his carious teet
and a knife dripping blood in his hand.

'That *salar*!' He swore obscenely in Hindi. He had settle
accounts with the hotel-keeper.

Chandra Sen shouted from the room next door. Na
wheeled and plunged inside. He saw the splintered door. F
saw wire starting out of the wall, a metal-clad amplifier of
British Army pattern—all these as a confused blur. He saw th

room's window wide open; the space crowded with his lieutenants. Gupta looked down, pointing excitedly.

Gopal vaulted over the sill and dropped out of sight like a stone. Chandra Sen threw up a hand holding a gun, and fired. Distantly, police whistles shrilled.

'Come on!'

Nath was at the window, too, now—seeing who Sen was firing at and what Gupta was shouting about, and jumping away.

Three men were running down the narrow street below the window; pursuers and pursued. One was a tall, lean, black-haired European—plainly the man whose room this was, the man who had been using the amplifier and headphones, the spy. The others were the two impetuous ones. Dil with a revolver. Gopal with a knife.

'Come on!' Nath shouted again.

He went out of the room at a spindle-legged run, the others following him. They crashed down the stairs to the street. They burst out into the brilliant, blazing sunshine and heat hit them like a blow. The sound of the police whistles was nearer.

Five hundred yards away, the tall, lean European was still going strongly, but Gopal and Dil seemed to be gaining on him. The others made to plunge after their comrades and the quarry, but—'This way!' Nath threw at them.

From memory he could have drawn an accurate map of this warren of streets. He knew each one of them by name. He knew where they led, and how deviously they twisted this way and that. He ran into the mouth of an alley with the others at his heels. As always, he knew where he was going. One hundred and ten seconds later they arrived.

They spewed out of the alley on to another street, blocking it. They did so just as the European blundered around a corner with Gopal and Dil only yards behind him.

They had him. He was trapped.

He was certainly trapped, and Nath knew it. But the end was not yet. For the European would not admit he was doomed and as good as dead. He dared not admit it.

Desperately he flung himself across the street to where a

passage opened between tall tenement blocks. It was his only escape route, and it was no escape route at all. Two hundred and fifty feet on it ended in a plain of cement littered with garbage cans and rotting refuse. All this Nath knew, and his companions knew it, too. They could afford to draw breath and take their time in following.

Then, inexorably, they moved down the passage and round a dog-leg bend. They reached the plain of cement—and their quarry had disappeared.

It was impossible, but it had happened.

Mahdu Nath remembered it now.

On the cement plain, amid the garbage cans, a small child lay on a string *charpoy* and coughed endlessly. Other children played nearby, a slow and solemn game which ended with Chandra Sen's rough-spoken question :

'Where is he? The Englishman? Where did he go?'

They looked at him in fear and did not answer. Sen seized one of them, a sloe-eyed girl, and shook her fiercely.

'Where? Tell me!'

And then Nath knew.

Beyond the string bed of the coughing child there was another heaped with *champa* blossom gathered for an evening cremation. And, even as Sen spoke, the blossom moved.

Three short, urgent strides took Nath to the *charpoy*. The champa blossom was swept away and trampled on. The Englishman lay there. Chandra Sen struck him with the butt of his revolver.

'He made his bed, now he can lie on it,' Mahdu Nath said, smiling as the Englishman slumped under a second blow. It pleased him beyond words to be able to quote an apposite, English saying.

'Burn him?' said Chandra Sen.

'Burn him—but first let's find out who he is.'

Fumbling fingers soon found papers to tell them. A military identification card and other documents were in the unconscious man's pockets.

His name was Blake. A name Mahdu Nath knew. Sexton Blake. A name to be feared. But he would soon be dead.

Chandra Sen hit him again—though there was no need. And the children stood in silence, watching and wide-eyed.

* * *

All this Mahdu Nath remembered as, with the cold wind blowing, and Blake dead on his funeral pyre behind him, he cut quickly through the mean streets away from the river and was swallowed up by the night.

CHAPTER THREE

Ninety minutes before midnight, a sleek black police car sped down the road past Calcutta racecourse. Its headlights blazed over the empty enclosures and barred gates, and wheeled over a wilderness of blown newspaper, discarded cigarette packets and tote tickets as the car turned again at Kidderpore Bridge to enter the Hindu quarter of the city.

It carried a man called Craille on a sad mission.

Once over the bridge, the streets were narrow and noisome, and the car slowed. On either side, pavements were thronged with people and gutters choked with fresh, wet rubbish. A leper lay against a wall and his hands were scaly and white in the light of the headlamps. His eyes were milky and blind. He carried no warning bell to ring—life was too short. Rats were coy in the stark shadows around him, and as fat and well-fed as pampered tabbies.

Pressure-lamps hissed incandescent at wayside cookshops as the car edged its way on. Jangling discordant music fell from loud-speakers; a raucous tangle of sound as unnerving and insistent as a nightmare. The spilled silks in the bazaars were like red waterfalls of blood.

In the back of the sleek black car Eustace Craille saw everything and heard everything—expressionlessly. In his thin, old, heavily-wrinkled, almost aristocratic face it was only the cat-amber eyes that moved.

Three minutes and forty seconds later, in the mortuary behind the police *thana* in Bentinck Street, the cat-amber eyes looked down into the burned, but still horribly recognisable, face of the dead Blake.

*   *   *

'That him?'

The man who had stepped in front of Craille to whip the sheet away from the incinerated face had all the slickness of a seedy conjurer performing his *pièce de résistance*. He seemed to savour the shock produced by the first glimpse of the corpse's pain-distorted features; the dead, agonised eyes, the brittle mouth that snarled into eternity like that of a trapped dog.

He seemed to enjoy it.

He was a greasy-skinned, olive-complexioned, paunchy, middle-aged Eurasian called Mawgan. Inspector Mawgan, in charge of the Bentinck Street *thana*. He had the moist, concupiscent lips of a sensualist.

'That him,'—he repeated, and then added—'sir——' very quickly as Craille's eyes, bitterly bleak, stabbed into him.

'Yes.' Craille looked down.

The eyebrows had been burned off. The eyelids were cinders. The widow's peak of sleek black hair was only a dusty shadow. But the corpse was that of Blake all right. There was no doubt of that. Craille had known the dead man too well ever to be mistaken.

Craille led Britain's counter-espionage service, and Blake had been one of his operatives.

'But just to be sure, we took his fingerprints,' Inspector Mawgan said. He produced a squared card. 'We got some good ones. You can check them?'

Craille's voice was toneless. 'Of course.'

He produced a record card too. Blake's record card, extracted from the files and brought with him precisely for this purpose.

The fingerprints on both cards matched exactly. They were identical.

* * *

Mawgan jerked his head towards the corpse. 'You want to see the woman who told us where to find him?'

'Who is she, and what is she?'

Mawgan sneered and uttered an obscenity. 'That's what she is. If you can believe it, she's English, and she goes about with natives....'

'Goes about with them?'

'Sleeps with them. She's almost one of them——' Mawgan's voice was savage with contempt.

It was contempt for all things indigenous, and it was indicative of an almost pathological frame of mind. Mawgan seemed to hate Indians with a blazing, unswerving hatred. It was as if, in this way, he sought to banish the bitter knowledge of the native blood that flowed through his own veins, and the unholy memory of a grandmother whose skin had been brown.

He bared his teeth. He said: 'If you want to see her, we've got her in the cells. Picked her up for questioning. And'—he added with a grim satisfaction—'I soon got *this* out of her. She was almost pleading to tell me by the time I'd finished with her.'

Craille could believe it. He said: 'What's her story?'

'She was in the Kashmiri Hotel when the balloon went up. She saw everything that happened there and got out before my men arrived. She lost the man she was with.'

'And——'

'She met up with him again early this evening,' Mawgan said. His mouth twisted sneeringly. 'I gather he thought they had some unfinished business. He told her what had happened to Blake and she told me—under questioning.' Suddenly he shook with an outburst of anger as violent as desire. 'We're holding her, and she's going to be in trouble. Real trouble!' He almost spat the words out.

Craille eyed him. Then: 'Does this—this Indian have a name?'

'The one she was with?' Mawgan shrugged and his eyes were cold. 'She says she doesn't know it. It could even be possible.' He laughed sardonically.

'And the men who did this to Blake? Do they have names?' Craille wanted to know.

'Only one of them. The leader, Mahdu Nath.'

Craille nodded slowly. 'And we'd guessed that already.' He looked up. 'What about the woman herself? What's her name?'

'Rose.'

'Just Rose?'

'Rose of England.' Mawgan laughed again, bitterly. 'A fine example for British prestige in India.' Then he said: 'Do you want to see her?'

'No,' said Craille.

*   *   *

There was truly only one person Craille wanted to see at this moment—and couldn't—for the man had not yet arrived in Calcutta.

Long hours had to pass.

Dawn found Craille pacing the concrete apron in front of the control tower on the military strip at Dum-Dum—waiting. Another thirty minutes went by.

And then the distant sound of aircraft engines—beating nearer and nearer with every passing second—heralded the arrival of a Dakota transport and the man Craille most urgently wanted to see.

The 'plane landed. It taxied around the perimeter track.

And Craille went to meet it.

*   *   *

Later, in the glassed-off privacy of the back of a hired Rolls-Royce limousine being driven at speed towards Calcutta, Craille reached for his briefcase and extracted the day's newspapers. Without speaking, he opened them one by one, and folded the pages back. Then he handed them to the man who sat by his side—and waited.

'*What!*'

Craille's companion jerked bolt upright, staring at the headlines.

INTERNATIONALLY FAMOUS DETECTIVE MURDERED! they screamed. SEXTON BLAKE DEAD! DOYEN OF BRITISH PRIVATE INVESTIGATORS PERISHES ON FUNERAL PYRE!

'Dead . . .?' Craille's companion echoed, almost dazedly. 'Murdered? When?'

'Last night.' Craille's eyes were very watchful. Suddenly—strangely—his companion began to laugh.

'What is this?' he said. 'Some kind of a joke?'

And then, abruptly, he stopped laughing. He had seen Craille's face; caught sight of his expression. He said sharply:

'Who died? Who was it? Somebody died—someone was burned to death. Who?'

He had a right to know.

This was Sexton Blake talking.

'It was your brother Nigel,' Craille said, softly and slowly. 'He was working for me . . .'

'Nigel!'

Blake slumped back against the seat of the car and the word came out in a whisper. For a moment his face was grey and old and defeated.

Then he said : 'Who did it?' and his head came up sharply.

His eyes were steel-blue and cold as ice.

CHAPTER FOUR

'Nigel'—Sexton Blake said—'was always the black sheep of the family. Never out of trouble. He nearly broke my father's heart.'

Restlessly he paced the thick-carpeted lounge in Craille's luxury apartment atop a mansion block in Calcutta's Park Street. The sedate sound of early morning traffic in this exclusive, expensive district came discreetly through the sun-drenched windows. It was less than two miles and yet more than a world away from the mortuary behind the Bentinck Street *thana* where Blake had looked into the savagely contorted face of his dead brother and felt grief as a dull, empty ache in his breast.

'He nearly broke my father's heart,' he repeated.

Craille sat, almost motionless, in an armchair, smoking the inevitable Egyptian cigarette through a long black holder. He was silently watchful.

Blake paced restlessly on, then turned abruptly, shaking his head. He said, wonderingly: 'He was my own brother and I would have called him a scoundrel! I never knew...'

'He didn't want you to know,' Craille said.

'But *why?*'

Craille shrugged.

Blake said: 'You tell me now that he started working for you right at the outbreak of war. Two and a half years he was working for you, and I didn't know. I never heard from him...' He moved moodily '... and to be truthful, I was glad. I thought if I were to hear from him it was bound to mean trouble. The tight corners I've wangled him out of—criminal corners. He should have gone to jail ten times over.'

He broke off sharply, then went on: 'So I didn't hear from him, and I didn't want to. I never dreamed he'd turned over a new leaf. I never thought he could. If only I'd known——'

'It was his wish that you shouldn't know until he was ready to tell you himself,' said Craille. 'I think he felt he had to prove himself before you knew. I humoured him. It was his secret.'

'How did he come to be working for you?'

Craille said: 'September, nineteen thirty-nine, found your brother here, in India, and on the very day that war was declared he volunteered for the British Army. He tried to enlist as a private. Unfortunately'—Craille's voice was dry—'the kind of life he'd been leading had played merry hell with him physically. The Army turned him down flat at his very first Medical. But he wouldn't take no for an answer. He started to badger the life out of the authorities—and that's when I first heard about him.

'He'd offered his services in any capacity and he'd knocked around a lot and spoke some useful languages. He interested me. Additionally, though he himself had never laboured the point, he was your brother. So...'

Craille paused. He said: 'Of course, I soon discovered that he had a criminal record, but, knowing the rest, that didn't worry me. I reasoned that, as you yourself remarked a few moments ago, he was obviously trying to turn over a new leaf. He seemed determined to do so. His patriotism had apparently succeeded in reforming him where everything else had failed. Well, almost...'

Craille smiled fleetingly. The smile faded. He said, soberly: 'When I realised that I signed him on, and he never gave me any cause to regret having done so. He was a first-class operative. The best I had here in India. Certainly the most wide-awake. He kept his ear pretty close to the ground. It was he who heard the first whisper of rumour about a man called Mahdu Nath, who'd got something big on the boil. It was he who followed that rumour up. And, with his first report, when he realised that he was on to something very big indeed, it was he who suggested that I should send for you.'

Craille eyed Blake squarely.

'The reason he gave was simply that he felt out of his depth and wanted help. But he named you specifically as the help he wanted, and I think his motives went deeper than he was willing to admit. I think he was ready to let you know—actively— that the black sheep of the family had changed the colour of his coat, and I think he was seeking your approval. I don't for a minute believe he would have confessed it, but I fancy he prized your good opinion of him more than anything else in the world. He was certainly looking forward to meeting you again, and to be working with you—for once on the same side, the right side.'

'It should have worked out like that,' Blake said. His voice was empty.

'Yes....' Craille looked at him. 'And meantime,' he went on, after a pause, 'meantime he suggested that it mightn't be a bad thing if we let people think you were already here in India. He credited Mahdu Nath with a first-class intelligence organisation, and believed that he was bound to find out sooner or later that you were going to take a hand in the game. He reasoned that if Nath thought he had a chance of killing you before you got here, he'd find that chance and take it. So...'

Craille's old, frail shoulders moved in a gesture of resignation.

'So for the last few days he assumed your Christian name,' he said. 'And he let word leak out that Sexton Blake had already arrived in Calcutta. He looked reasonably like you, so that part of it was easy. He was a decoy duck, if one was needed, so that you could arrive here safe and sound. It was his own idea.'

Craille cleared his throat.

'So, your brother died bearing your name. Do you understand now? Officially, it's you who are dead. And Nigel—Nigel's just moved on. That's how it came about that you read your own obituary in the papers.'

'I see....' Slowly Blake nodded. Then he said soberly: 'Perhaps, in the end, he did the name more honour than I ever shall.'

'Perhaps.'

Both men were silent for a very long moment. Then Blake said:

'Tell me the rest of what you told me on our way here in the car. About this man Nath—about his plans—about everything. At the time I couldn't quite take it all in.'

'That's understandable,' Craille said quietly.

*　　*　　*

Craille lit a new Egyptian cigarette from the stub of the old one; his tenth cigarette of the day. He said suddenly, firmly: 'The first thing you should know about Mahdu Nath is that none of us have ever seen him.'

Blake's eyes narrowed sharply with surprise. 'What——?'

'That's right,' Craille nodded. 'You heard me correctly. None of us knows what he looks like.'

'But I thought——'

'You thought,' said Craille sagely, 'that I must know everything there is to know about him—his height, weight, age, coloration, even his size in hats and shoes—after the way I talked about him in the car. Right?'

'Yes.'

Craille sighed gustily. 'Well, I don't. I can tell you *what* the man is, but not *who* he is. I know the name he's using—Mahdu Nath—but I can't put a face and body to it. Come to that, I can't even say with certainty that the name Nath is the one he was born with, and as for nationality, he might be Indian, Burman, Singhalese, Persian, Eurasian or—or even renegade British for all I know.'

He went on: 'But I said I could tell you *what* he is. And I'll do it now. He's an accomplished rabble-rouser. His name has cropped up time after time in connection with riots in recent years. He can hold a mob in the hollow of his hand, and he's an organiser of no mean ability. And he's something more. He's a megalomaniac. He's mad for personal power. He means to get it at any price. It's plain in his record. That, basically, is why I'm here, and why I sent for you, and why Nigel Blake was murdered.'

He paused briefly and then said: 'And we've got to stop him seizing the power he craves for. And not even knowing what he looks like, it isn't going to be easy!'

'That,' said Blake, 'sounds like the understatement of the year!'

Craille nodded. He exhaled aromatic smoke through his nostrils. He leaned forward.

'To understand just how Mahdu Nath hopes to satisfy his
…aze for power,' he said, 'all you've got to realise is that he's
…orking for the Japanese—Nigel got proof of that—and also
…at the Japs have four armies less than six hundred miles from
…re at this moment. They're coming closer every hour. It's a
…im thought!

'They're going through Burma like a hot knife through
…tter, and our troops are going to have their work cut out to
…lt them on the borders of India. I think we will halt them,
…t it's going to take every man, every aircraft and every gun
…e've got to do it. The next two weeks are going to be decisive.'
…is voice was bleak. 'Now, consider …

'Consider what happens if, within the next two weeks, Mahdu
…ath stirs up trouble for us here in Bengal. And by "trouble"
… mean the real thing. Not just a small-scale riot or student
…monstration—Nath had only been organising those for prac-
…e. But big trouble. Trouble with a capital "T".

'What happens if, within the next two weeks, we have a
…al live insurrection on our hands—something comparable in
…ze with the Indian Mutiny or, more likely, even bigger. What
…ppens then?'

Blake's eyes narrowed. 'You think Nath can do it?'

Craille nodded grimly. 'I think he can do it, and he's going to
… it—unless we can stop him. And it's no good waiting until
… happens, because we certainly wouldn't be able to stop him
…en. To quell a second Indian Mutiny would take more time
…d more men than we could possibly afford. But you haven't
…swered my question. What happens in Burma if a second
…dian Mutiny breaks out here in Bengal?'

Blake's voice was bleak: 'It would be the end,' he said
…mply. 'And not only in Burma. Lines of supply and com-
…unication to our troops defending India would be the first
…ings to be cut. Our troops would be overwhelmed. The Japs
…ould pour in across the frontier. There'd be no stopping them.
…hey'd take Bengal within a week, and the rest of India in a
…onth——'

'If they bothered,' said Craille.

Blake looked at him sharply. 'What do you mean?'

Craille stood up. He motioned Blake to follow him across the

room to where a large globe stood in a book-lined corner. H
rotated the globe with skeletal fingers.

'Look. See for yourself. Here is India——' He pointed witl
his long, black cigarette-holder. 'Now,' he said, 'imagine th
plight of our armies after a Japanese invasion. They'd fight, o
course, but how long do you think they could go on fightin
without supplies, and with two powerful enemies to conten
with: the Japanese in front and the mutineers on every side

He answered his own question. 'Not long! As effectiv
forces they'd soon cease to exist. And the Japanese might we
think that the Indians themselves could more than adequatel
take care of them. I've no doubt Nath would do his best t
reassure them on that point. So...'

The thin finger moved swiftly across the face of the globe
jabbed down.

'... so the Japanese would hold Bengal as a base which the
could easily supply by sea from Burma, Siam and Malaya, an
they'd strike west. They wouldn't bother their heads abou
central and southern India—not at this stage. They'd appoin
Nath as their Viceroy, give him the use of a brigade, and leav
it at that. They'd go west across northern India to reach th
eastern frontier of Persia, and most of the way the going woul
be easy. They'd be ranging over India's great northern plair
and they'd be able to travel at speed. They could be in Delh
in ten days, and over the frontier into Persia in another ter
and I shouldn't have to tell you what a hellish situation tha
would produce!'

Again the finger jabbed down.

'The Japanese would pour into Persia here, from India. An
here, only five hundred miles to the north, is Russia—reelin
under German hammer-blows. Von Bock is in the Caucasus—
less than seventy miles away from the Russo-Persian borde
himself! It wouldn't take Von Bock and the Japanese long t
link up, now would it? And then——'

'Russia can be attacked from every side,' Blake said. 'At th
same time, Von Bock could spare a couple of divisions to strik
west through Iraq, Transjordan and Palestine, and Auchir
leck—already hard-pressed in Egypt—would be caught betwee
the hammer and the anvil. Between the Afrika Korps on on

hand, and Von Bock on the other.'

'Exactly,' Craille said. 'One move opens the way, relentlessly, to the next. Events must follow each other in a remorseless, logical progression.'

His mouth was a thin and bitter line.

'We could lose the whole war here in Bengal. One man could make us lose it—Mahdu Nath.'

The room was very quiet; very still. Craille's voice rang through it challengingly.

'And unless we can stop Nath doing what he plans to do, we *will* lose it. There's nothing more certain. We'll lose it in the next two weeks.'

CHAPTER FIVE

'All right,' said Blake presently. 'What *are* Nath's plans?'

Craille didn't answer.

Blake eyed him and then asked the same question again
Craille shook his head, a bitter expression on his thin-featured
face. 'I don't know,' he replied.

Blake stared at him incredulously.

'What——?'

'You heard me!' Craille snapped with a sudden flash
anger. 'I said I didn't know!'

'But——'

Craille interrupted him. 'Oh, I know what's bothering you
His voice was savage. 'You're just like all the others. Qui
suddenly you think I've become an alarmist in my old age, isn
that it?'

Still his anger showed through.

'I spoke of Nath stirring up trouble for us here in Benga
Something bigger than the Indian Mutiny, I said. And yo
asked me if he could do it. Yes, I said—for, believe me, he can
And now, just because I don't know exactly *how* he plans to d
it, you're beginning to discount everything I've said——'

Blake opened his mouth to voice a protest but Craille cu
him off with a peremptory gesture.

'Right at this moment you may even have a sneaking su
picion that I've been grossly exaggerating the danger. Well'-
he put the question harshly—'did I ever do that before?'

'No.'

'And I'm not doing it now. Nath is a spell-binder. A
organiser of the highest order. This his record proves. He's
very dangerous man. He's incited mobs to riot before. He
inflamed passions to fever-pitch——'

'There's never been a second Indian Mutiny, though,' Blak
put in quietly.

Craille glared at him. 'I know it!' He added, bitingly
'That's exactly the kind of asinine remark I got from the to

brass at Fort William when I went there to beg Army Head-quarters for troops to hunt Nath down. They can't spare the men, and they won't take the threat seriously. They think I'm an alarmist. I tried to warn them, the fools——'

He broke off, controlling his anger with an effort. There was a brief silence, and then in a quieter, calmer voice he said:

'Listen to me carefully, Blake. Mahdu Nath is dangerous. He can whip up a mob to a killing fury in next to no time at all. This his record shows. All right, I grant you that in the past he's only provoked local riots which have been brought quickly under control. But this, you must understand, is because he's never before been able to get Moslems and Hindus to settle their differences and turn on us together. Now he has a plan which will enable him to do this. I know, because your brother told me.

'But just what Nath's plan is, I don't know—because your brother didn't know. He died trying to find out.'

His voice strengthened.

'However, there is one thing of which I am quite sure, quite certain—because Nigel himself was certain of it, and he was no alarmist—and because all the indications are that Nath too is very, very sure. The plan is foolproof. It *will* unite Moslem and Hindu against us, and then what happens——'

He stopped, leaning forward, his eyes bright and glittering under their hooded lids: 'We can't let it happen,' he said. 'It mustn't happen. We've got to find out what Nath's plan is, and scotch it. We've got to get Nath himself—identify him, flush him out, arrest him or destroy him—and there's so little time. The balloon is going up in the next two weeks. It's got to. So we have only fourteen days at the most to do all that we have to do.'

His eyes bored into Blake's and his voice became suddenly steely, cutting like the edge of a knife across his own words.

'*You've* only got fourteen days,' he said.

And then, as Blake stiffened, Craille said, simply, relentlessly:

'Yes, Blake. This is *your* job.'

There was a long pause, then Blake said: 'Fine!'

He said it grimly and he meant it.

Nigel was dead. He had died horribly. Flesh of his flesh, Blake thought, cried for vengeance. And there was urgent work to be done.

It was vital work. Work on which the outcome of the whole war might well depend. But . . . where to begin?

'Do I have to start "cold"?' he asked. 'Or is there some lead you can give me?'

Craille shook his head. 'No. Nigel worked alone.'

'You mean that all he knew and all he suspected died with him?'

Craille demurred. 'All he knew for certain he told me, and I've already passed that information on to you. His suspicion, except for the earliest one, the basic one, that something big was brewing, he did not share with me. We dealt only in facts.'

'It's a pity there weren't more of them,' Blake commented tersely.

'True.'

Blake frowned. He was thoughtful. He murmured, almost to himself: 'Nigel must have shared his suspicions with somebody. He wouldn't be Nigel if he didn't.'

Then, suddenly, his brow cleared. He snapped his fingers.

'Of course! A girl-friend! Nigel had a girl-friend here in Calcutta.'

It was a statement rather than a question, but Craille answered it just the same. 'Yes, he had.'

'Of course he had! And they were close, I'll stake my oath on that. He would have confided in her. Who is she?'

'An Anglo-Indian girl. Rather beautiful, if you like the type. Her name is Caroline Perkins.'

'There you are then!' Blake's voice was lighter. 'I know my Nigel. Reformed or not, I knew he had to have a girl-friend tucked away somewhere.'

Craille said shortly: 'She knows nothing.'

Blake stared at him, frankly sceptical. 'Nigel didn't confide in her, you mean? Not once? Not ever? Not once in the long, still watches of the night? Is that what she told you? And you believed her?'

'I didn't say that.' Craille's voice held a faintly petulant note.

'In that case——'

Blake did not finish. There were footsteps in the hall outside the apartment, and a murmur of voices.

Then, heralded by a sharp tap on the door, a woman came into the room.

*   *   *

She was young and generously curved. She was blonde and business-like, but she was also very attractive.

Blake placed her instantly and infallibly. He placed her even before she began to speak in a voice which vibrated with a certain sexual huskiness. Eustace Craille liked to have beauty about him. This young woman, Blake judged, was the latest in a line of very personal and very private secretaries.

He was right. The blonde spoke directly to Craille: 'Colonel Maitland is here to see you, sir.'

'Maitland? Thank you, Molly. Have him come in.'

And then, as a tall, lean, military figure hesitated briefly in the doorway, Craille called out to him:

'Come in, Maitland. Meet Sexton Blake. And tell him the result of your interrogation of Caroline Perkins. He won't believe me.'

'The result,' said Maitland, 'was completely negative.'

He came briskly into the room and shook Blake by the hand. He had the timeless, ageless face of the professional soldier. He carried a short, leather-bound cane, with silver mountings, underneath his arm. His eyes were of the palest shade of blue. He sported a small, precisely-trimmed moustache and his speech was just as carefully clipped.

'I got nothing out of her,' he told Blake. 'Nothing at all, old man. Not a thing for any of us to work on. Sorry.'

'You interrogated her?' Blake asked.

'Colonel Maitland heads a branch of Military Security,' Craille told him. 'His services have been placed at my disposal.'

'I help in any way I can,' Maitland said. 'Glad to. But with the Perkins *bibby* I couldn't help at all, I'm afraid. I tried. Got to her as soon as I could after ... after—er—your brother's death was reported, and gave her the shock treatment. Rather brutal, really. Told her where your brother died, and how.

169

Spared her no details. She was horrified, of course, and I'm sure if she'd known anything at all that might have helped us get the devils that did for Nigel, she couldn't have held it back.'

'All the same, she must know something,' Blake insisted stubbornly.

'I tell you, it would have spilled out of her,' Maitland said. His moustache bristled slightly as he added, with the faintest touch of asperity: 'I'm a pretty experienced interrogator, Blake.'

'I don't doubt it, but...' Blake's voice was slightly cynical '...I'm a pretty experienced brother. I knew Nigel. He and this girl Caroline were pretty close, weren't they?'

'I suppose you could call it that.'

'Knowing Nigel,' Blake said, 'that's exactly what I'd call it. He had quite a way with the ladies. And he was never one for half-measures.'

'So...?'

'That was the way he was,' Blake said. 'It's strictly in character. And also strictly in character was the way he had of confiding in his women. He couldn't help himself. The confidences had to come out. I know.'

Maitland shrugged, and his manner had stiffened. Without appearing hostile, the mask of friendliness slipped a little, as though he disliked having his ability as an interrogator doubted.

'You may know your brother, Blake, I only know what Caroline Perkins said, and what she didn't say. And I only know what my training has taught me. I still say she knows nothing, but'—again he shrugged—'if you still doubt that, you can always interrogate her yourself. She has a flat in Alipore.' He named a street, a block and a number. 'Go there yourself. Find out for yourself.'

His lips were thin. Still his moustache bristled. The man himself bristled.

Craille sat very still in the background, watching, listening, saying nothing.

'All right,' Blake said calmly, nodding. 'I will.'

*   *   *

Alipore was space and sunlight, ordered peace and shade.

The pavements were noticeably cleaner. The roads were tree-lined. The district contrasted sharply with the dirt and squalor and gimcrack glitter of those other parts of Calcutta Blake had had to pass through to reach it. He drove a hired car.

Here, in Alipore, beyond the old Viceroy's house at Belvedere, heavy palms fanned their fronds against the cobalt blue of the sky, and white sugar-cake flat-blocks bulked large in their own green grounds. Blake stopped the car before one of them and got out. He walked over broad, bleached concrete flagstones to reach the dim and dusky coolness of the empty and echoing entrance hall.

A self-operated lift carried him up three floors in thick, humming silence to a landing and a door. He pressed the bell-push by the side of the entrance, and waited.

A bell rang distantly within the flat beyond the door, but nothing else happened. Time passed. Time punctuated by the far-off sound of sprinklers sighing over the green lawns beyond and below the open windows on the landing. A fly droned in out of the sunlight. Blake pressed the bell-push again.

There was still no response. Now Blake put his thumb on the bell-push and kept it there for a full half-minute.

Nobody came to the door. Miss Caroline Perkins was evidently not at home—or was she? Blake wasn't altogether sure that he liked the deathly silence which brooded over the flat beyond the door.

Nigel had been brutally done to death, and Caroline Perkins had been Nigel's girl. He himself had come here to ask her questions—following in Colonel Maitland's footsteps. But suppose someone else had come here, after Maitland had left ... someone determined that the Anglo-Indian girl should never, ever, provide any answers?

Blake didn't care for the images that crowded into his mind.

He turned quickly and took the lift back down to the entrance hall. It still echoed emptily. He went in search of a porter or a caretaker, anybody with a pass-key and authority to use it if necessary. He found a small, bespectacled Bengali clerk in an ill-fitting white suit industrious in a littered estate office at the rear of the block.

'Miss Caroline Perkins...?' The Bengali clerk's voice was

high, a little nervous as he echoed the name Blake had uttered. His weak eyes moved uneasily behind thick lenses. He said: 'Two men came for her. Military policemen. Security officers, I think. They took her away.'

Blake was startled. 'When?'

'Some hours ago. She was still sleeping when they arrived. I had to let them in to her apartment. They had a warrant.'

'You mean they arrested her?' Blake demanded. 'On what charge?'

But it was plain the little Bengali clerk neither knew nor wanted to know. It was enough that a scrap of official paper had been waved under his nose and that one of the occupants of the flat-block for which, it transpired, he was responsible, had been taken away like a thief or a murderer.

He seemed to bear the shame of it personally, like a weight bearing down on his thin shoulders. He was at this moment penning a report to his superiors about the incident. He said blindly, uncomprehendingly:

'But she had such good references when she came here——' and was prepared to expand this theme when Blake interrupted abruptly:

'Can I use your phone?'

A moment later he was speaking to Craille, telling him what had happened.

He heard surprise in the old man's voice. Plainly, Caroline's arrest was news to him. Blake went on to ask some short, sharp questions. Anger was stirring within him.

Who had authorised Caroline Perkins' arrest, and on what charge? If what the little, bespectacled Bengali clerk had supposed was true—that the military policemen who had made the arrest were Security men—then Colonel Maitland's department was undoubtedly involved, and Maitland himself must have been aware of what had happened. Why hadn't he spoken of what he knew?

Why—Blake demanded roughly of Craille—had Maitland said nothing to prevent him embarking on an utterly useless journey to question the girl? Why had the Colonel given him her address if all the time he had known she was no longer there?

And where was she now? This was the vital question and Maitland presumably had the answer. Where was Caroline Perkins?

Craille heard him out, and then tersely promised to ring him back soon. Colonel Maitland had left to return to his office, but he could and would be reached.

Blake put the phone back on its rest and, with bleak satisfaction, imagined the wires beginning to hum red-hot between Craille's apartment and Maitland's headquarters. Harsh words were about to be spoken.

Time passed. A very short time which Blake spent in asking the estate clerk a few pertinent questions about Caroline Perkins. Then the phone shrilled clamorously. It was Maitland himself on the line. Maitland dismayed.

His voice fairly leapt out of the telephone, urgent and anxious. 'Craille's told me what's happened. Believe me, Blake, until he did I knew nothing at all about it! What's more, no one else around here knows anything at all about it—nor does the Provost Marshal's Headquarters. Those weren't military policemen, Blake!'

'What——!'

'I don't know who they were, or what they were, but they weren't military policemen!' Maitland reiterated tautly. 'And no warrant has ever been issued for the girl's arrest. It looks like——'

Blake knew what it looked like, and he didn't relish the thought. Maitland put his fear into words.

'It looks as though she's been abducted. And we know why. You were right. Your brother must have confided in her. She knows too much for somebody's peace of mind.'

'We've got to find her,' Blake said. 'We've got to find her quickly. We must—before she goes the same way as Nigel. We've got to find her—before it's too late.'

CHAPTER SIX

What remained of the morning was lost in the blaze of noon. The afternoon passed and, for the second time in twenty-four hours, photographs of a missing person were rush-printed and circulated, and Redcaps and civil policemen again combed the native quarters of the city—all to no avail. Caroline Perkins had vanished. She was not to be found anywhere.

Meanwhile, the dead demanded a Christian burial, and in the golden light of early evening a bell tolled from the high tower of Calcutta's English cathedral. Sexton Blake walked bare-headed behind a coffin in the nearby cemetery. The body of Nigel, his brother, was soon to be laid to rest.

'*I am the Resurrection and the Life ... whosoever liveth and believeth in Me shall never die ...*'

The solemn words of the priest pacing before the coffin were caught and carried by the same light wind that stirred the white folds of his surplice. Out over the heads of the people lining the path they went. So many people, Blake thought. So many friends. A score or more. There were well-dressed Indians among them. One stood beside Craille, head bent as the coffin passed him. All had come to say a last goodbye.

'*For since by man came death. By man also came the resurrection of the dead.... Man that is born of woman hath but a short time to live ... suffer us not, at our last hour, for any pains of death, to fall from thee....*'

The coffin was lowered on to the ground at the side of the grave. The priest intoned the first words of the committal. Then the coffin went into the ground, and sprinkled earth fell soft against the lid.

'*...Ashes to ashes ... dust to dust; in sure and certain hope of the Resurrection....*'

Blake looked up. All around, marked by row upon row of headstones, those who had run the race and gone before—the soldiers, the law-givers, the creators of British India—slept out their hallowed sleep. Adventurers all to one degree or another, and neither certain saints nor unrepentant sinners. Nigel, Blake thought, would rest easily in their company. Basically he, too, had been an adventurer; one of their kind.

So Blake mused as the priest spoke the final words for the Order of the Burial of the Dead. And then, caught by the slightest of movements on the fringe of the crowd at the graveside, his gaze shifted—to focus instantly in fierce surprise. He was so startled that, for one split second, he even refused to believe what he saw.

Then he knew he had to believe it. There was no doubt about it, none at all. He was looking into a face on the edge of the crowd. A grief-stricken and beautiful face; the face of a woman. A woman whose photograph he had seen many times in the last few hours. At this very moment one of those same photographs reposed inside his wallet.

It was the face of Caroline Perkins.

And then, even as he made a small and totally involuntary movement towards her, the crowd shifted fractionally, and she was gone.

At that moment Blake was mentally torn in two. One half of him demanded that he should go after the Anglo-Indian girl; find her, stop her, question her. The other half of him insisted that he should remain where he was, out of respect for his dead brother.

But Nigel had been murdered—and the clue to his murderers might lie with Caroline Perkins. If he allowed this chance of finding her go by, he might never get another. He might never have the opportunity of bringing the killers to justice.

But how could he rush off now, in the very moments when Nigel was being laid to rest? There were no other members of the family there to mourn him, only Blake, his brother. No matter how great the need might be, could Blake leave now? Would he ever forgive himself, in later years, for having done so?

Blake made up his mind. He stayed where he was, by the graveside.

It was not only the blood bond which kept him there; it was the affection he felt for Nigel—and something more than affection—the sad, quiet pride he was experiencing. Nigel had redeemed himself at the end, and he deserved in full measure the respect he had earned.

The dead, deserving all honour, took priority over the living.

* * *

It was over. Blake turned slowly away from the graveside and looked for Eustace Craille. He found him standing quietly some distance away. The crush at the graveside had dwindled and only a handful of people lingered. The dead had been buried and life went on, perpetually posing fresh problems.

Craille looked up quickly as Blake approached him. He sensed an urgency in the other's movements. Without preamble Blake said bluntly:

'Did you see her?'

'Who?' asked Craille, staring.

'Caroline Perkins. She was standing there, on the edge of the crowd. When I moved she disappeared.'

Incredulity showed on the old man's face. 'Are you certain, Blake? After all, you've never seen the girl and——'

'I've seen her photograph. I've got one right here in my wallet.' He opened the wallet and took out the head-and-shoulders photograph, studying it closely. 'I wasn't mistaken,' he said. 'It *was* Caroline. I couldn't mistake that face.'

Craille said slowly: 'Then if you're certain—absolutely certain—it would seem she hasn't been abducted after all. And in that case, it would be perfectly logical for her to attend Nigel's funeral. Just the same, the circumstances under which she left her flat seem to demand some kind of explanation.'

'Exactly,' said Blake. His voice hardened. 'Who were the two men who posed as military policemen? And *why* did they? Why did they encourage the estate clerk to think they had come to arrest Caroline? And how did they persuade her to go with them? Where *did* she go with them?'

'A lot of questions,' said Craille.

'They all need answers,' said Blake. 'Every one of them. And I've a few more, too. If Caroline *was* taken from her flat in order to be questioned, for what reason was she afterwards released? Because she told them what they wanted to know, or because she had nothing *to* tell them?'

176

Craille sighed. 'It's a great pity you had to let her disappear,' he said. 'If she hasn't returned to her flat, we may have great difficulty in finding her again.'

'She's got to be found,' said Blake harshly. 'I want some answers to my questions. And if there's the faintest possibility that Caroline Perkins can give us a clue to those devils who murdered Nigel, then I want that information, too.'

'Of course,' murmured Craille. 'I'll try to have the military and civil police continue to help, but I don't hold out much hope. Not now.'

Blake's raised eyebrows made him feel he had to explain. He said, half-apologetically:

'I'll have to tell the authorities that you've seen her, and I think I know what the immediate official reaction will be. Obviously she hasn't been abducted, as we feared, so she can't be in any danger. In these circumstances I'm afraid that the authorities are going to tell me they can't spare men to continue to search for her—particularly as Colonel Maitland has already interrogated her, with purely negative results. I think you're going to have to go it alone, Blake.'

Blake nodded. 'That suits me,' he said.

Craille eyed him, measuring his confidence. 'And how will you go about finding her,' he asked. 'Where will you begin—if she hasn't returned to her flat?'

Blake frowned. 'I'll try to identify her friends first. Find out who they are, and what they know. Try to trace her through them. Someone must know where she's hiding—if she *is* hiding.'

'I'll help you all I can, of course,' said Craille.

'Of course.'

'And ...' the old man turned slightly, as though looking for somebody '... here's somebody else who might be able to help us. He'll certainly try.' He raised his voice slightly: '*Mr Dutt*——'

And the well-dressed Indian Blake had earlier seen in Craille's company at the graveside came slowly and solemnly forward.

*   *   *

He was neither a large man nor an exceptionally tall man,

nor was he old. But he had a certain unmistakable presence. He was in his mid-thirties or early forties, and his well-tailored European suit fitted him to perfection. He had a good brow, wide and intelligent, but the purposeful line of his jaw jarred with his deep brown eyes, which bore a perpetually wistful expression. A small moustache crowned his upper lip.

'Mr Sohan Dutt—meet Mr Sexton Blake,' Craille said, and the Indian's handshake was vigorous. Even a trifle too vigorous, Blake thought, as though he wanted to do all things well. 'Mr Dutt,' Craille went on, 'is a politician.'

'One of the responsible ones, I hope,' said Sohan Dutt, and smiled quickly. Then his face was serious again. The fleeting smile was like a trick he had learned. 'And as a responsible member of Congress, Mr Blake, I have to tell you with what horror and disgust I heard of what happened to your brother. Actually, it was only a few hours ago I learned that it was your brother and not you yourself who had died. I am here today as a mourner to publicly demonstrate my feelings in this matter.'

He spoke firmly, frowning to give his words weight.

'I am as much a Nationalist as Nehru or Gandhi, and I tell you frankly, Mr Blake, that I will rejoice with all my countrymen when the last Englishman has been driven from Indian soil. But I have no time for the extremists who say that now we should do it. They cannot have India's best interests at heart. First we should win the war and then the peace. That is logic. A man who fights two enemies at one and the same time by choice is a fool—isn't it?'

He was very earnest.

Blake nodded. 'I couldn't agree with you more. And I'm glad you see the Japanese as India's enemies, Mr Dutt. But of course, I can't agree that we British come into the same classification.'

'Of course not!' The quick smile came and went, switched on and off like an electric light. 'On this we agree to disagree as you English say.'

'We'll agree to disagree,' Blake affirmed, and nodded. 'Until the "night of the long knives" at least.'

Sohan Dutt laughed delightedly. This was a great joke

e'll deal with the Japanese first,' he said. 'Then with the
tish.'

Craille spoke up. 'I was just telling Mr Blake that you might
willing to help him investigate his brother's murder,' he
d to Dutt.

But naturally! Anything I can do.' The politician's tone was
ite but hardly enthusiastic. It seemed clear that while he
precated the manner and circumstances of Nigel's death and
plored the extremism which had prompted the killing, he
s not overly keen to have a hand in bringing the English-
n's murderers to justice. They would undoubtedly be Indians,
er all.

Nevertheless, he repeated, more vaguely this time: 'Anything
all I can do ...' He gave Blake his card. 'I am on the tele-
one. Feel free to call on me.'

With equal studied vagueness he gave a short bow. 'I must
now ... business.' The smile flashed on and off in farewell.
en he was walking away.

Blake glanced at Craille. 'He's not quite as enthusiastic as
a thought he'd be, eh?'

Craille shrugged. 'Oh, I don't know. After all, you can't
pect him to be truly enthusiastic—not in taking our side
ainst his own people. And that is how he sees this, after all.
t in the end he'll help, if you need him. He's helped in the
st in a number of small ways.'

Have you told him anything about Mahdu Nath?' asked
ake.

Nothing. He knows that Nigel died at the hands of extrem-
s, and that's true. But which extremists and what the deeper
tives were behind his murder are things I haven't shared
th Sohan Dutt.'

Blake was curious. 'Why not? You seem to have a fair degree
confidence in him.'

That's beside the point. The point is that I seek to avoid
sonalising such issues with Indians,' said Craille. 'In my
perience it only complicates matters. In many ways, you
ow, these people have a broad, irrational streak. They can
d do loathe principles in the abstract, and yet they can be
ught and held by the glittering personality of those same

179

principles' advocate. That is what I feared might happen i
mentioned Mahdu Nath's name to Dutt, and it is also wh
was careful to introduce *you* to him. He liked you, I thir
You impressed him. Therefore he will help you if you need hi
On the other hand, the reverse might be true had I mention
Mahdu Nath.'

'You think it makes so much difference?'

Craille nodded again. 'This is one thing you've got to und
stand about these people, Blake. They are a nation purpose-bu
for hero-worship. If and when we leave India, they'd do w
to beware of the strong man, the spell-binder, the demagog
One such man will rule here one day. India is ripe for
dictatorship.'

'You think Gandhi will rule—or Nehru?'

'Not as dictator,' Craille said quickly, 'though one or t
other of them may come quite close to it. But it is not
account of either of those two men that I fear for India's sa
Both of them, basically, are Moderates. I fear somebody else.

'I fear an unknown ... perhaps. Someone who hasn't be
in the public eye a lot. Someone new to the great mass of
people. Someone who can capture the public imaginatic
Someone whose name has not become so familiar as to bree
little contempt. ...'

'Mahdu Nath?' asked Blake softly.

'It could be Nath. It might well be Nath,' Craille agre
soberly. And then he laughed. It was a dry sound, with
humour. ' "If and when we leave India" I said ... as thou
it might not be for another twenty years—and it could hapr
tomorrow. We've not much time, Blake. We've hardly a
time at all.'

CHAPTER SEVEN

Blake parted from Craille at the cemetery gates. The old man's black car sped away, accelerating in the direction of Park Street. Blake watched it go.

And then he was conscious of someone standing beside him. He turned his head quickly.

'Mr Blake ...?' The man beside him spoke. He was olive-complexioned and paunchy. He was an Anglo-Indian police officer in a khaki drill uniform. 'It *is* Mr Blake, isn't it? There's ... a family resemblance. I missed you at the *thana* this morning.'

Blake gripped the soft, well-manicured hand which was offered to him. 'You must be Inspector Mawgan.' He had heard of the inspector from Craille.

'That's right.' The inspector moved his head slightly, almost deprecatingly. 'I tried to get away for the funeral, but I couldn't. Not in time. Just the same, I wanted to see you to offer you my sympathy. Anything I can do ...'

'Thank you.'

There was nothing in Blake's reply to indicate anything except appreciation of the other man's offer, but inside he was aware of a feeling of guardedness. Something else—something unspoken—lay between them. The inspector was eyeing him coldly. Was it only a desire to express formal sympathy that had brought him here?

Then Mawgan laughed; a small, self-conscious sound as their eyes met. And Blake knew.

'Yes, I was curious. ...' It was Mawgan speaking, as if he could see into the innermost recesses of Blake's mind. 'At first I was told it was *you* who had been murdered. Nobody mentioned your brother. I didn't even know you had one. And I've followed your cases; I know quite a lot about you.'

'So you wanted to see both of us?'

'Yes,' Mawgan admitted. Then he added; 'But there was something else. I'm not just indulging in *idle* curiousity, you know.'

Blake said nothing. He waited. Mawgan went on: 'I ha
something for you. You'll be investigating your brother's dea
of course.' He said it as if it was a foregone conclusion. Th
he went on: 'We're holding the woman who told us where
find your brother's body. I thought you might like to questi
her.'

'Rosemary Medwin?' Blake said quickly. Craille had to
him about Rosemary, too.

Mawgan nodded.

'She *says* the information was given to her by an Indian. S
says she doesn't know the Indian's name. She *says* she pass
the information on to us just as soon as she got it.'

Each emphasised word hammered another nail into the cof
of Rosemary Medwin's credibility. Each was intended to. Bla
surprised an expression of sheer, naked malice on Inspect
Mawgan's face.

'You don't believe her, then?' he asked.

'I know her,' the inspector replied. It was an answer. 'Bu
can't get her to change her story. I've tried—oh, I've *tried*!'

Was it the sweet after-taste of evil enjoyment that no
lurked around the corners of Mawgan's mouth, Blake wo
dered. The moist, concupiscent lips were savouring something

'I thought you might like to talk to her, Mr Blake,' sa
Mawgan deferentially. 'I'm sure she knows more than she
tell. *You* might be able to break her down.'

*　　*　　*

With Inspector Mawgan at his side, Blake crossed the dra
grey asphalt square enclosed by the barrack-like buildings
the police-station. Voices rang and boots trampled somewhe
beyond the edge of his consciousness as a sergeant drilled
squad of constables in the early twilight.

In the far corner of the yard someone was tinkering with t
engine of a motor-cycle and a woman came out on to t
balcony of the Married Quarters to call out something in
high, shrill voice as they passed. The man working on t
motor-cycle put down his tools and went inside.

Blake and Mawgan climbed steps to the narrow hall of t
thana. An Anglo-Indian sergeant stopped gnawing his cutic

and stood up behind his desk as Blake and Mawgan entered the inspector's office.

'I've been trying to reach you, sir,' he said. He was speaking to Mawgan and he was speaking with just a hint of apprehension lurking in his voice. He was the bearer of ill news, the teller of bad tidings—so much was plain.

'What is it?' Mawgan asked the question roughly.

'The woman prisoner——'

'Medwin? Rosemary Medwin?' The words leapt like bullets out of Mawgan's throat and he was half across the room in an instant. 'What's happened? She's not done away with herself——?'

'No——'

It was something worse than that, the sergeant's expression said.

'What then?'

'We've had to release her.'

'*What!*'

For an instant Mawgan stood transfixed—immobile—as if struck by lightning. His face was drained of colour. Then, all at once, it returned.

It came back in a great, angry flood. And he swelled visibly, like a bull-frog, in his choking fury.

'What?' he repeated again. 'You've had to release her? And on whose orders?'

His voice was harsh. The sergeant quailed before it.

'On Colonel Maitland's orders, sir....'

'Since when has Security had anything whatever to do with the proper functioning of the police?'

'But he came here personally, sir ... and he had a Release Order signed by the Commissioner. I had to let her go at once. I tried to delay things but ...' the sergeant was washing his hands, the one with the other, in his anxiety '... but Colonel Maitland insisted, sir. I had to let her go.'

'Maitland!' said Mawgan furiously—explosively. 'Damn him!'

And then he voiced the question which was uppermost in Blake's mind:

'But why the devil did he do it? Why?'

CHAPTER EIGHT

There was only one way to find out, and Blake took it.

Half an hour later he was in a position to put the question to the one man who could give him an answer. Colonel Maitland.

The day had slipped towards dusk and the stars were out, glimmering faintly. Lights burned bright along the broad bustle of Chowringhee. In the bare-walled, spartan, first-floor office there, Blake sat on the other side of Colonel Maitland's desk and asked his question.

'Why was Rosemary Medwin released, Colonel?'

'Because she shouldn't have been detained in the first place!'

The spare, soldierly Maitland spoke forcefully. The words came out like bullets; with real feeling behind them. He was not only annoyed; he seemed to be extremely angry and upset.

One of Blake's eyebrows quirked upward a little. 'Does Security frequently concern itself with the way the Civil Police use, or misuse, their powers?' he asked mildly.

Maitland looked at him grimly. A stocky staff-sergeant to whom he had been dictating orders prior to Blake's interruption stood woodenly by.

'Does Security frequently concern itself with such things?' Maitland echoed. Then he went on, more quietly: 'No, not often. But sometimes it has to. And in this case it has to. Of course, you want to know why?'

Blake nodded. 'I must confess I'm interested,' he said.

'Well, I'll tell you. It's simple. It's because we can't treat informants this way. We should thank them—not gaol them. Heaven knows we need them! We ought to give them encouragement, not treat them as criminals. Do you think Rosemary Medwin will ever help us again, after this?'

'Mawgan thinks she could help more than she has done,' said Blake slowly.

'*Mawgan!*' Maitland burst out. He uttered the name like a curse. He demanded: 'What do you know of him, Blake? Do

184

you know what he's done to Rosemary?'

'He told me he'd questioned her.'

' "Questioned her!" And did he tell you *how* he questioned her?' Maitland's mouth was twisted into a thin, bitter line. 'That man should never be allowed within a mile of her.'

'It's like that, is it?' asked Blake thoughtfully.

'Exactly like that! For some reason he seems to have it in for Rosemary Medwin. He hates her. He's detained her again and again, on the flimsiest of pretexts.'

'Without cause, you mean?'

'Without cause or reason. She's never committed any sort of crime. Of course, she's no saint——'

'I heard about that.'

'——and her kind is anathema to Mawgan.' Maitland bit off the name. 'But that's no indictable offence in itself. She's certainly more to be pitied than persecuted. She's had a rotten life.'

'I'd like to meet her,' said Blake.

'Why? On account of what Mawgan has said? That she knows more than she pretends?'

'Perhaps.'

'You can't believe that, Blake. Not after what I've told you.'

'I've got to make up my mind for myself,' Blake said quietly. 'And to do that I must talk to her. Do you know where she is?'

'At her usual address, I suppose.'

'She isn't,' said Blake. 'Before I left Mawgan he'd already checked on that.'

'Why can't the swine leave her alone?' swore Maitland.

'I think perhaps I could make him,' Blake said, 'but I want to talk to her first. Can I have her address? Will you give it to me?'

Maitland hesitated. In the background the stocky staff-sergeant's face was expressionless.

'Oh, all right,' Maitland said at last, grudgingly. 'But you won't give it to Mawgan?'

'No.'

'That's a promise? I don't want him hounding the girl from pillar to post——'

'It's a promise,' said Blake.

The colonel wrote the address quickly on an old scrap of card. He handed it over. 'But I don't think she can help you.'

Blake said determinedly: 'Well, I can but try.'

He went from Maitland's office, conscious that he had left behind him a man who was angry as well as annoyed. Maitland was emphatic that Rosemary Medwin could not help him; Mawgan was equally emphatic that she could.

The truth must lie somewhere between.

*   *   *

The address which Colonel Maitland had given Blake was a tenement block in a mean, narrow street. Light spilled out from the windows. Jangling music frayed the nerves. Men in dhotis squatted on their heels on the pavement in front of the entrance and talked, and chewed betel and spat. The six steps up to the main doorway were blotched and greasy with spittle the colour of blood.

Blake went up the stairs. He felt certain that Rosemary Medwin could easily be in possession of some small scrap of evidence, some vital information she did not know she had. She moved in the right quarters to have heard whispers of Mahdu Nath; and maybe, in any case, she really did know more about Nigel's death than she pretended.

It was possible she did—and there was only one way to find out.

Blake traversed a hall which was narrow and noisome, and then, abruptly, an Indian came out of the shadows to meet him. A sharp-eyed man, small and ferret-faced. The chuprassi, the watchman, guardian and caretaker of the tenement—armed with an iron-shod stave.

'You seek something, sahib?'

'Someone,' Blake corrected and asked for Rosemary Medwin's room.

Something moved quickly behind the little man's eyes ·and was as quickly gone. 'The third floor,' he told Blake and gestured towards more steps. They were stone steps, and dirty. They too were betel-blotched. They echoed as Blake climbed them.

He climbed to the first floor, to the second, to the third. He went up them quickly.

He came to Rosemary Medwin's room just as an Indian came out. He was a big man and bald, fumbling with buttons. He was dressed in well-worn but flashy European clothes, stained with sweat under the armpits. He moved in a rank aura, partly compounded of toddy. He had been drinking and his eyes were glazed. As he passed Blake he swayed—and then stopped. For a second he seemed to hold himself upright by sheer effort of will. He turned and stared. He looked at Blake and his mouth worked. Then he was gone. He went quickly, blundering down the steps, and Blake watched him go, narrow-eyed. A thought moved in his mind. He would remember that face.

Blake knocked on the door and a voice called from within, the words slurred. Then there was nothing. Blake knocked again.

This time there was movement and a sullen complaint. The door opened a fraction and then veered wider. A woman stood there, holding a stained dressing-gown tightly round her throat. Her face was flushed and her golden blonde hair was disordered. Her dark tan silk stockings were laddered. The high heel of one of her black court shoes was cracked and gave her a slightly lop-sided stance. There were small beads of sweat on her upper lip.

'Yes. . . . Who're you? Wadder you want?'

Blake looked at her. Her breath, too, had the smell of the Indian he had passed on the landing; the rank smell of the fermented sap of the palm. She hiccoughed:

'Well?'

Blake could see that, sober, this woman could still be very attractive. There were unmistakable lines of breeding in her face and in the way she held herself, despite the influence of drink. And her voice, under the slurred consonants, was educated, even trained.

'Miss Medwin?' he asked.

'Thass me. Who're you?' She moved closer, peering at him. Then suddenly her eyes snapped wide open. She lurched back from him—afraid. The colour had gone from her face now

187

and her eyes stared unbelievingly.

The hand at her neck faltered and fumbled and the dressing-gown gaped, unheeded. She said hoarsely:

'*You!*'

She tried to push back into the room behind her. She tried to shut the door, but Blake already had his foot against it.

'*You!*' she repeated. '*But you're dead . . .*'

Blake shouldered the door and was in the room with her. She continued to back away from him, white and shaking.

'Nigel——'

She began to sob hysterically. Blake seized her by the shoulders and shook her, not gently. 'Listen to me!' he snapped. 'I'm not Nigel—I'm his brother. My name is Sexton Blake.'

'His . . . brother?' she panted, struggling in his grasp.

Blake kicked the door shut with his heel. He continued to keep his hands tightly on the woman's shoulders. He steered her across the room towards the tumbled bed in the far corner.

'Yes, Nigel's brother,' he repeated. 'You knew him, didn't you? I've a feeling you knew him very well. And I've a feeling you know a lot more about the way he died—and who killed him—than you pretend.'

He pushed her from him and she fell across the disordered bed. She sprawled there, staring up at him, her expression stricken, her fingers groping at her mouth.

Blake stooped over her. His expression was hard and relent-less, almost cruel.

'You and I, Rosemary Medwin, are going to have a nice long talk,' he said.

CHAPTER NINE

She was sobbing again now, breathlessly. Blake stood back and looked at her for a moment and pity struggled with the grimness on his face. He put his hand into a back pocket and took out a silver flask.

Unscrewing the cup-cap he poured out some of the contents. 'Here, drink this!' he commanded sharply.

'What . . . what is it?'

'Brandy. Better than the muck you've been tossing off lately.'

Her hand trembled so violently that she could not hold the tiny cup. Blake helped her, and his touch was not unkindly. He sat down beside her upon the sleazy bed and held the cup to her lips.

'Better now?' he asked when she had finished drinking.

'Yes . . . yes, a little.' Her breathing was easier and the glance she shot at him now held curiosity as well as the aftermath of shock.

Blake said, on a note of warning: 'Don't imagine this is a respite for you to think up a lot of lies. I want the truth from you. All of it. You knew Nigel Blake, didn't you?'

'I—I'd seen him a few times.'

'Where and when?'

'With Caroline Perkins——' The words came out falteringly.

'You know Caroline?'

'Yes. We're friends, Caroline and I. And I saw him with her.'

That might be the truth, Blake thought, but not all of it. And he wasn't going to be satisfied with less than all of it.

'Where is she now?' asked Blake.

'Who . . . Caroline?' Rosemary Medwin spoke hurriedly, as though anxious to continue playing around the name and not be forced further afield.

'You know quite well I mean Caroline,' said Blake sternly. 'Now, tell me where she is.'

'At her flat in Alipore, I suppose,' said Rosemary.

'She is *not* at her flat in Alipore,' said Blake. 'She's left it. Gone. Disappeared.'

Rosemary's eyes registered astonishment. Her eyes opened to their fullest extent. It was a good act, but not good enough to fool Blake. His mouth tightened.

'If she isn't there, I don't know where she is,' she said—but she was lying. Blake wondered exactly what she had to hide and was all the more determined to find out.

He said: 'I have to find her. It could be very important.' And even as he uttered it, he recognised the phrase as coming perilously close to being the understatement of the year.

For, distantly, he could hear a reminder of the urgent nature of his assignment—if any such reminder were necessary. Somewhere a news broadcast interrupted the day-long jangle of music from All-India Radio; the music that, in this part of Calcutta, was as omnipresent as the very air one breathed. The news broadcast was in Hindi, but Blake understood enough of the language to be able to grasp the meaning of the opening phrases.

The Japanese were advancing again. They were driving closer and closer still to India's borders. British armies were engaged in 'strategic withdrawals'.

'Where is Caroline Perkins?' Blake demanded: 'You must know. You *do* know.'

He had to know—and there was so little time.

*   *   *

Rosemary persisted in her denials, cringing away from him as he grew angrier, almost inviting him to shake her, to strike her, to beat her in order to get at the truth. She wore an oddly exalted expression.

It was then Blake caught and held himself in check. Strangely, he was trembling.

For some women, he thought, invited violence as blotting-paper invites ink. They were made for it They could not fulfil their function without it. They whimpered and cowered and cringed, and they would cry out in the grip of pain while all the time, semi-subconsciously, they welcomed it like the embrace of a lover.

He believed that Rosemary Medwin was such a woman. And

the thought instantly coloured his attitude towards her. It had to. And his attitude had to change.

Rough demands for information would earn him nothing. He might threaten, even strike her, and she would hug her secret still.

Impatient as he was, desperately aware of the compelling urgency of the situation as he was, Blake could not question and cross-question this woman in any conventional way. He could not brow-beat her into speaking. She would merely continue, tearfully and tremulously, to deny the knowledge that he was now certain she possessed; and she would offer herself up—willingly, longingly—to the sharp lash of his tongue.

Threats would not move her. Even blows—if he could have brought himself to resort to violence—would only provoke in her a delicious *frisson*. Mawgan had tried. He had tried all this, and more if everything Maitland had told him was true. He'd tried—and he'd failed. Maybe Mawgan had never understood Rosemary Medwin.

And Blake thought he did understand her.

Quite suddenly Blake changed purpose, direction and tone. He moved a little closer to where she sat and his hand closed on her own, gently, without any sexual implication. His voice was kind.

'Tell me about yourself,' he said. 'How did a woman like you get into a mess like this?'

Rosemary's eyes instantly filled with tears. Here was a shoulder to cry on—a warm, comforting man's shoulder. Here was somebody who wanted to give, rather than take from her.

Blake knew that women like Rosemary yearned after pain and suffering and if none were inflicted, they must inflict it upon themselves. Mentally and psychologically, they were masochists. And this was just what he was inviting Rosemary to be.

Let her beat herself with the birch of harsh memories, let her pile remembered degredation upon degredation. If she talked long enough something must surely emerge; the truth he wanted.

He produced the flask again and found the bottle from which she had been drinking before he'd arrived. He took a small measure of brandy himself before giving her the rest with a measure of toddy. It would be good for her tears. Then he seated himself next to her again.

'Tell me all about it, Rosemary,' he said. 'All about your life. I may be able to help you. . . .'

Then she started talking and once started, she could not stop. She savoured every hateful, hurtful memory and cried as she talked.

Blake listened.

CHAPTER TEN

He heard a strange, compelling story. Her own story. The story of a girl with a guilt complex so great that it demanded endless efforts at atonement. It gave her no peace. It had harrassed and hounded her through thirty-one years of life. It had driven her on relentlessly—almost inevitably—to this time and this place; to this sordid, sleazy room in Calcutta.

Words spilled out of her. The room was hot and her speech, although still faintly slurred, had begun to take on a different timbre and intonation. An expensive boarding school, and possibly some exclusive finishing school abroad, thought Blake and wondered still more.

Rosemary bowed her blonde head and wept above the stained tumbled sheets; the disordered ruin of her bed. This was her life.

Rosemary's guilt complex had started almost from the moment she was born. Her birth had killed her mother and her father had never forgiven her for it. He never mentioned it, never reproached her, but she knew all the same. Her parents had been married only two years when Rosemary's forthcoming intrusion was announced; and they were still passionately in love. Neither of them had wanted a child so soon.

But Rosemary was born and Jennifer Medwin died. And by killing her mother, Rosemary had robbed her father not only of the woman he loved but the sons he had hoped to have one day. He had suffered a double loss—and Rosemary was the cause, the destroyer of his happiness and his hopes.

He might have reconciled himself to Jennifer's death, in time, if Rosemary had been a boy. If she had been one of the sons he had hoped and planned to have. A son to inherit the wealth he had accumulated and the name he had made for himself.

The twin accidents of her mother's death in childbirth and of her own sex lay like sins upon Rosemary's soul. She had nobody to whom she could confide her fears and her secret, growing complexes. While her father was not unkind to her, she knew that he cared nothing for her; that the only time he felt at ease in his own house was when she was not there. When he sent her away to school—ostensibly to receive the best education his money could buy—she knew that he was not doing it for her sake, but for his own. He wanted to rid himself of the incubus and continual reproach of her presence.

It was not until she had left school, at the age of eighteen, that Rosemary had discovered the exact source of her father's wealth. She knew that he owned vast factories; that he was 'something in steel'. What she discovered was that he had made his fortune during the First World War, in munitions.

The fact that the arms and explosives had been supplied to the French and British troops made no difference to Rosemary. Her father had made his fortune out of the war—the war which had brought death and disfigurement to tens of thousands of human beings. Profiteering in the price of blood. And she had added his guilt to her own.

She had turned her back on her father and his fortune. It was blood-money and she wanted none of it. In search of salvation, she had embraced socialism and the Left Book Club, and vigorously flagellating herself with tracts by Professor Laski and G. D. H. Cole, she had thrown herself heart and soul into The Movement.

'I went on Protest Marches,' Hunger Marches, everything,' she said. 'I even picketed Downing Street in the company of unemployed Welsh miners, and once I knocked off a policeman's helmet. I had to appear in Court, and my father got to hear about it. He was furious, but by that time I'd lost even the little affection I'd had for him. I suppose I felt, in a way, that I was getting my own back for everything he was and represented. Also for the way he'd treated me.'

Later on, Rosemary had bared her soul to intense young men in Bloomsbury drawing rooms redolent of red-hot Fabianism and cold, weak tea. Soon her attempts at virtue had reaped their own reward.

For then, as now, Blake knew, plain and politically-conscious young women were ten a penny; but attractive ones were as rare as orchids on a midden and just as noteworthy. And the socialist cause of that time had less than its share. Consequently, it hadn't been long before Rosemary had come to the attention of a certain middle-aged Member of Parliament about to embark on a fact-finding tour of rebellious, strife-torn India—a night in Bombay, a day in New Delhi, two days in Calcutta, and the same in Madras—and the more he had seen of Rosemary the more he had wanted to see. His intention had hardened.

'He offered me a job as his secretary on the tour,' she said. I was longing for the chance to get away from everything, especially out of my father's reach, and I accepted. I really believed at first, you see, that it was just a secretary he wanted. I'd had a fairly good education; I could speak both French and Spanish, and I simply jumped at the chance to go.'

He had hinted, during the voyage out, at what he wanted of her, apart from her secretarial duties, but she had been too innocent—or too obtuse—to understand. The seclusion of her long years in the boarding-school, though they had sent her out armed and equipped with all the necessary educational qualifications, had not thought fit to acquaint her with the facts of life. In those days of her early emancipation it was, perhaps, that innocence which had saved her.

But her new-found employer knew what he wanted. He began by taking her into his confidence to an even greater extent; telling her how much they could accomplish together on this tour. She had, through his words, bled for the penniless millions of India; the Outcasts, the Untouchables, the Great Unwashed. She had visualised herself as a Mission, rather than a missionary; a second Florence Nightingale, bringing relief where there was pain, light where there was darkness.

'He was so kind to me,' she told Blake, and Blake nodded sympathetically. He knew well enough what kindness had meant to her.

She went on: 'I suppose I looked upon Austin, at first, as a kind of father-figure—the father I'd never really had. I felt I was helping him to do great things. I didn't really know, until we actually reached India, what he had in mind. . . .'

He had shown her what he had in mind during the course of the night in Bombay, and had persisted after the day in New Delhi. He had planned it very carefully—dinner, soft lights and sweet music; the arm around her shoulders, the fatherly kiss. She had been surprised, thrilled, and then flattered; perhaps she had even led him on a little, revelling in a strange new sense of power.

'That night Austin came to my room,' she said. She spoke slowly and hesitatingly, with sidelong glances at Blake, yet he got the idea that she was enjoying the telling. It represented a further flagellation; another sin to add to those she already carried. 'I tried to resist him—at first; but I was a little drunk and too tired, and he was so kind and understanding. Then, too, I think I felt guilty. He made me feel that it was my fault; that I'd purposely led him into thinking I cared for him. You know what I mean. . . .'

'I know,' said Blake gravely.

'That was in Calcutta,' she said. 'It lasted for three days and then I seemed to wake up, to come to my senses. I saw the whole thing for what it was—not a romantic attachment, but a sordid little intrigue with somebody who wanted me only for one thing and not for the ideals I believed in at all. I ran away. . . .'

She had, she recalled, been shamed and shocked not only by what she had done but because at the time she had enjoyed doing it. It was her final act of rebellion against her father; against all the old moral conventions he upheld. It was the ultimate sin. Then once more the feeling of guilt had leapt out at her, and this time it had been stronger than ever. She had left the hotel and taken the first boat back to England.

Her sense of guilt had followed her all the way, pressing more and more heavily. She wanted to disappear, to hide herself away where nobody could find her. So she answered an advertisement as companion to an old lady who lived in Sussex, deep in the heart of the country. Here, she thought, she could atone.

But the old lady had proved demanding and irritable, and she had grown lonely. She had longed for her old friends once more and although she could not see them, she could at least write to them. She had done so—and to one in particular—a young man named Adrian whom she had known since childhood. Perhaps, with his help, she could recover some of her ideals as well as her self-respect.

Adrian, who she had not seen in years, was at this time serving with the British Army in Egypt, as a captain. She remembered that he had always been fond of her, in a brotherly kind of way; and very sympathetic. So they began to correspond. And their letters became longer and more frequent and friendship began to give place to affection.

'Of course, I didn't tell him about Austin,' she said. 'I felt that was all in the past—over and done with. It never occurred to me that Austin and I would ever meet again.'

But they had, with shattering unexpectedness. The old lady whose companion Rosemary was, had a nephew and he had written asking if he might bring a friend down for the weekend. They had arrived on the Saturday—and Rosemary had found herself face to face with the man whose secretary—and mistress—she had been during that brief, eventful stay in India.

Importunately, declaring that if she did not do as he asked he would tell the old lady everything, and thus make certain she was thrown out, bag and baggage, Austin had come to her room again. And, weakly, shamefully—yet at the same time subconsciously hugging to her a renewed sense of guilt—Rosemary had yielded.

But Austin, having conquered, had only too obviously boasted to the old lady's nephew of his conquest. And the nephew, who was nearer the Member of Parliament's age than Rosemary's, had speedily decided that if any *ex gratia* hospitality was being offered under his aunt's roof, he was legitimately entitled to it.

So he had crept into Rosemary's room the following night— and had emerged much more quickly than he had entered. She had left him in no doubt as to her opinion of him; and the nephew, as he stood at the door shaking with fury and frustration, left her in no doubt as to his opinion of her. He made it quite clear that he intended to let his aunt know the kind of girl she was harbouring under her innocent roof.

Rosemary did not give him the chance. She got up at dawn, packed her belongings and left—leaving the explanations to him. She had managed to save some money and now she travelled back to London and got herself a bed-sitting room—

and a job as a typist—near Victoria.

But she still kept up the correspondence she had started with Adrian and now their friendship, although somewhat restricted, began to blossom apace. He had now been posted to India and he wrote asking if she would join him there. He asked her to marry him and Rosemary's heart, which she had believed was empty of all emotion, was filled with happiness.

So Rosemary threw up her job, left the bed-sitter with no regrets and took passage to India. The fare swallowed up most of her savings, but money was her last concern. She was going to Adrian, and she was going to be married. He would love and protect her and they would be happy for ever afterwards.

When Rosemary had reached this stage in her story she took a final pull at the bottle of toddy and let the tears flow unchecked.

'I might have known something would happen,' she wailed, 'I might have known it was too good to last.'

For by the time her ship had docked in Calcutta a number of things had happened.

In London, the long-suffering wife of the Member of Parliament had finally filed a petition for divorce—citing Rosemary Medwin.

And, in Cawnpore, Adrian had been bluntly informed of this by his dour Commanding Officer who—to add yet another quota of ill luck to Rosemary's already overflowing proportion —had been a friend of her father's. He had told Adrian a number of things about Rosemary which Adrian had not known; one, that she had broken with her father and was, in consequence, penniless; and two, that she had been kicked out of her job as companion to the old lady because she had attempted to seduce the old lady's nephew.

To Adrian, upright, clean-limbed, 'pukkha', Conservative— and chronically hard-up—the first fact undoubtedly weighed more heavily with him than the second. In fact, the blow was devastating. A Socialist, an adulteress; moreover, an adulteress without a penny to her name! Thank God he'd found out in time.

He hadn't bothered to meet the boat.

'I couldn't understand what had happened,' Rosemary said,

her eyes brooding into space. 'I thought at first he hadn't been able to get away—that his leave had been cancelled. I sent him a wire—he was in Cawnpore—and booked in at a hotel to wait for him.'

'But he never came?' asked Blake sympathetically.

'No. Then I wrote to him, and the letters came back to me unopened. I nearly went out of my mind wondering what had gone wrong; what had turned him against me. You see, I hadn't seen the papers; I didn't know what Austin's wife had done. If I had known I could have tried to explain—to have let him see that it wasn't entirely my fault. I don't suppose it would have made any difference, but if I'd been honest with him. . . .

'Instead I kept on writing, asking him what had happened, why he didn't want to see me. And in the end he replied. He said he wanted nothing to do with the kind of woman I was and he thanked God he'd found out in time. And just in case I thought I could continue to pull the wool over his eyes, he said, he was enclosing a copy of the newspaper cutting. He also told me what his Commanding Officer told *him*.'

She went on, her voice tightening: 'So that was that! It finished me in India before I'd even got off the boat. Not so much the fact that I was a "bad woman" who'd been caught out, but because I was associated in the minds of the so-called "British society" with Austin. In their minds he was a fact-finding, trouble-making crank, one of those whose missions of "Enlightenment" made it so difficult for the governing classes to govern. It put me beyond the social pale.

'And then . . .' Now Rosemary's voice faltered and she turned her head away from Blake's penetrating gaze. 'Then I discovered something else. I discovered I was going to have a baby. Austin's baby. It had, of course, happened that night in the old lady's house.'

Suddenly she was crying again, burying her head in her hands, sobbing so that her shoulders heaved convulsively. And these tears were different; they were tears of mental and physical agony as well as guilt.

Blake's hand closed reassuringly over her own. All his anger and condemnation of her fused into compassion. He said:

'Don't tell me if you don't want to.'

'I do,' she said. 'I must! I've never told it to anybody else. Perhaps it will help—if it's not too late.'

Penniless, ostracised, unwanted by the people of her own kind and her own country, she had not known where to turn. In the end she had obtained a job as waitress in a second-rate hotel, where a small back room compensated for most of her wages. During her spare time—and there was little enough of that—she did sewing.

'I was always good at needlework,' she said. 'And even if some of the women didn't want to recognise me socially, they didn't mind employing me as cheap labour. Even a Chinese coolie wouldn't have worked for what they paid *me*. But I had to have it. I had to have every penny I could lay my hands on— for the baby.'

She turned suddenly and glared into Blake's face. 'I suppose you're wondering why I didn't get rid of it?' she demanded. 'Well, believe me or not, just as you like, the idea never occurred to me. Never. I wanted my baby, not because it was his, or even if it had been Adrian's—but because it was mine. It belonged to *me*. It was something I could love and who would love me in return. I would work for it until my fingers fell off.

'Well, I had my baby. A girl. I got to the hospital just in time—I was up all night, putting the finishing touches to some old dowager's party-dress—and I only just made it. She was lovely—exquisite; the prettiest baby in the hospital they said. Afterwards the manager of the hotel let me have my job back— and my room. He was the only really *good* man I've ever known. The only man who didn't try to make me.' She gave a short, bitter laugh.

'And the baby?' asked Blake gently.

'She died. Oh, not straight away; perhaps I could have borne it better if she'd died before I really got to love her so much. Before she came to mean everything in the world to me. No, she was two years old when it happened—toddling around, beginning to ask questions. She was in and out of everything like quicksilver. That was how she got hold of the bottle of disinfectant——'

'Disinfectant?' repeated Blake, hollowly.

200

'That's right. She followed me into the kitchen where I was doing the washing-up. And when my back was turned for a minute she found this bottle—pushed into a cupboard. It was carbolic, used to wash down the yard and the drains.'

Blake did not speak. He moved his hand from Rosemary's and placed his arm across her shoulders. He knew there were no words which could bring her comfort.

She was silent for a long time, then she said. 'It was my fault. I'd put the bottle there. I'd put it there and forgotten about it. And she found it. I rushed with her to the hospital, holding her in my arms, but it was too late. There was nothing they could do for her. She died . . . and it was *my* fault.'

'It was an accident,' murmured Blake. 'You mustn't blame yourself——'

'I killed her,' said Rosemary, and her voice was suddenly ice-hard. There were no tears in her eyes now. 'She died because of me. And after that I didn't care any more—not about anything. I didn't care whether I lived or died.' She looked at him. 'I don't have to tell you the rest, do I?' she asked.

'No,' said Blake, quietly.

'First it was drink—and then men. Then it was drink *and* men. Sooner or later one or the other will kill me—and I don't particularly care which.'

Suddenly, almost violently, she wrenched herself away from him and swayed across the room. She grabbed a bottle from where it stood on a rickety table and wrenched off the cork. Blake saw that it was almost full.

He got up and moved swiftly after her. But he was not quick enough to stop her lifting the bottle to her mouth and gulping greedily, recklessly, at the contents. When he pulled the bottle away from her, so forcibly that some of the liquid spilled down the front of her robe, he saw that she had swallowed at least half of what it had held.

'Snap out of it!' he said, and now his voice was purposely harsh. 'You haven't finished telling me——'

'There's nothing more to tell,' she hiccoughed.

'Nigel——'

'To hell with Nigel! T' hell with all men! T' hell with *you*——!'

She swung a blow at him with outstretched arm and as it missed she lost her balance and toppled forward. Blake caught her as she fell. Her face was suffused and her blue eyes glazed and unfocused. Through her parted lips her breath came in little puffs.

'Damn all men . . .' she muttered. 'You and Nigel and Maitland and Mawgan—damn 'em all. . . .'

Blake lifted her up bodily and carried her across the room to the disordered bed. She was senseless, unheeding, uncaring, before her head touched the pillow.

CHAPTER ELEVEN

Blake left her then. He left the sleazy tenement and went out into the cool night air of the native quarter. He hailed a taxi and told the driver to take him to the police *thana* in Bentinck Street.

The Anglo-Indian sergeant on duty greeted him without enthusiasm when he revealed the purpose of his visit.

'We have records, certainly we have, but this "big, bald Indian" you saw leaving the Medwin woman's room—it could be any one of a hundred answering to the same description.'

'You have photographs, haven't you?' Blake insisted.

'We have. But it will take hours to——'

'Just let me see the files,' Blake said. 'I'll do the rest myself.'

The sergeant brightened visibly then and led the detective into an adjoining room. He left Blake alone with the files and returned to his office. Fifteen minutes later—it took no longer—Blake had the photograph of the man he was looking for.

The name of the bald man he had seen coming out of Rosemary Medwin's room was Chandra Sen. And underneath the square reserved for fingerprints was written: *Believed connected with proscribed political group. Cf Indian Office Publication 'Internal Security—Calcutta GS/436/Sec, 1940.'*

The publication, thought Blake, could wait. He was now satisfied that Rosemary's visitor was one of Mahdu Nath's lieutenants.

He left the police *thana*, and hailed another taxi. He ordered it to take him back to Rosemary Medwin's apartment. He hoped that by this time she might be in better condition to finish her story—at least in so far as it dealt with Nigel and how she had come to meet him.

He felt tremendously sorry for the woman. Life had given her a raw deal, which had culminated tragically in the death of her child. If the baby had lived, Blake thought, Rosemary might have succeeded in struggling free of her unhappy environment; she might even have managed to return to England

and start a new life there for herself and Carol. But since the child's death it was obvious she had not cared what happened to her. She lived as best she could, obsessed with guilt, numbed with grief, frequently and gratefully stupefied with drink. The only money she had now was the money she took from the men who came to her bed.

But now Rosemary had to tell him what he wanted to know. She *had* to. There was so little time left.

He reached the tenement block, paid off the taxi and once more climbed the slippery, dirty steps. There was the usual huddle of scabrous beggars and sore-eyed children standing around the entrance. Blake climbed the last few steps over the body of a sprawling drunk and knocked on the door of Rosemary's room.

He knocked again, but there was no reply. He had not really expected one. He sighed, wondering how long it was going to take him to rouse Rosemary into some semblance of soberness and elicit from her the information he wanted.

He put his hand to the knob and turned it. To his surprise the door was locked. Apparently Rosemary had recovered during his absence to the extent of crossing the room and locking her door. He wondered why.

Then a thought struck him and his face paled. He remembered her state of mind while she was talking to him—her tears, the anguish in her voice as she spoke of all the things which had led to her downfall. She had been depressed, strung almost to breaking-point, and the flood-gates of her grief had been released anew when she spoke of the death of her little girl. Had she, during those dreadful moments of struggling back to consciousness from her drunken stupor and finding Blake gone, taken that final, irrevocable step? Had she, in fact, found the courage and desperation to kill herself?

Blake hesitated no longer. He lifted his right foot and sent it crashing against the door. But the wood was thicker than he had thought. He took two swift paces back and then launched himself forward, and his shoulder struck the panels with all the force he could muster. He hit the door and the wood splintered beneath the jolting impact. The next instant Blake was inside the room.

The room was in darkness, save for the moonlight filtering in through the uncurtained window. But Blake's keen nostrils caught the smell of a lamp which had been hurriedly extinguished, and he breathed a sigh of relief. That lamp could not have been blown out more than a half-minute earlier.

He stood in the darkened room and called her name:

'Rosemary? Are you there——'

There was a faint movement from the corner of the room. Blake turned and in that instant two dark shapes leapt at him simultaneously. He was borne back beneath their weight and as he instinctively twisted to one side he caught the downward flashing gleam of a knife.

He had not time to reach for his Luger. As the first shape, carried forward by the impetus of its own movement, stumbled past Blake into the wall, the second man closed with Blake. His arms gripped the detective in a bear-like hug, one arm around his chest, the other across Blake's throat. He hung on, pulling Blake backwards, trying to pull him down.

Blake stood quite still, took a deep breath, and then suddenly stooped. The figure gasped, lost its hold, and went flying over Blake's back. Before the man could recover, Blake launched himself forward and his foot crashed savagely into the other's ribs. The man gasped and fell back, winded.

Blake whirled to meet the rush of the first attacker once more, and this time the knife, ripping downward, cut through the shoulder of Blake's jacket. He reached up and grasped the man's wrist with his left hand, while his clenched right fist thudded into the man's chest. Back and forth across the disordered room they wrestled, and all the time they struggled Blake was putting his full weight upon the hand that held the knife. He wrenched and twisted, his grip like steel around his opponent's wrist.

Suddenly, with a yell, the man opened his fingers and the knife dropped to the floor. Blake's foot caught it and sent it skidding across the room. Then he turned to tackle his adversary once more. His clenched fist took the man squarely beneath the chin and he staggered back, striking against the wall. Then, shaking his head like an enraged bull, he hurled himself forward and his fingers clawed for Blake's throat.

Blake dodged him easily. Again he struck out and this time he turned his hand so that the blow descended, karate-wise. It was aimed for the man's neck and if it had fallen there it would have killed him. But the man dodged just in time and the deadly blow caught him across his shoulder. There was the dull sound of snapping bone and the man, with a yell of agony, fell to the floor.

He slithered between Blake's legs, scrambled to his feet, lurched towards the door and disappeared down the stairs, his shoes clattering on the stone steps. Halfway down he apparently saw the drunk—but too late. There was another yell, a wild flurry of activity, and the noise of two bodies hurtling clumsily down the steps to the hall below.

The other man was just getting to his feet as Blake turned back into the room. He saw his companion dive towards the door and decided that one against one was disproportionately unfair. As Blake moved towards him he aimed a wild blow at the detective's head, skidded past him and rushed for the open doorway. He went through it like a bullet from a gun and when Blake ran out to the head of the stairs he was just in time to see both men scuttle through the street door and disappear outside.

He wondered why Rosemary had not called out during the brief fight, and a sudden uneasiness filled him. He found the lamp and lit it, turning the wick up high so that the yellow light played around the room. As he raised the lamp above his head he saw Rosemary's figure outlined in the open doorway which divided the room from another, smaller one.

She was standing quite still, her face turned towards him, and in the smoky light from the lamp he saw it only dimly. She was a shadow among shadows.

'Rosemary?' said Blake again.

Still she did not reply. He put the lamp down upon a table and moved towards her. Then she turned, but without speaking, so that her face was half-averted from him and he could see her profile etched against the grimy white wall behind her.

Then, joltingly, with a sudden terrible, violent contraction of his heart, Blake knew the reason for her silence.

* * *

Rosemary Medwin was not standing in the shadowed doorway between the two rooms. She was hanging there. Hanging, and gently gyrating, on a hair-thin steel piano wire which had momentarily caught the light as she moved. Blake saw it gleam and for a moment he hadn't known what it was. But he knew now, and jumped forward. His hands went out instinctively towards her—and then recoiled.

She was beyond all help. She was dead, and death had come as a friend. She had been gagged, and beneath her thin dressing-gown her skin was bruised, splotched with purplish-yellow stains. A knife had been used upon her—and it had been used while she was still alive. She had almost bitten through the gag and her eyes were terrible to see.

After that she had been hanged. Hanged on a piano-wire.

Blake swung round and plunged for the door. The police would have to be called—immediately, before he could touch her.

Then he saw the telephone. It seemed to strike an incongruous note in that cheap, untidy room. It was standing on the floor, half-covered by a dropped cushion, and as he moved towards it Blake wondered why—if there was a telephone—there had been no electric light. He looked up at the ceiling and saw the remains of a smashed bulb hanging from the gently-swaying pendant. Beneath it, on the floor, was one of Rosemary's shoes. During the struggle which must have taken place between her and her murderers, she had hurled it at them in a last futile, frantic gesture. She had missed and hit the swinging light bulb.

What they had done then they had done in the smoking yellow light of an oil-lamp.

Blake shivered and just as his hand reached out towards the telephone it began to ring.

He lifted the receiver then, slowly. He didn't speak. He waited. And whoever it was who was calling didn't speak, either. For a long four seconds there was no sound on the line save that of faint breathing.

Then the four seconds passed and without a word spoken Blake heard a sharp click. The other receiver had been replaced. Tautly, Blake called the operator.

He asked a sharp question and, after a few minutes, received an answer. The telephone exchange was manually operated and calls could be traced. He had traced this one.

A frown formed between his eyes.   didn't touch the telephone again.

He had intended to call the police, but they would have to wait. He blew out the lamp and went out of the room, closing the door behind him. He couldn't lock it, but it stayed shut.

The body of Rosemary Medwin hung in the grey light which filled the room, moving silently in a grim *danse macabre* as the draught from the open window struck her.

Blake went down the stairs two at a time. He was a man in a hurry. The last few minutes had answered one of the questions already in his mind. Now he could be certain that Rosemary Medwin had possessed dangerous knowledge. She could have helped him, and he could have saved her life, if only Maitland hadn't intervened; if only he had been able to make her talk sooner.

Instead, she had been killed to ensure her silence, and in place of the one question answered, others now came crowding into Blake's mind.

Who had killed her? Or rather, who had caused her to be killed? For Blake sensed that the men who had actually murdered her—the men he had disturbed within minutes of finishing their grisly work—were merely paid hirelings, sent to do the job. The man who wanted her dead would not have risked being seen or caught.

Had it been the bald Indian whom Blake had seen on the stairs? Blake remembered the look in his eyes as he came face to face with the detective—as though he'd seen a ghost. Perhaps he'd thought he had!

Perhaps he had had a hand in killing Nigel. Blake knew that he looked sufficiently like his brother to confuse and frighten a man drunk on palm-toddy. Had the big, bald man sent the two thugs to kill Rosemary? If he had done so, and if he had had a hand in Nigel's murder, then he must be one of Mahdu Nath's principal lieutenants. He had acted on Nath's orders.

He had to be found. Where was he? The killing of Rosemary, following so closely upon his departure from the room and his meeting with Blake, had not been coincidental.

There was another question which demanded an urgent answer. That silent, four-second telephone call. Who had made it—and why? And why had the caller remained silent?

Blake could think of a reason. It could have been the bald man calling—checking up on his victim—trying to discover if his killers had done their work. Or perhaps the caller had been Nath himself, also checking up.

Both thoughts were equally disturbing, for this reason. Blake knew where the phone-call had come from.

Mahdu Nath was a shadowy shape, an organiser of insurrection, and no one knew what 'cover' he might employ to cloak his real activities. No one save those around him knew what he looked like. Blake certainly didn't. All he knew was what Craille had been able to tell him.

But now a new suspicion formed in his mind. For the silent, four-second phone call had been made from the Bentinck Street *thana*—Inspector Mawgan's station. That was what the telephone operator had told him.

CHAPTER TWELVE

When Blake went out of the room and down the slippery, betel-stained steps, he found the tenement entrance strangely deserted. Not a beggar remained in sight. Either the noise of the fight had frightened them away or—like animals—they had sensèd trouble and removed themselves temporarily from the scene.

But Blake was not going to give up easily. He went in search of the chuprassi again, whom he found lurking in his little office. He said, bluntly:

'Two men came running down the stairs a few minutes ago. Who were they? Did you recognise them?'

The chuprassi shook his head. 'I saw nobody,' he said. 'I was here, in my office.'

'But you heard shots?'

'No, sahib. There is always so much noise—shouting, screaming, quarrelling, cars back-firing. . . .'

Blake could have struck him. Instead he said, curbing his anger: 'What about the man who left here just after my first visit? You must have seen him—a big, bald-headed man. Do you know him? Has he been here before?'

The chuprassi's eyes flickered. 'What man, sahib? So many come and go.'

Blake said impatiently: 'I told you. A big man—bald. An Indian. Wearing European clothes, striped suit, checked shirt, a gaudy tie——'

The chuprassi was shaking his head. 'I saw no such man, sahib!'

'But you must have seen him. You must have seen him both coming in and going out. He was leaving Miss Medwin's room, just as I got there. He came down these stairs——'

'No, sahib,' the chuprassi said, shaking his head again, and his crafty ferret's face seemed to have grown more sharply pointed and sly than ever. 'The sahib must be mistaken. I saw no such man.'

He was lying. Of course he was lying! Blake stared at him

stonily, controlling his mounting anger with difficulty. Outwardly he was cold and calm; inwardly he raged. The watchman had obviously been bribed to see nothing, hear nothing—and say nothing. Blake wanted to reach forward and shake the truth out of him, but there was no time for that now, and he knew it.

Later there would be time, and he promised himself that he would do it, and more, if he had to. But for the moment he contented himself with saying harshly:

'Don't think you're deceiving me—don't think it for one moment. You'd be a fool if you did.' And so much of his fury showed in his eyes that the chuprassi quailed and took a nervous step backwards. But he still kept on shaking his head.

Blake said, with deadly emphasis: 'Listen to me. Nobody is to go up to Miss Medwin's room, do you understand? Nobody. Neither you nor anybody else, until I return. Is that clear? If you disobey me, I promise it will be the worse for you.'

The chuprassi believed him. This time he nodded.

Blake turned on his heel. He went on down the hall and out into the night. He walked until he saw a cruising taxi.

Mawgan now, he thought.

Inspector Mawgan was there to meet him. Fat, paunchy, olive-skinned and effusive, the police inspector rose from behind his desk.

'Good to see you again. Did you find out anything about the Medwin woman?'

Blake eyed him narrowly. What he had to say in the next few moments would, he thought, wipe that welcoming smile clean off the inspector's face.

He came out with it bluntly—and he was right. 'I found out one thing,' he said. 'Rosemary Medwin has been murdered.'

'What——?'

Mawgan looked staggered; completely bowled over. But Blake still watched him closely. Surprise was easy to feign.

So when Blake spoke again it was in a cynically disbelieving voice, probably for a reaction. 'Then it's news to you, Inspector?'

Mawgan gaped at him—but only for a moment. Then furious colour flooded his face.

'Of course it's news! What the hell do you mean, man? How was she killed? Where?'

'She was hanged,' said Blake. 'Hanged on a piano wire in the apartment she took only a few hours ago in the hope that you wouldn't be able to find her again in a hurry—that you'd leave her alone. But that was a vain hope, wasn't it? Of course, you traced her——'

Mawgan burst out: 'So you think *I* killed her? You're out of your mind! Why on earth would I want to kill her?'

'I can guess why she was killed,' Blake said slowly. 'She knew too much about my brother's murder, and maybe she knew the true identity of a man who calls himself Mahdu Nath.'

Mawgan faced him.

'If Rosemary Medwin was killed because she knew too much, you're insane to suspect me. Didn't I try every trick I knew to get the truth out of her?'

His voice was shrill.

'Question for question,' Blake said quietly. 'You *did* succeed in tracing her after I left here, didn't you? You found out where she'd gone?'

'All right, so I found out. But——'

'There's still another question,' Blake interrupted, and now he was leaping straight out into the dark. 'Why did you spend four seconds on the telephone to her not more than a quarter of an hour ago? Four long seconds in which you never said a word! Why? What was the reason? Tell me, Inspector—if you really have got nothing to hide.'

It was a challenge.

Mawgan looked at him. 'You were there?'

Blake nodded. 'I was there, and Rosemary Medwin was dead. I picked up the telephone——'

'Then it was you——'

'Yes,' Blake said roughly. 'Of course it was me. Now stop stalling and tell me.'

The inspector sighed. He said heavily: 'You'll never believe this . . .'

'Try me,' said Blake.

'I'd find it hard to believe myself, if it was thrown at me.'

'I don't know what you're talking about,' Blake said. 'Supposing you tell me.'

Mawgan sighed again. He said: 'I rang Rosemary Medwin's number to begin putting on the pressure again. I wasn't going to give up. I was convinced she knew more than she was telling, and I was determined to make her crack. I heard the receiver lifted at the other end of the line and I thought it was her, naturally. But she didn't speak. I waited—was it really only four seconds?—but still she didn't say anything. So I didn't speak either. I couldn't—don't you see? I had to put the phone back. If it had been Rosemary there, and I'd spoken before she did, I . . .' His voice tailed off: 'It's hard to explain.'

'Terror tactics,' Blake said. 'That just about describes it, doesn't it? And if you'd spoken first you'd have robbed the call of its impact.'

'Yes.'

'And what made you think I wouldn't believe it?' Blake asked.

Mawgan looked at him quickly. 'Oh, it's not that I thought you'd find it hard to believe——'

'What, then?'

'The real reason I made that call was——'

'I thought you'd told me.'

'The *real* reason,' Mawgan insisted. 'The reason I didn't find her hard to trace whenever she moved "to get away from me" as you put it——'

'I'm afraid I don't follow you,' said Blake, frowning.

'It was Rosemary Medwin herself,' said Mawgan flatly. 'I've thought it all out, and now I know. She asked for everything she got. Consciously or subconsciously she made it all happen.'

Blake was frankly incredulous. 'Maitland hinted at the way you treated her.'

'I tell you, she asked for it,' said Mawgan roughly. 'Some women invite violence. They're made for it. They're not complete without it.' His tongue flicked out over his moist, red lips.

Blake said drily: 'She didn't ask to be murdered, did she? And even if what you say about her is true, that doesn't excuse your conduct.'

'No, but ...' The tongue flicked out over the lips again. It was like the darting tongue of a snake. Mawgan went on: 'I suppose I couldn't help myself. The life she led; everybody knew the kind of woman she was. It ... it inflamed me. A white woman! As British as you or me!'

Mawgan's voice had risen. 'Every time I saw her, it was like a red rag to a bull. In my mind's eye I saw other men——'

'Other men?' Blake echoed abruptly and his words cut short the inspector's tirade. Mawgan looked away from him.

Blake said: 'In actual fact you wanted her yourself, didn't you?'

'She'd sleep with anybody!' said Mawgan fiercely. 'Anybody with a few rupees in his pocket. ...'

'But never with you,' Blake said softly. 'That was the trouble, wasn't it?'

CHAPTER THIRTEEN

Fifteen minutes later Blake was back at the sleazy tenement where Rosemary Medwin had met her death, and Mawgan was with him.

The first thing Mawgan did was corner the chuprassi and haul him forth. He did what Blake had done—questioned him about the bald man and the two others who had been in the apartment when Blake arrived a second time—and he got the same result. He got nothing.

'Right!' he said shortly. 'Now let's go upstairs, shall we? Maybe you'll see something that will make you sing a different tune.'

He stepped in front of Blake and grabbed the man's arm, ignoring Blake's attempts to stop him. 'Let me handle this my way, if you don't mind,' he said, and his tone was pugnacious.

He dragged the man, frightened and protesting, up the stone stairs and opened the door of the woman's room. Blake stepped past him, groped for the lamp, and lit it once more. The bright yellow flame gushed up, revealing the hanging shape of Rosemary Medwin.

The man screamed. He screamed in a long, shrill whine, like a trapped rabbit. But for Mawgan's restraining hand he would have turned and bolted. He was not only horrified—he was terrified.

Showing him the body had been a cardinal psychological error on Mawgan's part, Blake thought grimly. Now the chuprassi would admit to nothing. He would lie his head off rather than get involved in murder.

And Blake was right. In spite of threats, bribes and even an uncontrollable slap across the face from the inspector's hand, the watchman refused to talk. He had seen nothing, he said. Nothing at all. Neither the bald-headed visitor nor the two men Blake claimed had run from the room and out into the street. Blake knew the reason for his continued silence—fear that he himself would meet the same end if he opened his mouth.

Mawgan couldn't have made a bigger tactical mistake, Blake thought. Or had it been a mistake? Every one of his earlier doubts returned as he found himself wondering whether Mawgan's action in dragging the watchman into the room had been deliberately planned to intimidate him into silence.

Something had to be done to make the chuprassi talk. But what? And who could do it?

Someone had to gain the man's confidence, persuade him that he could tell what he knew without fear. Could Blake himself do it? Hardly. Not now. In the chuprassi's mind he must for ever be labelled 'dangerous', along with Inspector Mawgan.

It was then he thought of Craille's friend, the Member of Congress he had met at Nigel's funeral. Sohan Dutt. Dutt had helped in the past, Craille had told him. He was a reliable man for all his Nationalist and mildly anti-British leanings.

Blake had his card and his telephone number, and a vague promise to help again. He left Mawgan still shouting abuse at the cowering chuprassi—and rang Sohan Dutt's number.

* * *

Sohan Dutt was not very enthusiastic—until he heard about Mawgan's treatment of the chuprassi. Then he came quickly.

Blake met him in the hall of the tenement block and told him the whole story. He told him what had happened and what he wanted Dutt to do.

Dutt listened grimly. He stood erect and stiff with indignation at Mawgan's behaviour as Blake's story unfolded. He had left his slick, trick smile behind him. It was nowhere in evidence now. And as Blake explained how it had been Mawgan's idea to confront the already frightened chuprassi with the sight of Rosemary Medwin's dangling corpse, his eyes narrowed into a frown.

'But why?' he asked, searching Blake's face with his dark eyes. 'Surely as a trained police officer he must know better than that? Indians are an introspective people. Their reaction to that kind of shock is not the same as a Westerner's. It was the worst thing he could have done.'

Blake nodded.

Dutt was thoughtful. 'When the milk is spilt there is no use to weep. . . . You wish that I should talk to the chuprassi?'

'There may still be a chance,' said Blake. 'But it depends on persuading this man that he has nothing to be afraid of.'

'Very well,' Dutt agreed. 'But before we go may I make a suggestion?'

'Of course.'

'I think you should send away the police inspector. The chuprassi is unlikely to talk with him still there.'

Blake nodded agreement and led the way up the dirty stone steps to the third floor. Even before they reached the room, the sound of Inspector Mawgan's voice, high-pitched and angry, reached them on the landing. The chuprassi was still being questioned.

Sohan Dutt frowned as they reached the door, but as Blake opened it, all thoughts of the police inspector were thrust from his mind. His gaze went towards the bed, to the still shape beneath the sheet. He stepped into the room and over to the bed, lifting the sheet from Rosemary's face. Horror and revulsion filled the delicate outlines of his smooth, dark face.

Blake and the Inspector had taken down the woman's body. They had removed the wire from about her neck and Blake had gently straightened the stiffening limbs and folded her hands across her breast. But nothing could hide the swollen, turgid face, the protruding eyes, the tongue thrust between the blackened lips.

For a moment Blake thought Dutt was going to be sick. But with a visible effort the politician took hold of himself and stepped inside the room. His nostrils quivered at the rank smell of palm toddy, then he looked around in silence, taking in the details of everything he saw, calmly, objectively, until his eyes came to rest at last upon Mawgan.

Mawgan was standing over a battered armchair in which the chuprassi sat cowering. He looked up with sullen anger as Blake and Dutt came in. The caretaker had obviously told him nothing.

Mawgan stared at Sohan Dutt and then at Blake. His eyes were demanding an explanation. Blake did not give it to him.

'We're going to need fingerprints,' he said. 'And photographs. Have you sent for your Murder Squad?'

'I'll do it now,' Mawgan said brusquely and stepped towards the telephone.

'No!' Blake's voice stopped him in his tracks. 'Phone calls are too easy to intercept. There's no point in laying ourselves open. You'd better go back to the police station yourself.'

Mawgan shrugged and picked up his hat. He glanced to the chuprassi before leaving.

'He won't tell you anything. He needs a couple of nights in the cell to make him remember—preferably with the corpse.'

With that parting shot the policeman left.

Blake glanced at Sohan Dutt and pulled up two chairs. They sat down and Blake gave the chuprassi a cigarette. He allowed him to take two or three deep breaths and then, with his eyes still fixed on the caretaker, Blake spoke to Dutt.

'Ask him what—and who—he's afraid of.'

Sohan Dutt did so. He spoke Hindi with a soft accent. He spoke quietly, persuasively, and with a gentle cajoling manner. The chuprassi relaxed and as soon as he spoke Blake realised that Dutt had won his confidence.

Dutt translated his reply. 'He says he's frightened of the police inspector. He's frightened of what has happened and he doesn't understand what is going on. I think he is frightened mainly because he is confused.'

Blake nodded. 'Now ask him if he remembers my coming here this evening—the first time.'

Dutt did so and translated. 'He says yes. About two hours ago. Then you went away and came back.'

Sohan Dutt put a series of questions and translated the answers back to Blake, who listened carefully.

The chuprassi remembered several people coming in and out. One of them might have been the bald man whom Blake had spoken of, but he wasn't sure. He had seen and heard nothing of the two men who had run from the room and down the stairs after Blake's second visit. He had been going into his office when he saw Blake go upstairs, and he had seen and heard nothing.

'What about the noise of the fight?' asked Blake. 'It seems

218

strange he did not hear that. Everyone else seems to have done —the hall was empty when I came down.'

The chuprassi's reply, through Sohan Dutt, was that when he was in his office he could hear nothing. It was practically sound-proof. If he had heard the noise he would have come out, naturally.

'I believe he is telling the truth, Mr Blake,' said Sohan Dutt.

Blake was forced to accept his summing-up, although he did so with mental reservations. He said:

'Ask him if he remembers anything strange which happened that evening. Anything which might have been connected with the murder of Rosemary Medwin.'

Dutt spoke again and this time there followed a long exchange of questions and answers. Then Dutt turned to Blake with a look of thoughtful interest.

'He says that Miss Medwin moved into the apartment early this afternoon. He helped her up with a few of her things. A short time afterwards two military policemen came. They shouldered their way in and went up to the third floor—this floor—and stayed about a quarter of an hour. Then they went away again.'

'Military policemen!' exclaimed Blake. 'Ask him what they looked like—their description.'

Dutt eyed Blake with a level glance. 'I've already asked him. Their description corresponds exactly with the two military police whom Mr Craille spoke of earlier today—the two who picked up Miss Caroline Perkins at her flat in Alipore.'

Blake leaned back in his chair and was silent for several minutes. He was very thoughtful. His eyes were narrowed into a frown of concentration as he considered the picture which was now forming in his mind.

Sohan Dutt said: 'I think, Mr Blake, that there is one reservation to be borne in mind. I hope you will forgive me for saying this, but I am familiar with many of the activities of the British military police in India, and I know that it is not uncommon for women such as Miss Medwin to have ... er, friends among them. There might have been a quite innocent reason for two of them to visit her.' He added: 'Or at any rate, a *comparatively* innocent reason.'

'You mean, they might have been visiting her in her—shall we say professional—capacity?'

'It has been done,' said Dutt apologetically. 'There have been at least two notable Courts Martial. . . .' He paused, then added: 'On the other hand, it is also possible that they were somewhat unkindly received by Miss Medwin and later returned, possibly somewhat the worse for liquor, and . . .' He looked at Blake significantly.

'You think they may have been the two men who killed Miss Medwin?'

'Is it not possible?'

Blake said nothing. He got up and began looking around the room.

The furniture was cheap and shoddy. It was no more than the kind of furniture one might have expected to find in such a place. A plywood chest stood in one corner and next to it a dressing-table. Striding over to it, Blake rummaged swiftly through the drawers. A few clothes were all it contained. Blake was looking for something else.

He went into the adjoining room and Sohan Dutt followed. It was a sitting-room and kitchen combined, and was equipped with the same poor quality furniture as the other room. A tray of unwashed cups and saucers stood on a small table in the centre of the floor.

Blake's eyes wandered to a painted sideboard in the corner of the room. He saw what he was looking-for. It was a sandal-wood box exquisitely carved by some nameless Indian crafts-man. It stood out immediately against the other contents of the room.

This box, Blake thought, could contain those of Rosemary's few possessions which she had kept and valued. Letters, memen-toes, photographs, souvenirs—sentimental objects, however few.

He was right.

A bundle of letters met his gaze as he lifted the lid. They were tied together with a piece of blue ribbon. All of them were written in the same firm handwriting which Blake guessed was that of the young Army officer, Adrian.

Underneath the letters were a few photographs. One was of an elderly woman, three were photographs of a small, curly-haired child. Underneath these was Rosemary Medwin's passport, some picture postcards of Calcutta and finally, two more snapshots.

The first was of Rose and Caroline Perkins, taken together in the *Maidan*, Calcutta's main park.

The second sent a sharp stab of recognition through Blake as he gazed at the familiar features of his brother, Nigel.

It was a recent photograph, taken in a club. Blake assumed it was a club. The photograph merely showed Nigel Blake and Caroline Perkins sitting at a table in a corner which was decorated with tropical ferns and palms. Two glasses and an ashtray were on the white tablecloth in front of them.

Blake showed the two snapshopts to Sohan Dutt. The politician clicked his tongue sadly at the photograph of Nigel Blake.

'Miss Medwin must have known them both, then,' he said with a look of enquiry.

Blake nodded. 'I was hoping we would find a lead to some of her other friends. There must be someone, *somewhere* in Calcutta, who can tell us where Caroline Perkins is.'

'She is not at her flat, then?' asked Dutt.

'No,' said Blake. 'I called there before I came to see Rosemary the first time. She hasn't been back.'

Dutt made no reply to this. He had heard the sound of feet approaching on the landing. He followed Blake back into the other room as the outer door opened and Inspector Mawgan entered, followed by a small retinue of policemen.

Mawgan barely acknowledged the presence of Blake and Sohan Dutt. Instead he began ordering a detailed and systematic analysis of everything in the room. Flashbulbs began to explode as a police photographer went to work. Fingerprints men began dusting the furniture with fine brushes. Mawgan gave orders and made notes.

It was routine police work. None of it would answer the questions which were uppermost in Blake's mind. He had pressing business to attend to elsewhere.

He threw a last compassionate glance towards the sheeted figure on the divan. Poor Rosemary. Well, at least her troubles were over and if death had come more kindly to her it might have been welcome.

Blake thanked Sohan Dutt for his help and left. In his pocket he took with him the photograph of his brother and Caroline Perkins. It was his one solitary lead.

Could the snapshot be made to yield a clue to the Anglo-Indian girl's whereabouts?

CHAPTER FOURTEEN

Six minutes later Blake was crossing the Kidderpore bridge in a taxi. He had left behind the narrow streets of the native quarter and was driving towards the mansion block in Park Street where Craille had his apartment.

Within the next quarter of an hour Blake hoped to have the answer to at least one question.

It was exactly ten-thirty when he stepped out of the lift on to the deep, luxurious carpet of the penthouse at the top of the mansion block. Craille's secretary had gone off duty and Blake went in.

Craille was standing in the middle of the room, and the air was foul with the scent of the Egyptian cigarettes. He did not seem surprised to see Blake.

'Retreats!' he greeted the detective, without any preliminary welcome. 'Withdrawals everywhere!' He stabbed the map of Burma with a vigour which dislodged three of the small flags which represented British Army formations. Blake noted grimly the change in position of the Japanese flags since the last time he had seen Craille—only a few hours before.

'The casualties are getting heavier,' said the old man dourly. 'Heavier casualties every hour and reports of retreat coming in like clockwork.'

He strode over to his secretary's table and unwrapped a packet of sandwiches which stood on a plate. He unscrewed the cap of a large, chrome thermos flask.

'Coffee?'

Blake shook his head. 'I'm looking for a magic lantern.'

Craille raised one eyebrow and looked at Blake over the thermos flask as he poured the hot liquid into a cup. 'A magic what?'

'Lantern,' repeated Blake. 'Or an epidiascope. A camera will do—or a microscope—any kind of optical equipment. You used to have a set of lenses in London, at your office. Did you bring them out here with you?'

For just a fraction of a moment Craille looked almost surprised. Then he said, with a cool edge of dignity: 'It just so happens that I did.'

Blake caught the faintest suggestion of a smile on the old man's face as he put down the thermos and went into the adjoining room. The smile told him that he had succeeded in dispelling Craille's gloom. He had aroused the old man's curiosity.

Craille came back with a square leather box. It was lined with crimson velvet and contained an unusual variety of lenses and coloured filters. They were all mounted on a standard-sized flange—hand-made to Craille's own specifications.

Blake had never been told what they were for, but he guessed that Craille used them for reading microfilm and secret inks.

The detective went to work deftly and in a few minutes had assembled, with the use of an old shoe-box and Craille's desk-lamp, a makeshift projector which threw a beam of light on one wall of the room.

When it was ready Blake crossed the carpet and snapped off the light. He returned to the desk and slipped something from his pocket into a slot prepared in the box.

The wall opposite the desk suddenly jumped to life with a larger-than-life-sized picture.

Magnified to sixty times its original size, the snapshot of Nigel Blake and Caroline Perkins was reproduced with startling clarity.

'Where did you get it?' Craille wanted to know. But Blake was already striding across the room through the beam of light.

'It was taken in a club,' he explained quickly. 'A club somewhere in Calcutta—and in a moment I might be able to tell you which one.'

He gazed closely at the table which filled the foreground of the picture.

'There!' he exclaimed, as Craille joined him. 'On the ashtray. The South East Asia Club.'

He strode to the door and snapped on the main light again. 'Nigel was always one for having a regular haunt,' he said. 'If he went to that club once he must have been there scores of times—and Caroline with him. It means that we now know where to start looking for her friends. And once we get a lead on them, it's only a matter of time before we find out where she's hiding—and why!'

Blake left Craille's apartment with only the briefest explanation of what had happened during the evening. He made no mention of the help he had received from Sohan Dutt, nor did he tell Craille about the two military policemen described by the politician. There would be time for that later.

At the moment he was concentrating on one thing—getting to the South East Asia Club in time to catch the regular customers.

Ten minutes later, when his taxi pulled up outside the massive portals of the club, Blake realised that he need not have hurried. The South East Asia Club was one of those places which took no heed of the marches of Time. Age could not alter it, and neither could a World War.

It stood aloof from the rest of Calcutta, isolated in its own formidable dignity, as though it were a very bastion of the Empire itself. It was a place where everything had been done according to deep-rooted tradition. A place where it would have been unthinkable for any member to show his face on the premises before nightfall.

Blake allowed himself a smile as he reflected that the same British subjects who upheld this tradition in Calcutta, would do exactly the opposite the moment they set foot on the soil of the United Kingdom—and see nothing incongruous in their behaviour.

The interior of the club had a calm, reassuring atmosphere. It mattered not—the Victorian decor and furniture seemed to say—that the Japanese armies were only a few hundred miles away.

Blake went into the bar. It was empty except for the English barman—a small, bald man in his fifties, who might have been a butler in one of England's stately homes. He was polishing a set of brandy glasses with loving care.

Blake took a stool at the bar and ordered whisky. The barman poured out a measure expertly.

'Have you heard the war news this evening?' Blake asked

by way of striking up a conversation.

'Yes, sir. I usually make a point of listening in at ten o'clock,' the barman said deferentially. 'The bulletin said that heavy fighting is still being reported from the front, but otherwise there was little change.' He placed the glass on the counter in front of Blake.

For a fraction of a second as he looked the detective full in the face, he hesitated. Then immediately the brief reaction of uncertainty disappeared as he covered his slip with the smooth, non-committal reserve of his profession. He went back to polishing his glasses with calm, studied care.

Blake had to admire the man's self-control, for he knew in that brief instant that the barman, like several other people that day, had thought he had seen a ghost.

When the polishing was finished and the brandy glasses stood upturned and gleaming in a row along the shelf, Blake produced the snapshot of Nigel and Caroline. He handed it to the barman and asked if he recognised the couple. The barman studied it for several seconds.

'I noticed the resemblance,' he said. 'You must be a relative.' He looked up enquiringly. 'I was very sorry to read about the gentleman in the papers—I knew him very well. Only by sight, of course, but he came in here very often. . . .' He shook his head sadly.

'What about the girl?' Blake asked. 'Do you know her?'

'I've seen her in here quite a lot, sir. A very charming young lady she is. Always very gay. I'm afraid I don't recall her name, though.'

'I'm trying to find her,' Blake explained. 'Have you any idea where she lives—or where I can find out? It's very important.'

The barman thought for a moment.

'There I can't help you, I'm afraid, sir.' He shook his head slowly, then added as a sudden afterthought: 'But if I may venture a suggestion, sir—there's a gentleman called Mr Ainsworth who comes in here quite often. He's a journalist, and I think he knows the lady quite well.'

Blake was interested. 'A journalist? How can I get in touch with him? Do you know which paper he works for?'

'He works for a Fleet-street newspaper,' the barman explained. 'He's a War Correspondent. He should be coming in shortly.' He looked at the clock above the bar. 'Any minute now, sir.'

'He's a man of regular habits, then?'

'Very regular. One of our best customers.'

Blake ordered another drink and waited for the journalist to arrive. In the meantime he talked to the barman about the club and its members. It was one of the oldest clubs in Calcutta, he learned, and its clientele had once been exclusive.

Before the war it had been reserved wholly for the elite of Calcutta's European society—civil servants in the India service, senior officers of the British Army and Navy and their wives. The outbreak of war had swelled the club's membership with engineers, Americans, Allied Service chiefs and lower commissioned ranks. But apart from the rise in membership, life at the South East Asia Club went on much as before.

It was ten past eleven when the first customer arrived. He was a large, flabbily-built, perspiring Englishman in an off-white lightweight suit. He carried a briefcase under his arm and made immediately for a corner table with a proprietary air.

He dropped the briefcase on the table and threw himself into the corner amidst the palms. Without so much as glancing towards the bar he called out:

'Start 'em rolling, Charles—I'm ten minutes late already.'

He unzipped the briefcase, pulled out a sheaf of papers and began to study them, tapping on the table with a pencil.

The barman poured out the newcomer's order—a large whisky —and as he did so he leaned over to whisper to Blake:

'*That's* Mr Ainsworth, sir.'

Blake nodded his thanks and paid for his two drinks. He waited until the barman had delivered the whisky, then left his stool and walked across to Ainsworth's table.

CHAPTER FIFTEEN

Ainsworth glanced up in the act of taking his first drink. Then, as his eyes fastened on Blake, sheer incredulity showed in them. His whole florid face seemed to explode into his glass. He choked, the whisky splashing across the table as he leapt to his feet.

He had moved with surprising speed for a man of his bulk. One of his hands was raised as if to ward Blake off. Two pallid eyes bulged beneath his sweat-beaded brow. The colour had gone dramatically from his face.

Then, staring wildly, he realised his mistake. He groped for the table with a trembling hand to steady himself.

'For Pete's sake, man'—he got out—'you scared the living daylights out of me! I thought the DT's had started! I thought I was seeing things. I thought——'

'You thought I was Nigel Blake—my brother.'

Blake introduced himself. He nodded towards the spilt drink. 'Let me buy you another.'

Ainsworth shook his head. 'No, no, the privilege is mine.' He was still a little unsteady, but fast recovering from his shock. He sat down. He managed to quip: 'Any brother of Blake's is a brother of mine, old boy, in spirit at least—that is, if you *do* drink spirits.' He mopped his brow as Blake nodded. 'Two doubles, Charles.'

He thrust out his hand. 'My name's Cecil Ainsworth.'

Blake gripped the hand and then sat down. Ainsworth leaned forward, hesitating. When he spoke again it was with a sudden, unaccustomed sincerity which he seemed to find it difficult to voice.

'I knew your brother,' he said. He stopped. It was as though the four words would explain all his feelings about the savage and terrible way in which Nigel had died, as though Blake would understand immediately how great was the loss he had felt.

The drinks arrived. There was a short silence.

228

Then Ainsworth said quietly: 'It was grim. I saw the papers and it was bad enough. Then I realised that they had all got it wrong; that it wasn't you who had died—that it must be Nigel. I could hardly believe it. What a helluva way to go.'

He broke off. Another thought was moving in his mind. His hand groped for his glass. 'We used to drink together. We used to drink a lot. And he used to tell me things he couldn't tell other people.'

The journalist looked up to give Blake a half-apologetic glance, then went on: 'I suppose I'm one of the few people in Calcutta who knows that your brother wasn't as bad as he was made out to be. I know he fell into the category of the black sheep of the family. He told me. But he was certainly one black sheep who made good.'

Blake nodded.

'You'll get the man who did it,' Ainsworth added. It was a statement rather than a question, and Blake made no reply.

Ainsworth picked up his glass, toyed with it fleetingly, drained it, and set it down. 'I only wish I could help you.' Then he added, as a wry afterthought: 'Perhaps it's just as well that I can't. I'd make as big a shambles of *your* job as I make of my own—if not bigger. But in any case, I've got my time cut out coping with the Burma campaign.'

He gestured towards the papers on the table and quoted:

'—the yellow flood. British troops fight back through the jungle against overwhelming odds. Our forces bloody but unbowed——'

One of Blake's black eyebrows arched enquiringly. 'You write all that here in Calcutta?'

Ainsworth looked at him and then looked away again—quickly. He shrugged. He said tiredly: 'Why not—Calcutta gives me free access to cable facilities. And I can find out as much about what's going on in the jungle as any front-line correspondent. More, in fact.'

'You don't ever see the things you describe?'

Still Ainsworth refused to meet Blake's gaze. 'I prefer not to.' He fingered his empty glass and brooded over it. 'In any case, there's nothing to see up there. Nothing except the wounded and the dying—the beaten and the dead. In Calcutta I can sit back, use my imagination and cable home the kind of story everyone wants to read. Gallant rearguard actions— orderly withdrawals—shining acts of heroism.'

Abruptly, he thrust the papers aside and shrugged. He looked at Blake again. 'I suppose you look on me as something of a stinker?' he asked.

'It isn't my place to judge,' remarked Blake.

Ainsworth called out to the barman. 'Same again, Charles.'

'Yes, Mr Ainsworth.'

An Indian waiter had come on duty, appearing from beyond velvet curtains with the grace of a girl. The barman set the glasses on a tray for him. The Indian brought them to the table.

'Thanks, Singh.' Ainsworth dismissed him, adding to Blake, as he watched the Indian move sinuously back to the bar. 'He gives me the creeps.'

'What about your editor?' Blake returned to the subject they had been discussing. 'Does he know your despatches are written here in Calcutta?'

'If he does, it doesn't seem to worry him.' Ainsworth drained his glass and stood up. 'Excuse me.' He crossed to the bar and spoke quietly to the man behind it. He returned to the table with a full bottle of whisky, opened it and began to pour. 'I can't stand that waiter, Singh. This way we don't have to use him.' He looked pointedly at Blake's glass. 'Want a refill?'

'Not yet, thanks.'

Ainsworth sat down. He took down half of the amber liquid in his glass with a wry-faced gulp. 'If you want to know the truth,' he said, 'my editor actually thinks the world of me.'

'He does?'

'Yes.' Ainsworth spoke almost defiantly. He tossed off the second half of his drink and filled up his glass again. He eyed it intently. 'Of course, he hasn't actually said so to my face. But Antonia—she's my sister—told me privately. And she ought to know. She and my editor are very good friends. Antonia's a beautiful girl, everyone says so. When the looks were being given out in our family, she got the lot.'

Ainsworth gulped more whisky. He was getting drunk now

and his words were beginning to slur.

'Very good friends,' he repeated and held out his hand, two fingers together. 'Just like that. Close. Just like that.'

He laughed, but it was a sound without humour. He filled his glass again. 'You want another drink?' he demanded.

'Not for me, thanks.' Blake again refused the invitation.

The journalist took another long gulp. 'Where was I?'

'Talking about your sister. . . .'

'My sister,' Ainsworth agreed heavily. 'My sister Antonia. Now, there's a fun-loving girl——'

'Does she work on the same paper?'

'Work? Who calls it work?' The journalist leaned forward confidentially. 'You know, my sister and my editor are the two best pals you could ever wish to meet. They think the world of me. Both of 'em. "Cecil"—that's me—"Cecil, William has been talking about giving you a rise." or: "I've asked William to get you better hotel accommodation." See——? They both think the world of me!'

'They must get on very well together,' said Blake drily.

'But they do!' Ainsworth exclamed. 'My dear ol' chap, they do! Like a charm. They've got so much in common—you've no idea.'

Blake marvelled silently at the remarkable *modus vivendi* of this amoral and unholy trio—Ainsworth, his beautiful sister and his editor. But he said nothing. He waited and listened to half-a-dozen of the journalist's anecdotes, and watched him drink five more whiskies.

Ainsworth would reach the stage, Blake knew, when the alcohol content of his blood-stream would achieve the point of saturation at which he was accustomed to maintain control when drinking. In another ten minutes the journalist would have drunk himself sober.

In the meantime he talked. He kept on talking, moving from generalisations to anecdotes. He told them with a complete lack of inhibition; they were forthright and jocular. And they were delivered with a masterly alcoholic *panache*. Some of the more outrageous stories concerned people in political life whom Blake knew personally.

Suddenly, in the middle of one of his most *risqué* stories,

Ainsworth suddenly broke off. He leaned across the table, fixing his bleared gaze upon Blake, with difficulty. Little puffing breaths came through his half-open mouth.

'D'you know something, Blake?' he hiccoughed. 'I'll shtell you something, shall I? Do you know why I d-drink sho much?'

'I've an idea,' said Blake quietly.

The journalist nodded his head. 'An' you're right, ol' boy, you're damn right. . . Rheason I drink so much is because when I'm shober I bloody well can't shtand the sight of myself. . . .'

* * *

Paradoxically, it was Ainsworth's free and frank confession of his own dishonesty which convinced Blake he could be trusted. As soon as he was satisfied that the journalist had reached the sober stage he taxed him with urgent questions.

'What do you know of Mahdu Nath?' was his first demand.

'Mahdu Nath?' Ainsworth shook his head. 'No, sorry, old chap. Can't say I ever heard that name before. Certainly old Nigel never mentioned it.'

Then Blake showed him the photograph of Nigel and Caroline Perkins. The journalist identified Caroline immediately, and outlined her history for Blake in a few succinct sentences.

'When I first met her, she was in the Wac-Eye. The Indian Women's Army Corps. That was a couple of years back. She's a beautiful girl. Damned attractive. And intelligent. Her father's an Anglo-Indian, a railways official at Allahabad. She was doing her service here in Calcutta, and she had a boy-friend who used to bring her to the club. He was a colonel in the Artillery; I think his name was Saunders. At any rate, it was he who arranged for her discharge. He got her out of the W.A.C. and fixed her up with a flat somewhere in town. About eight months later Saunders was reported missing in action—believed to be a prisoner of the Japs. And shortly after that she took up with Nigel. He was very fond of her—and I think she loved him.'

Ainsworth drained his glass again. He looked at Blake's. 'You're empty, too.'

He refilled both.

'And that's just about all there is to tell you about her,' he concluded. 'All *I* know, at any rate. I don't know what will happen to her now.'

'Do you know where she's living at this moment?'

'Do I . . .' Ainsworth frowned. 'Yes . . . Yes, I think I do. If I can remember where it was I saw her. . . .'

Blake's attention quickened. This was more than he had dared to hope for. The Indian waiter was moving around the tables, replenishing the iced water in the carafes. Ainsworth thanked him, absently, still thinking hard.

Then:

'Got it!' he said suddenly. He snapped his fingers. 'It was this morning. I was in Firpo's having myself a late breakfast before starting on my usual liquid lunch. Firpo's on Chowringhee, you know——'

Blake nodded. Firpo's was the one place in Calcutta that everyone knew.

'—and I saw her through the window,' Ainsworth said. 'I saw her coming out of a flat-block just over the way.' He made a quick calculation which gave Blake the address. The detective snapped his notebook shut and stood up.

'You're not going?' Ainsworth was disappointed.

'I've got to. But I want you to know that you've been of invaluable help to me. I mustn't keep you from your Burma campaign despatches.'

'True,' Ainsworth sighed. Moodily, he picked up his glass. He gulped whisky. 'I've still got to finish describing the fall of Mandalay.'

'*Mandalay!*' Blake was startled. 'Has it fallen already?'

'Oh, don't worry,' Ainsworth reassured him hastily. 'It hasn't fallen yet. But I may as well get my piece written, because it's going to!'

Blake left him refilling his glass; busy with the bottle.

He went out of the club with his mouth set in a thin, hard line. Ainsworth's attitude, however macabre, was a bleak reminder that time was running out.

He had to reach Caroline Perkins quickly and make her answer some very important questions. Already he knew the answers to most of the things which had been baffling him, but only the Anglo-Indian girl could supply the final vital link in the chain of evidence he had been forging. One question now puzzled Blake more than any other.

It was simply: Why, if Caroline Perkins was free to come and go as she pleased, which now seemed certain—had she not come forward before now?

Blake was so preoccupied puzzling over this as he left the club that he didn't notice that Singh, the Indian waiter, had followed him as far as the lobby and there slipped into a telephone booth.

Singh rang a number in the native quarter. When a voice at the other end answered, he repeated a snatch of conversation between Ainsworth and Blake, which he had overheard in the bar.

It was Caroline Perkins' address on Chowringhee.

CHAPTER SIXTEEN

Ten minutes before midnight the lights along the two-mile stretch of Chowringhee were starting to go out. The darkness which engulfed Calcutta's park, the Maidan, was beginning to spread out towards the hotels, shops and clubs which had been ablaze with lights and neon since dusk.

The taxi which carried Blake from the South East Asia Club swept past the Calcutta race-course and slowed down at the approach to a large block of modern flats. It drew up at the main entrance and Blake got out. He paid the driver and stood by to watch the taxi drive away.

As he turned to go in through the main door he brushed past three people coming out. Two of them were Indians in European clothes. A woman was walking between them and for a brief instant Blake saw them from the corner of his eye, merely as passers-by.

Then suddenly his brain registered something else, and it sent an immediate reaction through his whole body. He stopped almost in mid-stride. The woman wasn't walking between the two Indians. She was being supported!

And in that same instant Blake knew something else—something which was confirmed in two sharp paces back the way he had come. The woman they were with, the woman who was moving along between them, half-walking, half-dragging, was Caroline Perkins.

For the smallest fraction of a second Blake was poised on the steps of the entrance. Then suddenly the steps were a launching pad beneath his feet. It all happened with the speed of light. And it happened as swiftly and spontaneously as it did because into Blake's mind flashed a mental vision of Rosemary Medwin —as he had last seen her.

One moment there were two men walking along beside the Anglo-Indian girl, and the next moment there was only one. The other was outflung across the pavement, arms and legs splayed in a grotesque horizontal position. Blake had put him there with the full force of one heavy shoulder-blow in the centre of the man's back.

And long before the man knew what had hit him, Blake was back on his own feet and turning to deal with the second adversary.

Metal glinted, dully, from the Indian's coat pocket as he jumped back in fright and alarm. Caroline Perkins, released by her captors, stood for a bare half-second, then fell limply to the ground as Blake moved in to disarm the man with the knife.

It was the work of two short seconds and four sharp judo punches, and it sent the man crashing back against the flat-block wall as the knife clattered to the pavement, striking sparks as it fell.

From behind him Blake heard the sound of running feet and glanced over his shoulder in time to see the first man sprinting down the side of the block, running as though for his life. A car engine started up distantly and headlights lighted up the entrance as Blake turned his attention back to the man he had stunned.

Was this one of the men who had killed Rosemary Medwin? If so, Blake was not prepared to deal lightly or mercifully with him.

But the man was no longer stunned. Those four blows, which should have felled an ordinary man instantly, had shaken him —but he was still on his feet. He was on his feet, and moving on them. He should have been paralysed in four joints; and instead he had dodged from the wall with the agility of a cat— and was starting to run.

Blake went after him. He broke into a sprint and would have overtaken the running man within a matter of seconds. But even as he gathered speed to close with his quarry, he heard the roar of an accelerating car. A warning sounded in Blake's brain. He stopped, turned and saw the car bearing down on the entrance to the building.

It was a taxi and it had already picked up the first would-be kidnapper. Now it was roaring down the side of the block— and it was moving with a single, unmistakable, inexorable purpose.

Caroline Perkins lay on the concrete pavement in the full glare of the taxi's headlights. Unless a miracle—or Blake—intervened, she would be dead in a matter of seconds—flattened to a pulp beneath the wheels of the car.

Blake moved as though fired from a cannon. With arms stretched full out before him he swept across the intervening yards of pavement with the speed and leaping grace of a panther.

The girl was scooped up from the ground in two powerful arms as Blake crossed the driveway within inches of the taxi's front wheels.

Shouts rang on the night air as the taxi swung out, denied of its victim. Out on the main road the second kidnapper was lit up in the flash of its swinging headlights. A door opened, he leapt and was hauled inside as the vehicle, veering crazily, accelerated into the main highway.

Blake placed the girl gently down in the shelter of the wall and stooped to examine her. She was semi-conscious and a quick glance at the pupil of one eye told Blake that she had been drugged.

He lifted her to a sitting position and, with one arm around her shoulders, he began massaging her cheeks with fast, light slaps until her eyes came into focus. She looked at him wildly, not recognising him.

'Stay awake!' he ordered brusquely. 'You've got to stay awake! You've been drugged—you've got to tell me how. Was it an injection or——'

She was groaning. The words came out jerkily, punctuated with deep gasps.

'They made me drink something. . . .'

It was enough for Blake. If the drug had been given to her orally there was still something he could do about it.

He helped the girl to her feet and supported her as he asked the number of her flat. It was a number on the second floor.

He tried to make her walk, but her steps were clumsy and faltering. She hung, a dead weight, on his arm. There was no time to spare and with sudden decision Blake picked her up in his arms again.

Several swift strides across the carpet of the deserted entrance hall brought him to the foot of the main stairs. He took the steps two at a time and reached the door of her apartment fifteen seconds later.

The door was locked. Caroline had no handbag and the key was not on her. For several anxious moments Blake thought his own skeleton set was not going to help, for the lock was of an unusual local design. But the fifth key fitted.

He carried the girl into a spacious, well-furnished lounge. The lights had been left on and the disarray of cushions and furniture indicated that it had been the scene of a struggle. He laid the girl on a large, low-slung divan and went in search of the kitchen.

There was a cupboard above the sink, and Blake snapped the doors open. His eyes went swiftly along the shelves. Curry powder, cinnamon, spices, salt, mustard. . . .

Curry!

He took it down, turned on a tap, searched for a glass—searched for a teaspoon. Neither was to be found. The girl had obviously not been in the flat long enough to have unpacked her kitchen utensils and put them in their proper places. Blake's eyes scoured the contents of the kitchen desperately. Anything! Anything that would hold water.

He found it—a small flower vase on top of the ice-box. He threw the contents into the sink, rinsed it and scooped in a handful of curry powder. He added water from the running tap and stirred it with a pencil as he hurried back into the lounge.

The Anglo-Indian girl was unconscious, her eyes closed, her head thrown limply back, her hands trailing. Blake stooped down beside her and began to slap her face. He shook her and presently she opened her eyes dazedly and stared around her.

Blake heaved her into a sitting position and thrust the vase to her lips.

'Drink it!' he ordered. 'Quickly! It's an emetic.'

Something stirred in the girl's confused brain. She understood and did her best to obey. Her lips moved, quivering, without proper control. She gulped twice, then a spasm shook her. Blake made her finish the drink, then lifted her from the divan and helped her into the bathroom.

She was gasping and choking as she lurched towards the

wash-basin and supported herself with suddenly new-found strength as all her facilities became subordinated to the one urgent necessity of purging her system of what she had swallowed.

Blake left her and returned to the lounge. He stopped at the telephone and hesitated for a moment with his hand on the receiver.

In his mind he carried a full description of the two men who had tried to abduct the girl. There was little doubt that if he passed the details on to the police it would be only a matter of time before they were picked up for questioning. One of them, at least, could be one of the two men who had killed Rosemary Medwin. The other man, Blake remembered, had a broken shoulder as the result of his fight with Blake in the darkened apartment, so it was unlikely he had been involved in the attempted kidnapping. That meant at least three men were involved, and it should not be difficult to trace at least two of them.

But was that what he wanted? The important thing was to pick up, not Mahdu Nath's henchmen, but Mahdu Nath himself. To settle for less now might jeopardise the issue later. He decided against it—for the time being, at least. He left the telephone and walked across to the cocktail cabinet.

Like most of the other pieces of furniture in the room, the cocktail cabinet was new. It was also expensive. Altogether, the contents of the apartment must have represented a tidy sum, and the rent for such a place would be proportionately high. And Blake found himself reflecting that as far as he knew, Caroline Perkins was not working.

He poured two double brandies and carried them across to the low table which stood against the divan. As he did so the girl appeared in the doorway of the bathroom. She was weak, pale and considerably chastened by her ordeal.

Despite her condition and appearance, however, Blake was struck by her remarkable physical attractions. She had dark eyes—eyes possessing a depth and lustre which was matched by the fine black hair which had fallen in disarray about her smooth oval face. She pushed her hair back now with her free hand as she clung to the lintel of the door with the other.

She looked at Blake without speaking. She was wearing an emerald-green two-piece suit, and the slender line of her neck was accentuated by the high collar of the white cashmere jumper she wore beneath it. Her only accessory was a spray of jasmine pinned to one lapel. Altogether her appearance combined curves with elegance.

She was exhausted and unable to speak until she was sitting down and sipping the brandy which Blake gave her. He waited patiently for her to recover her composure.

CHAPTER SEVENTEEN

Presently Caroline Perkins said: 'You're Nigel's brother, aren't you?'

Blake nodded.

She went on: 'I saw you at the funeral. I should have stayed and spoken to you. I wanted to, only ...'

'Only what?' Blake prompted as her voice trailed off.

'I'm sorry, it's hard to explain. Complicated ... I wouldn't have known what to say, in the circumstances. You know ...'

'It doesn't matter now,' Blake said. 'But why did you run away?'

She shrugged. 'There were many reasons. I was frightened mainly, I suppose. Not without cause, either, judging from what happened. It's a good thing you came along when you did.' She paused, looking into his face with her dark, lustrous eyes. 'Thank you.'

Blake noticed that there was an ugly bruise, just coming to light, on the soft skin. A small cut marred the smoothness of her lips. He said:

'Who were those men?'

'I don't know. I never saw them before in my life.'

'Do you know where they were taking you?'

'No. They came into the flat about twenty minutes ago—I opened the door to them thinking it was somebody else. They tried to make me drink something. I struggled as best I could, but in the end they forced it down me.' She shuddered. 'It was horrible....'

'Do you mean,' said Blake slowly, 'that you have no idea at all why they attempted to kidnap you?'

'I was Nigel's ... girl-friend. Isn't that enough?'

'I don't follow,' said Blake, and frowned.

'Nigel had a lot of enemies. And I don't mean just those who used to run him down because they thought he was idle, and a waster. He wasn't. He was doing a job in a million, if people had only known. He worked for the Government and his work was important. *That* was why he made enemies.'

Her defence of Nigel was impassioned. Already the colour was returning to her cheeks and she spoke with rising animation.

Blake knew now that Nigel *had* indulged in pillow-talk, just as he had suspected. He said:

'What did my brother tell you about his work?' As he spoke he took out his cigarette case and offered her a cigarette. She shook her head and put her hand to her throat.

'No, thank you. My throat still feels as though it's on fire. That stuff you gave me ... curry, wasn't it?'

Blake lit a cigarette for himself and looked at the girl through the flame of the lighter. He did not speak and presently she said:

'You're a detective, aren't you?'

'Yes. You're quite free to talk. I know that if Nigel spoke to you about his work when he shouldn't have done, it wasn't your fault. And at the moment I'm hoping he did.'

He paused, then added quietly: 'Officially, Nigel's secrets died with him. He died because he possessed vital, valuable knowledge. Knowledge which could affect the whole direction of the war. I believe that you are now in possession of some of that information—that you are the only person alive who can tell us what we need to know. If you do know anything— anything at all—it is your duty to tell me.'

She returned his gaze with steady eyes. 'I'll do anything I can to help. What do you want to know?'

'I want to know about a man called Mahdu Nath.' Blake watched her face carefully. Recognition showed in her eyes for a moment, then she frowned.

'Mahdu Nath? The name's familiar—isn't he involved somehow in a plot to organise a mass insurrection?'

'He is,' Blake told her grimly. 'And more. It is a plan to unite all India—Moslem and Hindu—against the British Raj and sell out the sub-continent to the Japanese.'

'All India?' Her eyes widened incredulously.

'All India,' Blake repeated. 'And if we don't stop him it's going to happen. It could happen today—tomorrow—in three hours. It could happen at any moment. And Nigel was the

242

only man who had any inkling as to how it would start. You've got to remember what he told you, Caroline.'

'Could it be something to do with the transportation system?' she asked. 'Nigel mentioned the railways several times. He was worried about vital supplies coming into Bengal. He said something about the railways being a main artery. And something about a particular railway junction where that artery could be cut.'

* * *

'Famine,' Blake said quietly. 'So that's it. Mahdu Nath plans to cut off essential food supplies for Bengal. Widespread starvation would be followed by widespread riots—creating the very situation of revolt which Mahdu Nath needs for his talents as a rabble-rouser to stir up mutiny and seize power. Simple—but deadly effective.'

He turned to face Caroline with sudden urgency. 'Two things—there are two things which I have to know. *When* and *where?*'

Caroline concentrated with a deep frown. 'Nigel never said where it would be. I don't think he knew. But he said something about a train coming through on the fifteenth. A special train, I think. The one which could make all the difference if it were stopped. Sunday, the fifteenth.'

'Tomorrow,' said Blake quietly. 'That leaves only a matter of hours to find out where it's going to happen and stop it.'

Blake paced the carpet, his mind working desperately. He knew that if Mahdu Nath were still in Calcutta, he would be leaving the city no later than tonight. The railway junction was the key to the whole situation and Mahdu Nath would have to be there to start the insurrection.

Blake stopped pacing and looked at Caroline. He had to get back to Craille.

'How do you feel now?' He was wondering whether it was safe to leave her.

She managed a smile. 'Better,' she replied.

'Tell me something,' Blake said. 'Why did you leave your old flat so hurriedly and come here?'

She shrugged. 'I was frightened, I suppose. I kept thinking

243

about Nigel, and the way he'd ... died. All I wanted to do was get away somewhere.'

'Another thing,' said Blake. 'When I called at your flat the first time the clerk told me that you had left in the company of two military policemen—Security officers, he thought they were. But Colonel Maitland denied that he sent any of his men to see you. Who were those men?'

Caroline's face, turned towards him, expressed astonishment. 'You must be mistaken!' she said. 'Nobody called at my flat—nobody at all!'

'But the estate clerk states he let them into your apartment—that you were still asleep at the time.'

'He must be lying,' said the girl. 'Though I can't imagine *why* he should. Or else he was mistaken.'

'I don't think he was lying,' said Blake slowly. 'As you say, there was no reason for him to do so. But you were certainly not at the flat when I called to see you.'

'No. I was looking for another flat—this one,' said the girl. 'It's possible, of course, that somebody *did* call at my flat while I was away—just as you did—but I certainly did not see them.'

Blake let the matter drop, though he was far from satisfied. He said:

'Even though you moved your flat, those men found you, didn't they? And very quickly. What will you do now—move again?'

'I don't know. But not today—two moves in one day are more than enough. I'm quite certain they won't return, anyway.'

'Be doubly careful,' Blake warned her. 'Don't open the door to anybody, anybody at all. As soon as I get back to headquarters I'll arrange for some men to be sent over to stand guard. Then we'll see about other accommodation for you—though perhaps by that time it won't be necessary. We may have Mahdu Nath by then.'

'I sincerely hope so!' replied Caroline with a shiver.

Blake moved over to the cocktail cabinet and picked up an object which had caught his eye. It was a short piece of cane bound in leather with silver mountings.

He turned it over thoughtfully in his hands. He was silent

for a moment then turned back to face Caroline as she got to her feet.

'I'll be quite all right,' she said. 'Really I will.'

As she spoke she was moving towards the door. Blake sensed a kind of urgency in her voice and movements, almost as though she was anxious to be rid of him. He paused on his way to the door and looked at her:

'Remember—don't open to anybody,' he said.

'I won't,' she promised him.

She stood there while he left, then closed the door behind him. Blake stood in the corridor for a moment, frowning. He was still frowning as he made his way to the stairs.

A few moments later he was searching for a taxi on Chowringhee.

CHAPTER EIGHTEEN

Caroline Perkins waited motionless, listening to Blake's footsteps going along the corridor. Then she walked over to the window, drew back the curtain with a careful hand and looked out. She waited until she saw Blake hail the taxi and drive off before she let the curtain fall and moved back into the room.

Twice her hand went out to the telephone and twice she let it fall to her side. She went back into the bathroom, washed, then went into the bedroom and changed into a blue woollen dress. She walked over to the door and checked that it was locked, although she knew it was.

She seemed undecisive and ill at ease. Presently she went back to the telephone again and this time she lifted the receiver and gave a number. There was a moment's lapse before she got through, then a man's voice answered, speaking cautiously.

Caroline said urgently: 'I've got to get away from here—at once——'

Then, as the voice broke across her words, sounding angry as well as surprised, she related rapidly what had happened.

'They may come back,' she said. 'And Sexton Blake, too— I think he's suspicious. You must get me away from here at once!'

There was a prolonged silence from the other end of the line; then the voice said sharply: 'Very well. I'll be over there within the hour. In the meantime, keep your door locked and don't open it to anybody.'

The receiver clicked back at the other end and Caroline put down the handset slowly and reluctantly. She felt suddenly isolated—and frightened.

For the next twenty minutes or so she continued to stride uneasily about the apartment. Several times she went to the window and looked out. The street was in comparative silence and there were deep pools of shadow where the street lights did not reach. She made some coffee but when she had poured herself a cup she did not drink it but helped herself to another glass of brandy.

When the knock came it startled her. It was loud and peremptory—a knock which demanded instant admittance. She flung aside the magazine she had been glancing through desultorily and ran towards the door. She shot back the bolt and opened it, her mouth opened to frame a welcome.

Then she gasped and her hand flew to her throat. All colour drained away from her face and she opened her lips to scream. But the man in the doorway—big, heavily-built, bald-headed—gave her no chance to do so. In three swift movements he stepped into the room, kicked the door shut behind him and grabbed the girl. His hand went over her mouth, cutting off her cry before it had bubbled to her lips.

She felt the sharp prick of a knife at her throat, held in his other hand. She was too terrified to struggle; her mind a black abyss of anguish and despair. Still holding her he looked around for something to gag her with and his eyes fell on a silk scarf lying over a chair.

He picked it up, still holding the knife. He released his hold over her mouth for an instant then, before she could cry out, he whipped the scarf between her lips, pulling it so tightly that it cut into the soft skin.

From his pocket he produced a short length of rope which he twisted around her wrists, pulling her hands behind her first. In less than ten seconds, even before she had had time to recover her scattered wits, Caroline was helpless.

He stepped back, still holding the knife. 'If you do as you're told you won't get hurt,' he said. And then: 'Where's the bedroom?'

Caroline rolled her eyes towards the adjoining room. He hurried across the room into the bedroom and came out holding a green sari and another scarf, this time of green chiffon. He walked over to Caroline and tied the scarf in a square over her face, just below her eyes, knotting it at the back of her head. Draped that way it looked something like a yashmak.

Then he took the green sari and draped it over her head and around her shoulders. The long clinging folds effectively concealed the fact that she was bound and the improvised yashmak hid all sight of the gag. Caroline could have walked along the street in broad daylight and have excited no comment.

The Indian motioned her towards the door, which he opened. He placed himself at her side, slightly behind her, and in her back Caroline could feel the keen point of the knife, pressing against her spine.

'Walk,' he said. 'Don't try to escape or you'll be sorry. Go down the stairs and across the hall, quietly. There's a car waiting outside.'

Caroline could do nothing but obey. She was too frightened even to wonder where the Indian was taking her. At the back of her mind was an overwhelming relief that she had not been killed instantly. Obviously they wanted her alive—for the same reason that they had attempted to abduct her before. Only this time Blake would not be there to rescue her.

She went down the stairs and across the carpeted hall. The reception clerk was standing behind his desk; he glanced up, then looked casually away again. He saw nothing out of place—merely two Indians, a man and a woman, walking together out into the street.

Around a corner of the building Caroline saw a black car drawn up, with another man at the wheel. The bald-headed one opened the rear door and pushed her roughly into the back seat. Then he climbed in beside her. The man in the driving seat turned to give Caroline a derisive grin and she wondered if he was the same man who, earlier, had tried to kill her by running her down with the taxi.

Inside the taxi her captor suddenly pulled a handkerchief from his pocket and bound it around Caroline's eyes. Now she could see nothing; only intermittent light and darkness as they swept past neon signs and the lights from the buildings which lined the street. She crouched back against the upholstery, wondering desperately if this would be the last ride she would ever take.

The car travelled through the night for around fifteen minutes or so, as far as Caroline could judge. Then she felt the car slowing and the brakes being applied. The engine stopped and she heard the driver getting out of his seat.

The door next to her was opened and rough hands fastened upon her arms, jerking her from the car. She stumbled and almost fell, recovering her balance with difficulty.

Both men took hold of her now, one on each arm. She felt the hard paving of a courtyard beneath her feet, and their footsteps echoed back eerily from what must have been the buildings surrounding it. Then she stumbled against a short flight of steps and heard a door squeaking open in front of her. Another flight of steps and then a carpeted corridor. Half-a-minute later one of the men knocked upon a door and she heard it open.

She was pulled inside the room and heard the door close. A hand pulled the bandage from around her eyes. She stood there, blinking in the bright overhead light, the transition from darkness to light so sudden and so violent that for a moment she could see nothing at all.

Then her vision cleared. She saw a large, handsomely furnished room, tall windows with velvet curtains drawn across them; a big desk slanted across one corner. From behind the desk a man rose, facing her, his face wreathed in a smile of quiet triumph.

Caroline knew without words being spoken, who the man was. He was the man who had murdered Nigel Blake; the man who was plotting to overthrow the British and hand India into the hands of her enemies.

He was Mahdu Nath.

CHAPTER NINETEEN

It was fifty minutes past midnight when Blake arrived back at the penthouse atop the mansion block in Park Street.

Craille had gone out and Blake let himself in with his own key. He sat down at the old man's desk and began to use the telephone.

First he spoke to police headquarters and left instructions for two men to be sent around to Caroline Perkins' flat. Then he phoned 'Enquiries' at Howrah railway station and asked a number of questions. In three or four minutes a picture was growing in his mind—a mental map of train movements which reflected in a curious way the economic life of north-eastern India.

By the time he had all the answers he wanted, Blake knew exactly what Mahdu Nath's plan was. The conversation with the Howrah station clerk confirmed every detail in his mind—except one. He still did not know the name of the junction where the trains carrying Bengal's vital food supplies were going to be intercepted.

He turned to the map of north-eastern India which lay on Craille's desk. Slowly, by a long process of elimination, he could work it out. Yet time was against him.

The minutes passed and he was no nearer a solution. He heard the sound of footsteps and the click of lift-doors.

The door opened and Craille came in. His eyes were tired and his expression grim as he looked across at Blake.

'Well?' he asked. 'Did you manage to trace the Perkins girl?'

Blake nodded. 'Yes.' He told of the brief fight outside the apartment block and how he had put the two kidnappers to rout. 'She was very upset—naturally. I took her back into her apartment and after she'd recovered, I talked to her.'

'And Nigel *had* confided in her?'

'Yes. He knew what Nath was planning to do, though not in full detail, of course. But Caroline is as much in the dark as we are as to the identity of this Mahdu Nath.'

'And you left her at the flat, alone?' asked Craille.

'I had no choice. I told her to lock herself in and answer the door to nobody. I've just rung police headquarters and told them to put a guard on her.'

Craille frowned. 'I don't like it,' he said. 'Mahdu Nath is dangerous and ruthless—he's already proved that. I think you should have brought Caroline Perkins away with you.'

'Where to? Here?' asked Blake, and he spoke irritably. 'I doubt if she would have come, anyway. And no matter where she went, those men would have found her. They seem to have a well-placed informer somewhere. She hadn't been in the place long—scarcely longer than Rosemary Medwin had been in her new flat—yet those men were able to trace both of them within the hour. I think they would have found Caroline wherever she was taken.'

Craille nodded, grudgingly. 'Perhaps you're right. But I'm not very happy about her story of the two military policemen. Why should that estate clerk have lied? There was no logical reason for him to do so.'

'I've been thinking about that, too,' said Blake.

Craille drummed with his fingers on the desk. 'I think we ought to bring the girl in for further questioning,' he said. 'As well as for safe-keeping. We'll have her taken somewhere where only *we* know where she is.'

'Very well,' said Blake. His hand moved towards the telephone. 'I'd better ring her, just to check that everything is all right.'

He lifted the receiver and gave Caroline's telephone number. Long seconds, running into a minute, passed as the number rang—and rang unanswered.

Blake put the receiver down and looked at Craille. 'I was with her less than an hour ago,' he said.

Craille said slowly : 'What I find puzzling is why Nath's men *killed* Rosemary Medwin—but *kidnapped* Caroline—or tried to. Both girls knew Nigel; they were both of them, possibly, in possession of information dangerous to Mahdu Nath. But only Rosemary is killed. *Why?* Why wasn't Caroline also killed? For what reason does Mahdu Nath want her alive?'

Blake was pacing up and down the room, his hand to his chin, his grey eyes cold and steel-hard. He said harshly:

'Well, at least we've found out what Mahdu Nath's plan is. My theory that Nigel would have confided in Caroline paid off, after all. Nath's plan is to intercept vital food supplies bound for Bengal. The idea is to create widespread famine——'

'Famine!' Craille's features hardened. 'We should have guessed! Famine, followed by an offer of food supplies from the Japs—with a rabble-rousing fanatic encouraging the Indians to let the Japanese army come through! To come through and feed them! When is this due to happen?'

Blake's eyes were bleak. 'Almost immediately. And all I know at this moment is that the train is going to be intercepted at a railway junction. It could be anywhere in north-eastern India.'

He dropped slackly into a chair and closed his eyes in despair. 'Do you know,' he demanded bitterly, 'how many likely points there are in northern India? Hundreds. Literally hundreds.'

He opened his eyes and glared at Craille, who was lighting one of his aromatic cigarettes. 'How would *you* find out which one it was?' he demanded.

'I don't know,' replied Craille, and his voice was as tired as his eyes. 'As you say ...'

Suddenly, explosively, Blake leapt to his feet. His eyes were wide open now and filled with excitement. He leapt forward and thumped his clenched fist down upon Craille's desk with such violence that the heavy cigarette box skidded across it and bounced to the floor.

'Of course!' he shouted. 'Why didn't I realise it before? *Allahabad!*'

Craille stared at him in complete stupefaction. 'Allahabad? But how can you——'

'Don't you see?' demanded Blake. 'You asked me just now why Mahdu Nath *kidnapped* Caroline instead of having her killed, as Rosemary was. The answer to that question is because he needs her—he intends to use her as a hostage!'

'A hostage? But——'

'One of the railway officials at Allahabad is Caroline Perkins' father. That journalist—Ainsworth—told me. That's why Caroline has been kidnapped—that's why Nath was so desperate to get his hands on her. He's going to put an armlock on Caroline's father, using her as his lever. Allahabad is the junction. It *must* be!'

Craille's eyes were reflecting Blake's own excitement now. 'Are you certain about this, Blake?' he asked.

'I'm positive! It all fits—and it's the only way it can fit!'

'Then we've got to stop Nath,' said Craille with calm control. 'What do you propose we do?'

Blake was already reaching for the telephone. 'We've got to get hold of Maitland.'

'Colonel Maitland?' One of Craille's thin eyebrows moved in surprise. 'Didn't he tell you he wouldn't be available?'

Blake paused. 'What d'you mean?'

'He went on leave at midnight. That's why he was working late this evening.'

Blake replaced the receiver without saying anything. He looked at his watch and then at the pad on the desk.

'The only train for Allahabad is leaving in fourteen minutes from Howrah Station,' he said, and his voice was cold, his eyes a hard, steel-blue. He looked at Craille again. 'We haven't a moment to lose,' he said.

CHAPTER TWENTY

The main hall at Howrah Station was alive with movement. Arc lights burned down through a pall of thickening smoke to illumine a scene which spoke of desperate, last-ditch defensive war. Troops were everywhere, moving in two directions.

Squads of soldiers in battle order and fresh, clean jungle-green uniforms were moving one way. They were all fully equipped and healthy; only their faces were pale, for they were newly arrived from Britain. They were bound for the front.

The others were coming back; thin, emaciated, battle-stained and weary. They wore bandages that were stained with blood and many were being carried on stretchers.

Through the smoke which swirled thickly along platform five came the lean figure of Eustace Craille. He was followed by a Military Police lieutenant and six military policemen. There was a mixed-goods and passenger train waiting at the station. Steam rose from its giant locomotive and the banging of coach doors indicated its imminent departure.

Craille drew the military policeman into the shadow of a pile of munition crates, stubbing out his cigarette before doing so.

He was waiting for something.

A minute later Sexton Blake appeared from the direction of the stationmaster's office. Craille made a silent signal to him and the two men met on the platform.

'I've checked everything,' said Blake. 'It has to be this train. The only other one which stops at Allahabad left two hours ago.'

Craille looked at his watch. 'Only two more minutes. Are you sure they haven't arrived yet?'

'Positive.' Blake's voice was firm. 'Their coach is still empty.' To forestall Craille's question he said: 'The last coach has been reserved in the name of Deva Sal, but it can't be anyone except Mahdu Nath because the last coach is the only one actually released at the junction—the rest of the train goes straight on. So the man who steps into that train is the one we want—Mahdu Nath.'

Blake glanced at his own watch. 'We'd better get out of sight.'
They stepped back into the shadow of the munition boxes.

Passengers were still arriving on the platform from the booking hall. Tall Sikhs moved by with sinuous steps; American officers with suitcases, a party of British nurses; porters pushing trolleys and carrying bags.

Then Blake nudged Craille suddenly. A figure had appeared, stepping fast through the crowd. He was carrying a single suitcase and wore civilian clothes. 'Watch him,' said Blake quietly.

It was Colonel Maitland.

'Wearing mufti,' muttered the lieutenant. 'That's one charge against him for a start.'

Colonel Maitland reached the last coach of the train and paused to look over his shoulder.

For a moment he looked around and then at the door of the empty, reserved coach. He hesitated.

The men standing in the shadow of the munition boxes watched with anticipation. All of them knew now that the man who entered that coach would be Mahdu Nath. Could it be Maitland? Maitland, who headed a branch of Military Security here in Calcutta? It was incredible—but here he was, standing on the platform in civilian clothes—and looking around him nervously, as though afraid.

Why was he hesitating?

Moisture stood out on the foreheads of the watching men. Did Maitland suspect something? Did he know he was being watched?

One thing they all knew—and it stretched their nerves to an unbearable pitch. Mahdu Nath had to step inside the coach before they could be certain of his identity. They couldn't arrest a military intelligence colonel on mere suspicion. They had to know Mahdu Nath's identity for sure. If they made a mistake there would not be a second chance.

Maitland had turned and was looking towards the booking hall. For a bare fraction of a second he shot a glance in the direction of the munition boxes. Then he turned towards the coach.

He turned and carried on. He had not seen them. He continued walking down the platform—down the length of the train towards the locomotive.

'So it's not him,' whispered Craille.

Blake nodded confirmation and watched with narrowed eyes as Maitland went by.

The tension among the waiting men relaxed, but almost immediately it began to mount again. A shrill, sharp whistle from the locomotive echoed through the station. The train was ready to leave. At any moment it might begin to pull out.

Last-minute arrivals were crowding on to the platform now and already they were starting to run. What had happened to Mahdu Nath? Surely he should have been here by now? Could there have been a change of plan?

Blake looked around the group of men who were standing beside him. All of them were beginning to sweat freely. Blake guessed what they were all thinking. He was thinking the same thing himself.

What would happen if Mahdu Nath simply missed the train? It was the sort of thing which could happen to anybody. Could it happen here and now to destroy the last chance of catching the man who planned to sell India to the Japanese?

Crowds of people thronged the platform. Soldiers, airmen and nurses. Noise was omnipresent Movement was continuous. Authorised porters with metal brassards strutted spindle-legged and splay-footed beneath impossible head-loads. The inevitable *char-wallah* squatted in the dust, scratching himself beside his charcoal-fired brass tea-urn and his tray of sticky, sugary, fly-speckled cakes.

But everyone in sight could be identified and immediately accounted for. Heat lay like a damp blanket over everything. Light glared back from the railway tracks. Blake wiped sweat from his eyes. Where was Mahdu Nath?

A crowd of Indians appeared from the booking hall, blocking the view. Blake cursed under his breath. Then he looked at them more closely.

A woman in a sari led the group, walking steadily and looking straight ahead of her. A silk veil fastidiously shielded her mouth and nostrils from the dust and the polluted air. A well-dressed, high-ranking Indian was walking to the left of her and a little behind. Blake could not see the face beneath the turbaned head; for the woman shielded it. But something about the man and the way he moved made Blake's eyes narrow sharply.

Was it Nath? In a moment he would know. The party had almost drawn level with the empty coach.

Another whistle of steam blasted shrilly. Craille made an involuntary movement forward, but Blake stopped him.

The group had paused by the coach.

They had stopped, but was it only to discuss something? They seemed to be arguing among themselves. Was this the only reason they had paused? Would they continue walking in another moment?

Blake knew he could not afford to make a mistake. If he were wrong, the sudden sight of red-capped military policemen swarming across the platform would be a danger signal which Mahdu Nath would recognise wherever he was.

Blake knew that he had to be right first time. The trap had to snap shut on the right man. There would be no second chance.

It was swelteringly hot behind the stacked ammunition boxes. Men held their breath achingingly under the almost unbearable strain.

And then, suddenly, something happened. Blake's keen-eyed watchfulness was rewarded. Still arguing, the grouped party by the coach shifted their positions fractionally. Just that.

But it was enough. In that moment it was as if a jigsaw had been instantly unscrambled. The picture was plain to see.

Reaching up for the handle to open the coach door was Chandra Sen—the bald-headed man Blake had seen coming from Rosemary's apartment. Blake could see him clearly. And behind him were the two men who had fought with Blake outside the block of flats where Caroline Perkins lived. All three faces were visible and recognisable now that their owners had moved.

And then Blake recognised something else.

The high-ranking Indian whose face was still shielded from him had throughout maintained carefully a position to the left of, and slightly behind, the woman in the sari.

It was an odd position for any Indian male to take up in relation to a woman, as Blake had recognised in the first moment he had seen the group coming along the platform. In India, men took precedence. So the position had been a strange one.

But there was more to it than that.

The high-ranking Indian had moved with a certain stiffness. A certain awkwardness. And now Blake knew why.

Craille moved forward for the second time, and again Blake stopped him.

'He's got a gun.'

Craille froze.

Urgently, Blake beckoned the police lieutenant. Swiftly he outlined what he wanted him to do. The lieutenant nodded, stepped on to the platform, and walked towards the group. They were beginning to climb into the coach.

Blake watched tensely as the lieutenant drew alongside them, and stopped.

They were all there. Nath's confederates. And Mahdu Nath himself was the man who wore the turban—the man who had been walking awkwardly behind the woman in the sari. Walking awkwardly because he was holding a gun to her back.

He was holding a gun to her back because the woman in the sari was Caroline Perkins.

CHAPTER TWENTY-ONE

Blake stepped out on to the platform, his Luger in his hand.

This was the showdown, the moment of truth.

If Mahdu Nath's plans were to be countered, it had to be now. If justice was to be done, as Blake was coldly determined it should be, this was the time.

His gun jutted forward.

Then it happened.

There was a fleeting, scuffling movement as the man in the turban turned and saw the police lieutenant. In that same instant the policemen drew his Service revolver.

'No!' shouted Blake.

He leapt forward as the first shots blasted out. Chandra Sen, the bald-headed one, half-in and half-out of the coach, had also drawn a gun. The police lieutenant shot him through the throat.

The rest of the group scattered. More shots. Women screamed. Bullets richocheted down a platform cleared of bystanders as if by magic.

Mahdu Nath was caught between two fires.

For an instant of time he had seen himself confronted with a choice of two targets at which to aim—Blake or the police lieutenant. He had forgotten his hostage, Caroline.

Too late, as more military policemen raced over the platform, he remembered the girl standing beside him and turned his revolver towards her.

Blake cut him down with three successive shots before his hand could complete the movement.

He shot him down coldly, as he would have shot down a mad, dangerous dog. There was neither pity nor remorse in his eyes as he fired the bullets. This man was not merely a murderer— the killer of Nigel and of Rosemary Medwin—he was a fiend. Remembering how Nigel and Rosemary had died, Blake was in no doubt at all about that.

There was more shooting; a rapid exchange of fire between Mahdu Nath's remaining men and the police. Bullets sang past

Blake's head. Then, all at once, it ended.

Mahdu Nath was dead. He lay face down on the platform in a grotesque heap, blood oozing from three chest wounds. He was dead, and in that moment everything he stood for was dead, too. His supporters surrendered. They knew they were beaten.

Blake stepped over Chandra Sen, who—shot in the throat—was bubbling blood and gasping hysterically. He reached the body of Mahdu Nath and turned it over with his foot.

He looked down bleakly into the face of Sohan Dutt.

*　　*　　*

'Sohan Dutt?' Craille said dully.

He stood beside Blake with a small, pearl-handled Biretta still smoking in his hand. The lines on his old, parchment-like face were drawn into new patterns. He had lost his look of eternal calm and in its place was an expression of near-disbelief.

'Sohan Dutt . . .' he repeated.

'Hard to believe, isn't it?' Blake's lips drew back from his teeth. 'The man who went out of his way to be so helpful to the British authorities. The man who was always so anxious to profess political moderation. Sohan Dutt, the liberal-minded humanitarian.'

Craille nodded slowly. 'I would never have known,' he said. 'He had the perfect cover.'

A light kindled in his amber eyes. 'I would hate like hell to think there might be another one like him, Blake. He fooled me completely.'

'Don't blame yourself,' said Blake. 'He fooled a lot of other people, too. And he was all set to fool his own people as well.'

The Military Police lieutenant stared down at the sprawled body. Nearby, Chandra Sen was lifted, whimpering, on to a stretcher. The lieutenant looked down at Sohan Dutt for a long moment, then he said:

'He always seemed such a harmless chap. A bit cranky, but I'd have sworn he was straight.'

'He was a psychologist,' Blake said thoughtfully. 'It all fits, really—if you think about it. Only we didn't. We weren't meant to. We were got at—below the level of our conscious awareness. Sohan Dutt had planted himself in the British mind as a friend long before any of this happened. Maybe, at one time, he even was a friend. But that was before his innate lust for power conquered him completely.

'The only reason I kept an open mind was because I'd never met him before. If we'd known each other better he might have got away with it. It would have seemed grotesque them—impossible—that he could be a traitor. He had a plan that was almost foolproof.'

'It didn't do him much good in the end,' remarked a police corporal who was rubbing a grazed shoulder. 'Sen's being loaded into an ambulance. What do you want me to do with the rest of them, sir?'

'Take them down to headquarters,' Blake ordered. 'And I want two men to go and collect Colonel Maitland from the other end of the train.'

'Colonel Maitland, sir?'

'Yes,' said Blake. 'And they can tell him he's under arrest.'

*　　*　　*

A few minutes later Blake faced Colonel Maitland in the stationmaster's office. The Security Officer arrived blustering.

'What is this? I demand to know what's going on? I'll——'

'You'll do nothing,' Blake interrupted him. 'Nothing except stand there and take what's certainly coming to you. For you, Maitland, this is the end of the road.'

He half-turned to speak to the others in the office.

'Because of one man,' he said coldly, 'Mahdu Nath might have been in Allahabad by morning, implementing his plans for an insurrection which could have cost us the war. Because of one man we might have lost the war here in Calcutta, tonight. One man—and his wild, all-consuming, selfish infatuation for this woman!'

He pointed towards Caroline Perkins, who stood with Craille beside the stationmaster's desk, and swung round to face Maitland.

'That man,' he said harshly, 'was you!'

Maitland didn't answer. The blood had left his face now; he stood, chalk-white and staring.

'I don't doubt,' Blake went on quietly, 'that your Court

Martial will add a substantial number of other charges to the ones which I lay against you now. But, just for tonight, you'll have this much to think about. You almost succeeded in selling your country in your desire for one woman. I hope that makes you proud.'

Craille spoke up. 'Does it, Maitland? If it does'—his voice rose angrily—'take a look out at the platform. Take a look at your fellow countrymen who've been fighting and dying to keep it safe for you here in Calcutta!'

'For nothing more than your own selfish reasons,' Blake said, 'you withheld vital evidence. You could have jeopardised all our efforts to lay Sohan Dutt by the heels. You prevented a witness from speaking out—for no other reason than that you didn't want to be parted from her.

'So you kept her hidden in a flat you rented for her—telling her that it was for her own safety; that she must lie low until the hue and cry over Nigel's death had died down. And she believed you. Even when I found her tonight she was loyal to you. She didn't tell me that the flat she was living in was provided by you. She even lied about the two military policemen who called for her at the flat where she originally lived. The estate clerk hadn't lied; it was Caroline who lied—because she was afraid you might get into trouble. She thought you were her friend, you see.

'Tonight you were going on leave—and you planned to take her with you. You were afraid I was getting too hot on the trail; you knew I was getting closer to her all the time. It must have been a nasty surprise for you when you found she wasn't at her flat tonight, when you called for her. Unknown to you, she had been tricked by Mahdu Nath's thugs—for the second time—and taken away by them.'

Caroline Perkins stared at Blake wide-eyed. He turned and spoke to her.

'Your life was in danger, because of what you knew—and Maitland was very well aware of this fact. But when he offered you a new flat and promised you his protection, instead of letting you tell all you knew to us—it wasn't safety he was giving you. He was placing you in mortal peril.'

Caroline shivered involuntarily.

Blake continued: 'I only discovered all this this evening when I found an officer's swagger stick on top of the cocktail cabinet in your flat. For a moment I didn't see whose it was. Then I remembered where I'd seen it before—it told me all I needed to know.

'You lied about the two military policemen—and so did Maitland. He tried to make me believe that they were Nath's men, impersonating soldiers. Because it was on his instructions that those two men called at your flat in order to take you to another —which Maitland assured you was "safe".'

He looked back at Maitland.

'Another thing' he said. 'Rosemary Medwin might be alive today if you hadn't ordered her to be released from police custody. At least her life wasn't in danger while she was being held by Inspector Mawgan. But you went over his head and had her sent home—where she was butchered by Mahdu Nath's thugs. You didn't want her to be questioned in case she let fall any scrap of information about Caroline's whereabouts. So, indirectly, one might say, you sent Rosemary Medwin to her death. You've certainly got a lot to answer for.'

Blake turned to face the group.

'We caught Mahdu Nath in the end, but it was no thanks to the man in charge of Military Security. In fact, it was almost as the result of an accident. Mahdu Nath—or to give him his real name, Sohan Dutt—made one mistake. He made the mistake of thinking that I did not understand Hindi when he was questioning the caretaker, on the pretence of helping me. He told me that the caretaker had mentioned two military policemen, who had called to see Rosemary shortly after she moved into the flat. That was purely fiction. The caretaker did not even mention them.'

'But what was his object?' asked the lieutenant, puzzled.

'He had two reasons. One was to draw a red herring across the trail—he already knew about the military police who had called earlier to see Caroline—and the other was to create trouble within the organisation, so to speak. He must have known that thrown mud would stick, and where it would stick. He knew that our investigations would substantiate accusations of corruption against our Military Security. In spite of what he made us believe about him, he was very much anti-British, as you now realise.'

Here Blake paused, then he went on: 'It's ironic to think that Dutt's carefully devised plans could be overthrown as the result of any tiny mistake. On the other hand, it is in keeping with his grandiose ideas of power and ambition. He made the mistake of under-estimating an enemy; he thought that because I had been assured by others of his friendliness and good-will towards the British, I would accept him at his face value. Every man has his Achilles' heel—and in Mahdu Nath's case, it was his over-weening pride. He thought he had us all in the hollow of his hand; and his pride would not allow him to believe that he could be outwitted or out-smarted by one man.'

Blake paused. He paused for so long that his companions looked at him curiously. Then he said, very quietly and very slowly:

'I am not a vindictive man, neither am I a cruel one. But when I think of Nigel and Rosemary, and the way they died, I could wish that Mahdu Nath's death had not come to him as quickly as it did.'

Then he stopped again. There was only one other thing which remained to be said now, and he said it. He turned to the two soldiers who stood one on either side of Maitland. He spoke with finality, and with contempt:

'Take him away.'

*　　　*　　　*

Later—not long afterwards—Blake and Craille left the station together. They walked to where a car stood waiting for them. They were silent now; neither spoke. Each man was an island girded by his own thoughts.

Craille was thinking of the mistake he had made in trusting Sohan Dutt. He had never laid claim to any kind of infallibility, not even to himself. He was a man without illusions. Everyone made mistakes. All the same, throughout his life he had contrived to make very few of them, and now he trembled inwardly to think of what could have happened—if it had not been for the man at his side.

This time, he thought, he had been lucky. Luckier than he

deserved. He must not make another mistake like that, ever again.

Blake was hoping that he would never be given another assignment like this one. Not another job of work with such impossibly high stakes, nor one shadowed with such personal anguish.

Nigel Blake was dead. Nothing that he could do would change that irrevocable fact. He wondered how he would break the news to his father. How would the old man take it? He would have to tell him the whole story—though not *how* Nigel had died; that would have been too much for his father to bear—and stress the importance of the role Nigel had played. He must set the record straight.

Beyond the station, the Howrah Bridge flung its arches wide over the sludgy, silvery Hooghly. The girders were stark and black against the lighter, starlit sky.

A few hours ago, Craille thought at that moment, and the whole war could have been lost here in Calcutta.

The two men paused briefly on the edge of the pavement. Then Craille opened the door of the car and bowed gently. 'After you,' he said. The gesture meant something.

Blake looked at the older man and hesitated.

'Go on,' said Craille. 'This time you lead and I'll follow.'

Blake climbed into the car.

CHAPTER TWENTY-TWO

Dusk came early to the south coast of England.

It was March. A cold March. Nearly a year had gone by. This was March nineteen forty-three.

The daylight thinned into grey twilight. Mist crept up over the sea. Soon, in a small hotel on a promontory overlooking the Channel, the blackout curtains would have to be drawn. But in a room of this hotel, facing seaward, one man talked to another and both were heedless of the passage of time.

The one who listened was old and white-haired. He sat in a wheelchair by the window in the deepening dusk. His name was Doctor Barclay Blake. The man talking to him was the elder of his two sons.

Doctor Blake had been confined to his wheelchair for three years now. But the powerful pair of binoculars on the window-ledge behind him bore testimony to the fact that he was still mentally alive and active. It was his passionate hobby, on a fine day, to study the movements of ships out in the Channel. He watched the destroyers and mine-sweepers going about their work, and could identify coastal patrol aircraft on sight.

Counting the ships and the aircraft day by day, he would study the newspapers and listen to news bulletins, and make predictions to himself and to the friends who visited him, about the coming invasion of Europe.

But today he had spoken very little. Instead he had listened to one of his sons telling how the other had died in the service of his country. The old man had been deeply moved and now, at the end of his son's story, he was silent for a long time.

Then: 'What became of the girl?' he asked.

'She took a job,' Sexton Blake said. 'At the University of Calcutta. Teaching English. I think she'll be happy enough there.'

'Calcutta University. . . .' The old man nodded. 'I remember it well. I'm glad.'

He was quiet again for a while. Then slowly he moved the wheels of his chair.

He pushed himself over the carpet to a bureau. He opened the top drawer and brought out a fat file of papers. 'One thing remains to be done,' he said.

He manoeuvred his chair to the fire and picked up the poker. He stirred the dying embers into dull but glowing life. The file was flat on his blanketed knees. He said: 'We must do this together.'

Sexton Blake got to his feet. He joined his father at the fireplace. He knew what that fat bulky file contained. Sorrow and heartache. Here were press-cuttings relating to Nigel, his brother. Page after page of them. Page after page of pasted-up fraud, petty crime and deceit.

'I always hoped that one day Nigel would make good,' the old man said. 'So did your mother.' He sighed.

He said quietly: 'She used to pray for it. . . .'

There was silence.

What a pity she didn't live to see her prayers answered.'

Another silence.

'He did make good, didn't he?' the old man said.

'He made good,' said Sexton Blake.

Then the old man took the fat file of papers into his hands. He broke it open. He fed the pasted-up pages one by one into the fire, and his son helped him. The flames leapt up greedily —hungrily.

This fire mirrored another. As Nigel himself had perished, so did his past.

Sexton Blake went on helping his father until the last infamous page had dissolved into ash. Then it was dark in the room. Very dark. And the curtains had to be drawn.

Sexton Blake drew them.

He drew them on an assignment, on the past, on the life of his brother and on the memory of a narrowly averted storm over India.

Then, and only then, he knew the case was at an end.